T0158102

WANTING THE VAMPIRE

Without warning Locke was at her side, his arm wrapping around her waist to pull her tight against his body. "I'm not letting you out of my sight."

She tilted back her head, telling herself to be annoyed. He didn't have the right to manhandle her. If she desired a male to touch her, then she would ask him.

"Is that a promise or a warning?"

He lowered his head until they were nose to nose. "What do you want it to be?"

What she wanted was to throw him on the ground and strip off his clothes. She knew it. He probably knew it. But she wasn't going to admit the truth. Not until she was ready.

Which might be never.

He was, after all, threatening to kill her, she reminded herself.

"Do you seduce every nymph who crosses your path?" she demanded.

"Jealous?"

"Discerning."

He used the tip of his fang to outline her lips. "Discerning?"

The sensation of the sharp tip pressing against her skin was oddly erotic. Almost as erotic as the jolts of pleasure that darted through her...

Books by Alexandra Ivy

Guardians of Eternity
WHEN DARKNESS COMES
EMBRACE THE DARNKESS
DARKNESS EVERLASTING
DARKNESS REVEALED
DARKNESS UNLEASHED
BEYOND THE DARKNESS
DEVOURED BY DARKNESS
BOUND BY DARKNESS
FEAR THE DARKNESS
DARKNESS AVENGED
HUNT THE DARKNESS
WHEN DARKNESS ENDS
DARKNESS RETURNS
BEWARE THE DARKNESS
CONQUER THE DARKNESS
SHADES OF DARKNESS
DARKNESS BETRAYED
BEWITCH THE DARKNESS

The Immortal Rogues
MY LORD VAMPIRE
MY LORD ETERNITY
MY LORD IMMORTALITY

The Sentinels
BORN IN BLOOD
BLOOD ASSASSIN
BLOOD LUST

Ares Security
KILL WITHOUT MERCY
KILL WITHOUT SHAME

Historical Romance
SOME LIKE IT WICKED

SOME LIKE IT SINFUL
SOME LIKE IT BRAZEN

Romantic Suspense

PRETEND YOU'RE SAFE
WHAT ARE YOU AFRAID OF?
YOU WILL SUFFER
THE INTENDED VICTIM
DON'T LOOK
FACELESS

And don't miss these Guardians of Eternity novellas

TAKEN BY DARKNESS in YOURS FOR ETERNITY
DARKNESS ETERNAL in SUPERNATURAL
WHERE DARKNESS LIVES in THE REAL WEREWIVES OF VAMPIRE COUNTY
LEVET (ebook only)
A VERY LEVET CHRISTMAS (ebook only)

And don't miss these Sentinel novellas

OUT OF CONTROL
ON THE HUNT

Published by Kensington Publishing Corp.

Bewitch the Darkness

Alexandra Ivy

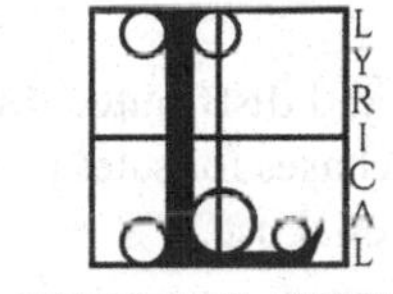

LYRICAL PRESS
Kensington Publishing Corp.
www.kensingtonbooks.com

To the extent that the image or images on the cover of this book depict a person or persons, such person or persons are merely models, and are not intended to portray any character or characters featured in the book.

LYRICAL PRESS BOOKS are published by

Kensington Publishing Corp.
119 West 40th Street
New York, NY 10018

All Kensington titles, imprints, and distributed lines are available at special quantity discounts for bulk purchases for sales promotion, premiums, fund-raising, educational, or institutional use.

Special book excerpts or customized printings can also be created to fit specific needs. For details, write or phone the office of the Kensington Sales Manager: Kensington Publishing Corp., 119 West 40th Street, New York, NY 10018. Attn. Sales Department. Phone: 1-800-221-2647.

First Electronic Edition: November 2021
ISBN: 978-1-5161-1096-4 (ebook)

First Print Edition: November 2021
ISBN: 978-1-5161-1099-5

Printed in the United States of America

To my fabulous readers. Thanks for taking this crazy ride with me!

Much love,

Alex

Chapter 1

Locke didn't encourage visitors. Just the opposite. He'd gone to a lot of trouble to promote his reputation as a churlish hermit who regularly feasted on the hearts of intruders.

And if his surly temperament wasn't enough to drive away unwanted guests, he'd chosen to settle in the remote mountains of Iceland. The landscape was stunningly beautiful, but it was a combination of jagged glaciers with sheer cliffs that plummeted to the distant bay below. Up here there were no prying human eyes and, best of all, the pesky sun barely bothered to make an appearance during the long winter nights.

Impervious to the brutal chill of the early December air, Locke poured himself a glass of the aged cognac that he imported from France and stepped onto a narrow ledge to savor the star-spattered sky that spread above him. It didn't matter how many nights he spent admiring the view, it always amazed him.

Taking a sip, Locke barely noticed when the ground shook beneath his feet. It was a common occurrence. You couldn't reside above a boiling pit of molten lava and not have a few tremors.

It wasn't until the thunderous power sent the nearby ice sprites dashing for the protection of their nests that Locke reluctantly turned to view the massive male who was stepping out of a portal.

Styx, the current Anasso, the official name for the King of Vampires, was an impressive sight. In his human life he'd been a proud Aztec warrior who stood at six-foot-five with skin kissed by the sun and angular features. His glossy black hair was pulled into a braid that hung past his waist and he was wearing black leather pants, thigh-high boots, and a black silk shirt.

It was his sheer presence, however, that made the earth shake and the local wildlife flee in terror. Oh, and the big-ass sword strapped across his back.

Easily loping down the jagged rocks, he halted directly in front of Locke. "Hello, brother."

Locke arched a brow. "You again?"

Styx smiled. Until a few years ago, the males had been fellow Ravens, the personal guards to the previous Anasso. But after that Anasso had gone batshit crazy, forcing Styx to kill him and take the throne, Locke had retreated to this remote lair. It offered him the privacy he craved, as well as allowing him to concentrate on the one reason he still existed.

"Just like a bad penny."

"I was thinking more like a pain in the ass."

"That too," Styx agreed.

Locke instinctively reached up to touch the star-shaped burn on the side of his neck. It was the only blemish that marred his traditional vampire beauty. Or at least that's what he was told by his various lovers. He had no reflection, so he had only their descriptions that his eyes were a pale blue and rimmed with gold. And that his strong Viking features were perfectly carved. He did know that he kept his dark blond hair chopped to brush his broad shoulders and that his hard body was currently protected from the elements with a leather jacket, jeans, and heavy black boots.

"What do you want?" he demanded in his usual blunt manner.

Good manners were for creatures who cared what others thought about them. He didn't give a shit.

"I thought I'd let you know that Ian is dead."

Ian had been a Raven as well. Only his allegiance to the previous king had gone beyond loyalty, to blind devotion. The obsessive male had been unable to accept the death of his beloved Anasso and had been plotting his revenge.

"I've heard that one before," he said in dry tones. There'd been rumors of Ian's death months ago.

"This time there's no doubt. I personally chopped off his head," Styx assured him.

"Did you come here for a pat on the back?"

Styx leaned forward. "Do you want to?"

"Hell no."

Styx folded his arms over his chest, regarding Locke with an expression that was impossible to read. "I'm just keeping you in the loop."

"We have a loop?"

Styx shrugged. "A loose loop."

"Mmm." Locke wasn't impressed. "How did I get in the loop and how do I get out?"

"Once a Raven, always a Raven."

Locke frowned. At one time this male had been a brother to him, but since Styx had taken the throne they hadn't seen one another. Probably because Locke never left this isolated area. And then Styx had shown up a few weeks ago asking him questions about the other Ravens.

"Fine. Ian is dead. I've been looped."

"Don't you want to know why I killed him?"

"Not particularly."

"What do you care about, Locke?" Styx demanded.

"My privacy." Locke pointedly glanced around the bleak, gloriously empty landscape. "Which you are currently ruining."

"Get used to it."

Locke perched his glass on a flat rock before fully turning to study the male. He recognized that edge in Styx's tone. He was about to dig in his size sixteen boots and nothing could change his stubborn mind. The question was what he was going to be stubborn about.

"Get used to what?"

"Since taking the throne I've been dealing with one disaster after another."

"Uneasy lies the head that wears the crown," Locke quoted.

Styx ignored Locke's deliberately mocking tone. "Something like that. Unfortunately, I've let things slip through the cracks." He paused for dramatic effect. "Like you."

Uh oh. Locke didn't like the direction this conversation was veering. "I didn't slip through the crack. I walked out of the Anasso's lair and never looked back."

"You never said why you left."

"It was time."

"Time for what?"

"None of your damned business," Locke snapped.

The male frowned, almost as if he was hurt by Locke's sharp rebuke. Something perilously close to regret touched Locke's heart before he was sternly dismissing the stupid thought.

Of course Styx wasn't hurt. The Anasso wasn't a touchy-feely sort of vampire. Thank the goddess.

"I want you to come stay with me and Darcy in Chicago," Styx abruptly announced.

It was Locke's turn to frown. "Why would I stay in Chicago? Are you in danger?"

"No, I simply want you to meet my new mate. And you could spend time with the Ravens. I have some recent additions who could use your training."

Locke shook his head. "Thanks, but no thanks."

"Locke, it isn't healthy for you to spend so much time isolated from others."

Okay. Maybe the male was more touchy-feely than Locke had suspected. Or maybe he was just a bigger pain in the ass. The two were the same thing as far as Locke was concerned.

"I like being isolated."

Styx tightened his jaw. "It's time to rejoin the world."

"No."

"Yes."

"No."

Styx stepped forward, his power sending tiny rocks cascading down the side of the mountain.

"Right now it's an invitation, *amigo*," he drawled. "That can change."

"Invitation declined." Locke released a trickle of his own magic. Tingles that were just short of painful crawled through the air like an electric current.

Styx narrowed his eyes. "Are you challenging me?"

Locke ground his fangs together. He could be as stubborn as the Anasso, but he wasn't suicidal. Only an idiot would directly challenge this male.

A soon-to-be-dead idiot.

"Shit, Styx," he muttered. "What crawled up your ass?"

Styx held his gaze. "I'm worried about you."

Locke had walked away from the Anasso's caverns almost fifteen years ago. Why the hell would Styx be worried now?

"Don't be. I'm fine."

"I—" Styx's protest was cut short by a loud buzzing sound. He glanced toward Locke with a frown. "What's that?"

Locke shook his head in genuine confusion. "I have no idea."

"Let's check it out."

Styx turned and bounded up the steep cliff with a speed and grace that no creature but a vampire could achieve. Locke was rapidly following behind, not entirely unhappy to have a formidable warrior with him as they rushed through the narrow crack that opened into the inner cave. The buzzing was louder in here. And annoyingly shrill.

Locke took the lead as Styx wisely stepped aside. No vampire left their lair unprotected and Locke was no exception. Anyone trying to force their way inside would be fried to a crisp.

Laying his hand on the rock wall to remove the web of illusion he'd paid the local ice sprites to create, he led Styx down a narrow path that zigzagged to the very center of the mountain. At last they reached a vast cavern that Locke called home.

It was barren and cold and his few possessions were tossed in a pile near the exit, in case he needed to make a quick getaway. It wasn't that he didn't care about his surroundings. He enjoyed his comforts like any other vampire. But this wasn't truly his home. It was just a place to stay until he'd completed his goal.

Then he would move on.

"Damn." Styx winced as the buzzing became a shrill screech, as if someone had set off a fire alarm. "Can you turn that off?"

"I would if I knew what..." Realization hit with the force of a sledgehammer. "Oh, hell," he muttered, rushing into one of the side caves that wasn't much bigger than a closet.

In the center of the floor was a granite pedestal and on the top of the flat surface was a delicate gold necklace that was surrounded by a halo of light.

Crap. He'd waited centuries and it had to happen now?

"Um." Styx halted beside him, staring at the pedestal in confusion. "Your necklace is glowing."

Locke glared at his companion. "It's not my necklace."

"Hey, I'm not judging."

"Argh." Locke clenched his hands, frustration vibrating through him. "Will you just go away?"

Styx paused, no doubt sensing the urgency that thundered through Locke. Then he reached out to lay a hand on Locke's shoulder, his face set in somber lines.

"Whatever drove you away from the Ravens, you know you can trust me, don't you?"

Locke glanced away. He wanted to blow off the male's words. This necklace and what it represented was private, something he didn't want to share with anyone. But he'd been too close to Styx for too long. The older male had not only accepted him into the clan, but he'd been the one Raven who Locke instinctively had known would always have his back.

Besides, he could use a little perspective.

"Yeah, I trust you," he warily conceded.

"Then let me help."

Locke moved to touch the necklace, thankfully cutting off the shrill alarm. At the same time, he considered his words. He hadn't lied when he said that he trusted Styx. The male would lay down his life to protect his brothers. But it was difficult to force himself to share the events that had nearly destroyed his life.

"Do you remember when I traveled to Greece to deal with the vampire challenging Leonidas?"

Styx tilted his head to the side, as if searching his mind. "Vaguely," he finally conceded. "It had something to do with a witch, didn't it?"

Locke nodded, his mind filled with visions of rolling hills dotted with olive trees that swept toward rocky beaches and the bitter pine scent of juniper. When he'd arrived in the area that had once been Thebes, he'd discovered Leonidas battling a ruthless band of rebels who were willing to cheat to gain control of the wealthy clan.

"Black magic," he said. "The vampire was accused of using a spellbound weapon to earn the right to challenge the clan chief."

Styx grimaced. Vampires were unable to sense or protect themselves against magic. Which no doubt explained their violent aversion to anyone using it in their presence.

"Nasty."

"I put an end to the challenger's aspirations," Locke said. It'd taken a few nights, but Locke had eventually located the traitor hiding in a crypt beneath Athens. Dragging the coward out of his lair, Locke had challenged him to a mano a mano battle. The vampire had tried to cheat with his magical sword, but Locke had used his power to draw the static electricity from the air and zapped the bastard until he'd dropped the weapon. After that, it'd been a simple matter of cutting off the traitor's head. "But before I left Greece I met Xuria."

Styx looked confused. "Should I recognize the name?"

"No. She was a nymph who was fleeing a band of trolls." A warmth flowed through Locke, easing the ice that coated his unbeating heart. Locke had been returning to Leonidas's lair when he'd caught sight of the fragile female lying in a pool of her own blood. "I found her badly injured beside the road."

"I assume you rescued her?"

Locke remembered that he'd hesitated. Vampires avoided petty disputes between other demons. Why would they care what was happening among the trolls or fey creatures? They had enough problems dealing with each other. But for some reason, he'd felt compelled to stop and bend down to scoop her in his arms.

Immediately he'd been enveloped in a sense of enchantment. As if he'd been waiting for this moment since he'd awakened as a vampire. With exquisite care he'd cradled her against his chest as he'd returned to Leonidas's lair and hidden her in the deepest chamber. He didn't want anyone near her. No one but himself.

"I took her inside and cared for her."

"She was beautiful?"

They both knew Styx wasn't talking about the female's physical appearance, although Xuria had been glorious with her cloud of golden hair and eyes so pale they appeared almost white. Vampires searched for the beauty of the soul.

"She was…" Locke struggled to find the words. He wasn't sure why. Perhaps because the sensations whenever he was with the nymph were like nothing he'd felt before. "Compelling," he at last decided on. "I sensed the moment she touched me that she was my mate."

Styx jerked in shock, his gaze lowering to Locke's arm despite the fact it was hidden beneath his leather jacket. A mated vampire possessed a crimson tattoo on the inner forearm. A visible mark of the eternal bond.

"You're mated?"

"No." Locke's tone was edged with a century's old bitterness. "We never completed the ceremony."

"Why not?"

Locke didn't want to admit the truth. That he'd urged Xuria to take his blood. Not only to heal her wounds, but to claim her as his own. But she'd insisted they wait until they could travel to her grove on Mount Olympus. She claimed she wanted to be surrounded by her tribe when they formalized their bond.

Instead he focused on what had happened after her refusal to accept his offer.

"One night I traveled away from the lair," he said. He'd had to feed and he preferred to do it away from the distracting scent of his beautiful nymph. "When I returned I discovered Xuria was being attacked by an unknown female."

Styx arched his brows. "A troll?"

"No. A nymph."

"How did she get into the lair?"

"She managed to open a portal."

Styx's brow furrowed in disapproval. "Sloppy. I expected better from Leonidas."

No one had been more shocked or furious than the clan chief that his considerable layers of protection had been penetrated. In fact, Leonidas had been in the process of replacing each illusion, curse, and web of lethal spells when Locke had left Greece.

"It wasn't his fault," he told Styx. "The nymph had a strange magic. I think it was human."

"Do you know why she was trying to kill your mate?"

"No idea." The air snapped with a sudden burst of electricity as the painful memory seared through his brain. "I walked into our private chamber and found Xuria dead with the nymph standing over her with a black dagger clutched in her hand." He paused, grimly leashing his power that was sizzling against the magical barrier around the pedestal. He couldn't risk disturbing the spell. Not after he'd waited so long for it to be ignited. "I assumed that she must have some connection to the vampire who I killed. He was, after all, dealing with black magic. What better way to punish me for killing her master?"

Styx eyed him with sympathy. "She's dead." It was a statement not a question.

Locke clenched his teeth, anger blasting through him. "Unfortunately, no. She stepped through the portal before I could rip out her heart. I had no way to follow her."

Styx was smart enough not to linger on Locke's failure to punish the female responsible for the death of his mate. It was still too painful for Locke to discuss.

"Does the necklace belong to your mate?" he asked instead.

Locke shook his head. "I grabbed it off the nymph as she darted into the portal. She was gone, but I managed to keep ahold of the necklace."

Styx leaned forward, studying the glowing object. "It looks like it has a charm."

That was Locke's thought as well. The chain was made of gold, but the amulet hanging from it was carved out of bronze in the shape of a tree. It reminded him of something a dryad would possess.

"I had an imp place a tracing spell on it," he told his companion.

Styx made a sound of surprise. "That must have been pricy."

Locke cringed. "You have no idea."

The truth was that he'd handed over the majority of his treasure that he'd managed to accumulate over the long centuries to purchase the spell. Imps were notorious for gouging their customers and not even the threat of ripping out the bastard's heart had made him lower his price.

Styx's attention returned to the necklace. "So why not use it to find her?"

"She must have been behind a magical barrier that prevented the spell from locating her," he said. He'd been infuriated when he'd realized that he'd spent a fortune on magic that was completely useless as long as his prey remained hidden. A hard smile curved his lips. "Until now."

"Do you intend to go after her?"

Locke grabbed the necklace. It felt warm against his palm, indicating the spell was working. According to the imp who created the magic, the metal would grow even warmer the closer he got to his victim.

"She's not going to slip away again," he growled.

Styx squared his shoulders. "I'll go with you."

Locke sent him a startled glance. "Bullshit."

"You shouldn't be alone."

"I've been alone a long time, Styx," he said dryly. "I don't need a babysitter."

"This could be a trap."

Locke scowled. "If it's a trap, then why wait a century to spring it?"

"What's time to an immortal?" Styx countered. "I'll send one of the Ravens with you."

"No." Locke held up a hand as the Anasso put on his obstinate-as-a-rabid-mule face. "This is personal, Styx. The nymph killed my mate. I need to deal with her in my own way, on my own terms."

"You need someone watching your back," Styx insisted.

Locke glared at his companion. "I didn't know you cared."

"I've always cared, Locke," Styx held his gaze. "I let you slip away once. I'm not going to let it happen again."

Locke didn't have a snappy comeback. As much as he hated to admit it, he'd missed being a part of the Ravens. The laughter, the danger, the excitement. Even the occasional spats that had always ended up with a night of revelry when they'd called a truce. There'd been a sense of brotherhood that had taught him the meaning of loyalty. And trust. And family.

Something that had been sadly missing during the first centuries of his life.

Once again he reached up to touch the scar on his neck. "I'll be back," he promised.

"Famous last words." Styx studied him for a long moment, then, seeming to accept that he'd done all he could to keep Locke from hurtling headfirst into an ambush, the older vampire turned to stroll toward the opening. "Don't forget. When you're done with the nymph, you're going to spend some time at my lair in Chicago."

"I don't remember agreeing to that."

"Well you are getting old." Styx flashed a smile over his shoulder, revealing his massive fangs. "They say that the memory is the second thing to go."

"You know you're older than me?"

Styx continued out of the cave. "I'll tell Darcy to have a room ready for you."

"Stubborn bastard," Locke muttered.

"I heard that," Styx called back.

"Good."

Chapter 2

The exquisite throne room of the mer-folk castle was exactly what a throne room should be. A long, sweeping space with lofted ceilings from which dazzling chandeliers splashed light over the marble floors. A crimson runner led the way to a high dais where a massive throne stood in all its glory. And the walls were decorated with dazzling murals that were so real they looked as if they were windows revealing the beauty of the ocean that surrounded the castle.

Troy, the Prince of Imps, looked perfectly at home among the splendors. There was a noble elegance in his muscular form that was enhanced by the fishnet bodysuit that shimmered with tiny diamonds. And a regal perfection to his pale features. His thick mane of scarlet hair cascading down only added to his dramatic appearance.

Inga, the current Queen of the Mer-folk, on the other hand, looked like a fish out of water.

In appearance, she took after her ogre father. She was well over six foot, with shoulders broad enough to ram through solid walls and tufts of reddish hair on top of her square head. They stood straight up, as if she'd stuck her finger in an electric socket. At the moment, her solid body was stuffed into a muumuu in a shocking shade of orange with splashes of lime-green flowers. The only hint of her mermaid mother could be glimpsed in her eyes. They were a delicate blue that only flashed red when she was in a temper.

Which was unfortunately more often than not.

Standing near the throne, Inga was clutching the Tryshu in her hand. The mighty trident was the symbol of authority among the mer-folk. Like

King Arthur's sword, only with the power to level entire cities. She was shuffling from foot to foot, clearly uneasy beneath Troy's accusing gaze.

"What do you mean they've cancelled the Royal Feast?" Troy demanded.

"They felt—"

"Who is they?" Troy interrupted her defensive words.

"Lady Perchella."

Troy curled his lips at the mention of the arrogant mermaid who'd made it her life's mission to undermine Inga's authority. The petty female had publicly snubbed Inga, started rumors that Inga had stolen the throne even though they'd all been present when the Tryshu had chosen Inga as the queen in this very room, and stirred up rebellions whenever Inga suggested a change in tradition.

"Who else?" he pressed.

"The others on the Queen's Council."

"Sycophants to Perchella." He snorted. "What do you call a group of sharks? A shiver? A herd? A pod of putrid poop-heads?"

"Troy." Inga struggled not to smile.

Troy stepped toward his friend. "You're the queen."

"I'm aware of that, Troy."

"Are you?"

The ogress deliberately glanced toward the trident gripped in her hand. "It's hard to overlook this."

"Then *you* get to decide if there's going to be a feast or not," he patiently pointed out.

Inga wrinkled her nose, reaching up to scratch a tuft of hair. Her hefty fingers knocked her crown to an angle, giving her the appearance of a drunken sailor.

"They were right," she said. "The mer-folk have suffered through too many changes lately to be in the mood for a party."

"Pfft. They're fey. Even if they smell a little fishy. And fey are always in the mood for a party," Troy insisted. "Those hags are just jealous."

"Jealous?" She blinked in confusion. "Of what?"

"You."

Inga sent him a fierce glare, as if assuming he was playing a cruel joke. "That's not funny, Troy."

"It wasn't meant to be."

"Why would anyone be jealous of me? I'm too large, too loud, too awkward. Too..." She waved her arms, nearly whacking Troy with her trident. "Too everything."

Ducking out of the path of the lethal weapon, Troy straightened and smoothed back his fiery hair.

"Because you're the queen and they're not."

Inga snorted. "I'm a terrible queen."

"You just started this gig." Troy shrugged. "You'll get better."

"When?"

"When you decide you actually want to be a queen."

Inga heaved a harsh sigh, turning to glower at the throne. Troy understood. Most creatures assumed being a part of royalty was a gift. All they saw was the lavish castles, the piles of treasures, and the fawning servants. They never bothered to consider the constant worry, the threats of war, or difficult decisions that usually managed to piss off everyone.

Or even the fact that someone was always trying to take your place. Usually by some gruesome plot that involved the removal of your head.

It only made matters worse that Inga had never been trained to take her place as queen. One minute she'd been an outcast, and the next she was holding the Tryshu in her hand. Not the easiest way to start her reign.

"What if that's never?" she muttered.

"A legitimate choice," he said, although they both knew it was impossible. As long as she held the trident, she was the queen. Period, end of story. Still, if she wanted to play the game of what-if, he was willing to indulge her. "I prefer to ignore the fact I'm a prince."

Inga turned back to eye him with a curious expression. "Why?"

"Once you take the title it comes with all sorts of strings that can choke a male who prefers his freedom." He lifted his slender hands to wrap them around his neck. "Like a noose."

Inga held up the Tryshu. "Or an anchor."

They shared a rueful glance before their privacy was interrupted when the doors to the throne room were shoved open. Troy turned, knowing who was going to appear from the outer corridor. He'd already caught the scent of granite.

"What is the meaning of this…" Levet waved his arms in a dramatic gesture as he waddled up the crimson runner to stand in front of Inga. The tiny gargoyle barely reached Inga's knees with large fairy wings that shimmered in brilliant shades of blue and red and strands of gold. The only gargoyley things about him were his ugly gray features and the stunted horns. He should have been a source of amusement, but amazingly the creature not only managed to bewitch the females, but regularly saved the world from disaster.

"Of what?" Inga asked.

"This tapestry."

Inga blinked. "What tapestry?"

Levet gave another wave of his hands. "The cancellation of the feast."

Troy arched his brows. "What does tapestry have to do with the feast?"

"Oh." Inga snapped her fingers. "Travesty."

"*Oui*, that is what I said. It is a travesty," Levet complained, his French accent more pronounced than usual. "Did you know that I have been practicing juggling my balls for weeks?"

"You...um..." Troy cleared his throat. "You juggle your own balls, do you?"

Levet sent him a glare. "My fireballs, you *imbécile*."

Troy snorted. "Is that supposed to make it better?"

"Bah." Levet stuck out his tongue.

"I'm sorry, Levet," Inga interrupted the brewing battle. For whatever reason, the Queen of the Mer-folk was bedazzled by the annoying gargoyle. "The council decided it would be best to postpone it."

"Best for who?" Levet demanded.

"Right?" Troy echoed the question.

Inga rolled her eyes. "For everyone."

Levet stomped his foot. "No roasted pig? Or piles of mashed potatoes smothered in gravy? And pie?" His gray eyes widened in horror. "What about the pie?"

"I have bad news gargoyle. Even if there had been a feast it would be lots of ambrosia and nectar, not roasted pig," Troy drawled.

Levet glanced toward Inga. "Is that true?"

Inga grimaced. She had enough ogre in her to appreciate a finely roasted pig. "Probably."

Levet's wings drooped in abject disappointment. "Party suckers."

"Party poopers or joy suckers," Troy corrected the ridiculous creature. "Pick one."

Levet clicked his tongue. "You are..."

Troy frowned as his words trailed away. "What?"

The gargoyle pointed toward the back of Troy's hand. "Being summoned."

Glancing down, Troy discovered a black tattoo in the shape of a crow etched onto his skin.

"What the hell?" he muttered.

Levet moved toward him, touching the tattoo with his claw. "It is Cleo's marker."

It took Troy a second to recall the dark-haired nymph they'd encountered in London. He'd been with Levet as they hunted down the crazed vampire who was seeking to bring back the previous Anasso.

"She marked me?" Troy shook his head in confusion. He couldn't remember the female touching him. "When?"

"When you agreed to her bargain to open a portal in London."

Troy glared down at the aggravating beast. "I didn't agree to the bargain. *You* did."

Levet offered a smile of pure innocence. "That cannot be right. You are the one being summoned, not me. So." Levet shrugged.

"You..." Troy reached out to grab the gargoyle. He didn't know what he intended to do to him, and in the end it didn't matter. A burning pain had him pulling back to cradle his hand against his chest. "Argh. It burns."

"It will only get worse the longer you resist," Levet informed him. "If I were you I would go see what she wants. You do not want her to lose her temper."

Troy hissed, the pain becoming unbearable. "When I return we're going to have a very long, very painful conversation, gargoyle," he warned between clenched teeth.

Levet glanced toward Inga. "I hear that a lot."

* * * *

Locke called on the services of a tribe of ice sprites to open a portal. He'd randomly chosen Greece since that was the last place he'd seen his prey. Astonishingly, as soon as he'd stepped out of the magical doorway, the necklace warmed against the skin of his palm.

Had his luck finally turned?

Perhaps it had, he decided, catching the aroma of bougainvillea as he wandered through the velvet darkness. The scent of his enemy. At last!

With a low growl, Locke shook off the lethargic disinterest that had haunted him since the death of his mate, flowing over the rolling hills outside of Athens with fluid speed. Anticipation sizzled through him, along with something else. Excitement? Euphoria? Dazzling impatience?

Perhaps a dizzying combination of all three.

He'd nearly reached a grove of cypress trees when he at last caught sight of the female. He instantly recognized her. Odd considering he'd only caught a brief glimpse over a century ago. Then again, it wasn't like they'd casually passed each other on the street. She'd just murdered his mate. That sort of trauma tended to linger in the brain.

Besides, she was remarkably different from other nymphs. Usually they had golden hair and pale eyes and the sweet prettiness of a ripe peach. This female possessed a lush tumble of raven black curls and eyes the color of aged whiskey. At the moment, she was wearing a tiny silk sundress that revealed her soft, feminine curves in all their glory. She was more like an exotic flower than a peach. One that bloomed beneath the silvery moonlight.

A strange tingle of anticipation raced through him. An intoxicating eagerness that he hadn't experienced in over a hundred years.

Waiting until she rounded a bend in the road, Locke stepped out of the shadows of the trees and blocked her path.

"Going somewhere?"

The female squeaked, leaping back in seeming fear. "Who are you?"

"You know who I am," he growled, stepping into the moonlight.

"I don't."

Locke narrowed his eyes at her terrified expression. There was no sign of recognition. Just blatant fear.

A weird emotion burned through him. Was he offended she didn't remember him? Yes. Yes, he was.

The realization pissed him off.

"Locke," he informed her. He wanted her to know his name before she died.

"Locke." She pressed a hand to her throat, as if assuming he was there for a quick meal. "What do you want from me?"

Locke's fangs lengthened at the mere thought of tasting that bougainvillea-scented blood. Would it be sweet? Tart? Enticingly addictive?

He squashed the image of his fangs sinking deep into her soft flesh. This female was his enemy, he fiercely reminded himself.

"Justice," he snapped.

"Justice? Justice for what?"

He stepped closer, allowing a trickle of electric energy to tingle through the air. They were far enough away from civilization not to attract attention, and he wanted her to understand her danger.

"For the death of my mate."

"Death of your mate? You can't mean that you think I..." Her eyes widened, a tiny gasp escaping her parted lips. "No. You've made a mistake. I could never harm anyone."

Locke ground his fangs together. Her air of innocence was annoying. He would have far more respect for the female if she admitted what she'd done. Even spit in his face.

"Are you claiming this doesn't belong to you?" He held out his hand to reveal the charm that was glowing from the heat of the spell.

An unreadable emotion rippled over her face before she was meeting his gaze with a wary expression.

"Where did you get that?"

He made a sound of impatience. "Playing games is only pissing me off, nymph. We both know that I ripped it off your throat when you fled from the scene of the crime."

Shaking her head she backed away. "You're mistaken. It isn't mine."

He narrowed his gaze. "That might be believable if I hadn't had a very expensive tracing spell placed on the charm." He dangled it in front of her face. The metal shimmered with magic. "It led me directly to you."

She took another step back. "There's something wrong with your spell. The necklace doesn't belong to me."

"Liar."

"It belongs to my twin sister."

"Twin?"

He scowled in disbelief, his gaze skimming over the perfection of her features framed by the raven curls and the stunning whiskey-gold eyes. No. She was utterly unique. Unlike any other female he'd ever encountered.

His mind refused to accept there could be two of them.

She nodded. "Identical twin."

Locke shoved the necklace in the pocket of his leather coat. "Convenient."

"Not really." Her expression hardened. "She's vain, temperamental, and ambitious to the point of madness."

There was an edge of sincerity in her voice that Locke found hard to dismiss. Instead he glanced around. They were standing in a shallow valley that was close enough to the sea to catch the scent of salt on the light breeze. Further away he could smell humans who were gathered in a small town and several fey creatures who were scuttling through the open countryside. None of them were nymphs.

"Where is this mystery sister of yours?" he demanded.

The female glanced toward the towering trees next to the pathway. "She just went into the grove to gather nectar. We sell it in the market."

Locke studied the grove. He couldn't sense her sister, but no doubt magic was woven through the dense cluster of cypresses. This was the land of the dryads. They were very, very protective of their trees. There could be entire tribes of creatures hidden within the dark depths.

A wise male would no doubt kill the female and return to his lair. Mission accomplished. But Locke found himself unable to strike the final blow.

Perhaps because he couldn't be one hundred percent certain there wasn't a sister who was responsible. What was the point of paying a fortune for a tracking spell if he ended up slaying the wrong nymph?

Or perhaps because…

He slammed shut a mental door on any other reason he might hesitate to bring an end to this female.

"Take me to her," he abruptly commanded.

Her eyes widened, then she lifted her hands in a pleading motion. "No, please. She'll punish me."

"Punish you for what?"

"For not trying to stop you."

"Trust me, she's not going to be punishing you or anyone else when I'm done with her," he assured her, the air sizzling as his power swirled around him.

"Just…" She struggled to form the words. "Just don't hurt me."

He pointed toward the grove. "Go."

Her lips parted to protest, but catching sight of Locke's expression, she heaved a resigned sigh.

"Fine," she muttered, jumping over the narrow ditch that ran beside the road and disappeared among the trees.

Locke hurried after her, determined not to let her out of his sight. Instantly the cool shadows wrapped around him, thick with the spicy scent of cypress. Unease slithered down his spine, but he ignored the voice of warning that whispered in the back of his mind. He'd come too far to fail.

Besides, he wasn't afraid. If there was a predator capable of matching him in deadly strength lurking in the grove, he would sense the danger.

Confident in his ability to overcome any enemy, Locke allowed himself to be led deeper and deeper into the grove. Like Hansel in that ridiculous human fairy tale. Only Gretel wasn't his companion. She was the witch in disguise.

He'd reached the center of the grove, where a small cottage with a thatched roof was built in the clearing, when disaster struck. Reaching out to grab the nymph's arm, he intended to make her call out for her sister. He wasn't stupid enough to enter an unfamiliar cottage. Even the fey were capable of nasty surprises to protect their lair. But just as his fingers brushed her shoulder, she was leaping to the side.

At first he assumed his touch had frightened her. She was obviously skittish and eager to be away from him. It wasn't until he heard the woosh of air that he glanced up to see the cage dropping from the sky. It'd been held up by magic and concealed behind a thick layer of illusion.

It could be a trap….

Styx's warning echoed through his mind as the cage landed with a loud thud, with him caught inside.

Turning back, she offered a smug smile. "Males. So predictable."

More aggravated than worried, Locke folded his arms over his chest. Okay, he might have been a little distracted by the sight of the silken sundress that clung to her luscious backside as they'd walked through the trees. And the long length of bare legs that were brushed with pollen from the wildflowers. And that rich scent of bougainvillea.

But he wasn't predictable.

He had a few tricks of his own, some of which he intended to use on this female. Just as soon as he lured her into believing he was well and truly defeated.

Chapter 3

Kyi kept her smile pasted to her lips even as her entire body quivered with the effort of pretending she wasn't completely freaked out.

She'd known that lowering the magical barrier around her grove would make her vulnerable to danger. But she'd been prepared to battle against family members, not a male who'd nearly captured her a century ago.

Thank the goddess she'd managed to catch the familiar scent before he'd stepped in front of her. She'd only smelled it once, but the mixture of copper and lightning was impossible to forget. Without that early warning she would have completely panicked. Instead, she'd managed to resist the instinct that urged her to flee. She could never outrun a vampire on the hunt. But she could hopefully trick him into following her to the cage she'd created when she'd first claimed this grove back in the days when the area was still called Thebes.

No one was more surprised than she was that her crazy plan had actually worked.

That didn't mean, however, that she wasn't still freaked.

She told herself that it was the male's blatant lack of concern that was unnerving her, as if he was confident in his ability to escape whenever he wanted. She didn't want to admit that it might be her stunned reaction to the sight of him. He was big and gorgeous in his leather coat and deliciously tight jeans. His hair was a rich gold that framed a face that might have been sculpted by the hands of an angel. He had a noble brow, a long, slender nose, and wide lips that demanded to be kissed. And those eyes. A fierce blue encircled in gold. They seared into her with the force of the sun.

Everything about him was irresistibly magnetic. Even the odd star-shaped scar on the side of his neck.

A Nordic warrior who had once rampaged across the tundra.

As if to emphasize the image of a ruthless predator, Locke folded his arms over his wide chest.

"What's your name?"

It was a command, not a question, and she answered before she could halt herself.

"Kyi."

"Kyi." He repeated her name, his faint accent giving it an exotic texture. "Let me guess. There's no sister."

Angry that she'd lost control of the encounter, Kyi sternly reminded herself what was at stake. She'd waited a long time for the opportunity to destroy her witch of a mother. The last thing she wanted was to risk allowing Xuria to escape with the fey she'd come to this world to enslave.

"There is a sister named Cleo." Kyi shrugged. "Just not here."

Locke shook his head in self-disgust. "Styx was right. I must be getting old. Borderline senile." He narrowed his eyes. "How did you know I was coming?"

She frowned at the unexpected accusation. "I didn't."

"You just happen to have a silver cage ready to drop on unsuspecting vampires?"

"It's a multipurpose cage. The bars have a mixture of iron, copper, and silver," she told him. The combination of metals could hold a vampire, fey creature, or a human witch. "A girl can't be too prepared."

"I suppose that's true for a girl like you." He ran a contemptuous gaze down the length of her body. "No surprise that you have lot of enemies."

Kyi was oddly offended by his words. "Why would you assume I have a lot of enemies?"

"Beyond the fact you're a homicidal maniac?"

She snorted. What a hypocrite. "You're a vampire."

"So?"

"If anyone is a homicidal maniac, it's a leech," she snapped. She'd done her best to avoid the bloodsuckers over the years, but a species didn't climb to the top of the demon food chain by being nice guys. They were ruthless predators who hunted their prey without mercy. "How many creatures have you killed?"

He waved away her words. "None that were injured and unable to protect themselves."

Kyi was confused. Was he implying that he was injured and somehow vulnerable?

Her gaze skimmed down his hard body. She couldn't see anything wrong with him. Nothing. At. All.

Sparks of awareness danced through her. It was dangerously easy to imagine running her hands over those chiseled muscles. Would his skin be cold? Would it warm beneath her touch? Would he taste like lightning?

Stop it, Kyi, she silently chided her renegade fantasies. She'd been cloistered for a century. Who could blame her for being hot and bothered? Especially when there was a gorgeous vampire available to sate her long-denied hunger?

But now was not the time. And this was not the male.

"You're not injured," she pointed out the obvious.

He arched a brow. "I was talking about the female nymph you murdered."

Murdered? What the hell…

"Oh." Kyi rolled her eyes. That was even more ridiculous than imagining this vampire as helpless. Her mother was like a hurricane. An unstoppable force that swept through the world, causing utter disaster before disappearing. "So that's how she did it," she muttered.

Locke frowned. "Did what?"

"Convinced you to take her into the clan chief's lair."

"She didn't convince me to do anything," Locke snapped, as if insulted by the implication he'd been manipulated. "I found her near death and made the decision to carry her to safety."

Kyi turned to pace from one edge of the cage to another. The last time her mother had returned to this dimension, she hadn't been prepared. The older woman had nearly managed to sneak up on her and slice out her heart with an iron dagger. It was only sheer luck that she'd managed to avoid the killing blow.

Surviving the attack, Kyi was determined to put an end to her mother's threat once and for all. Not only for her own safety, but to protect the fragile fey creatures she intended to capture.

But by the time she'd healed and followed Xuria's trail, the sorceress had managed to disappear.

"She must have sensed I was getting close." Kyi turned back to discover Locke studying her with a strange intensity. "It was clever to get into a vampire lair. It took me days to discover where she'd gone. And even longer to find a way inside."

His eyes flared with anger. "Are you saying that she allowed a troll to maul her and then crawled to a location where I would find her and potentially decide to take her into Leonidas's lair?"

Kyi swallowed a sigh. Her mother had many talents. A mysterious ability to extend her life. Traveling between dimensions. And manipulating the minds of demons. A rare power that would be a death-sentence if she didn't remain hidden most of the time.

"I'm saying she saw you coming and injured herself before collapsing in a spot that you would be sure to find her," she told him.

"No demon, no matter how desperate, would wound themselves like that."

"They would if it wasn't actually their body."

He scowled, appearing more impatient than troubled by her revelation. "Not her body? Have you been into the nectar?"

"The nymph who you were protecting wasn't…" The words dried on her lips as she noticed the pain that darkened his eyes. The feelings he'd had for Xuria had been magically induced, but they'd felt real to him.

"Beautiful? Enchanting? Utterly fascinating?"

Weirdly his words struck a nerve. As if she was…what? Not jealous. Of course not. Just annoyed, she assured herself. She didn't have time for this nonsense.

"Dead."

He stared at her with those stunning eyes, as if waiting for the joke. "Dead?"

"Yes."

A current of electricity crawled over her body, as if she was standing too close to a thunderstorm. It wasn't the first time she'd felt the sizzle since Locke had stepped from the shadows. It wasn't painful. In fact…

"As an unquestionable expert on the walking dead, I can assure you that she was very much alive." He thankfully interrupted her perilous thoughts.

Kyi grimly focused on convincing the male that he'd been tricked. "Her heart was beating and blood flowed through her veins."

"And she was warm," he added. "Gloriously warm. Especially when she was crying out my name."

"Yeah, I don't need any gory details."

The pain faded from his remarkable eyes, replaced by something dark and hungry.

"The dead are cold," he murmured, stepping close enough to the bars that he must have felt the poison leeching into his skin from the silver. "Open the door and I'll give you a demonstration."

She took an instinctive step back, unable to control the renegade heat that swirled through her body or the scent of desire that perfumed the air.

"Thanks, but no thanks," she snapped. Locke smiled with a flash of his fangs. It was a blatant taunt that revealed he could easily sense her fascination. Kyi sniffed, refusing to give him the satisfaction of trying to deny her awareness. What was the point? They both knew he was stirring up all sorts of yummy sensations. "The nymph's body was still functioning, but she'd been infected by the spirit of a sorceress," she informed him in tart tones.

"Yeah, right. I thought only humans enjoyed fairy tales," he mocked.

"You don't believe a sorceress could gain command of a nymph?"

He shrugged. "I have no idea. But I do know that I would have sensed that the nymph was under compulsion."

"It wasn't compulsion." Kyi shuddered. It was one thing to coerce a creature to obey commands. But her mother had once been human, which meant her body had disintegrated eons ago. The only thing left was her spirit. An essence of pure evil. "The poor creature's mind was crushed by a spell before Xuria entered the body. There was nothing left of the nymph beyond the hollow shell that the sorceress used to move around this dimension."

He was shaking his head before she ever finished speaking. "Impossible."

"I thought vampires couldn't sense magic?"

"We can't."

"Then why do you say it's impossible?"

"Because she was my mate."

Mate? Xuria had convinced this male that they were destined to be eternally bonded? The thought once again touched a raw nerve.

"No." Annoyed with her reaction, her voice was sharper than she'd intended. "She wasn't your mate."

"Ah. Of course not." His jaw tightened, as if he was gritting his fangs. "According to you she was the corpse of a nymph that somehow managed to inflict gruesome injuries on her dead body and was only using me to hide from you."

"You forgot the infected by a sorceress part," Kyi insisted. "She used a spell to bewitch you into believing she was your mate."

"Impossible."

She made a sound of impatience. Was Locke always this stubborn? Or was he just being an ass because she'd trapped him in the cage?

She was guessing the ass theory.

"You're fond of that word," she muttered.

"Hocus pocus doesn't work on a vampire."

Okay. Enough was enough. She'd tried to convince this male that he'd been tricked by Xuria. If he wanted to stick his head in the proverbial sand, then she hoped he choked on it.

Tossing her hands in the air, she turned away from the cage. Let him rot in there.

"Tell yourself whatever lets you sleep," she growled, heading toward the nearby cottage.

"Where are you going?" he called out.

"To kill my mother."

* * * *

Troy was in a mood.

Who could blame him? He'd gone from the luxurious comfort of the mer-folk castle to a dark, cramped alley in the backstreets of London. And since it was December, he was being pelted with a freezing rain that clung to his long braid and the faux leopard-skin cloak he'd had the sense to wrap around him. As an imp he could modulate his body temperature, but the effort pissed him off. He should be surrounded by warm opulence, not shivering in a dank alley.

Plus, he was an imp who'd spent several centuries flitting from one place to another, like a butterfly on steroids. He never let anything tie him down. Not family. Not friends. Not business.

Nothing was more important than his freedom.

So how the hell had he allowed himself to be marked by a nymph he didn't know?

"Levet," he groused.

If there was any fairness in the world, that idiotic creature would have been standing in the cold, not Troy. The gargoyle was the one who wanted to help the vampires avoid a rebellion. Troy personally couldn't care less if the bloodsuckers decided to destroy one another. Hell, he'd hold their beer while they did it.

But the world wasn't fair, and he was stuck in this place waiting for… actually he had no idea what he was waiting for. That only made it worse.

His dark thoughts were interrupted as magic sizzled through the air. Troy tilted back his head to study the brick buildings that surrounded the alley, not surprised to find that the roofs were suddenly lined with nymph warriors. Each soldier was clothed in a black uniform with gold trim and each one was currently pointing an arrow at his heart.

At the same time, a portal opened directly in front of him and a female stepped out.

Troy hissed. He'd seen Cleo before, when she'd helped them follow the treacherous vampire. But she possessed the sort of beauty that smacked a male in the face. It wasn't just the dark, glossy curls that framed her pale face or the eyes that were more cognac than gold; it was her vibrant sensuality and commanding presence that captured his attention.

She stepped forward, her long black-and-gold gown that matched the warriors' uniforms brushing the damp cobblestones, while the outrageous emerald that hung around her neck glowed in the darkness.

"You took your time," she chided.

Troy scowled. "Hey, you're lucky I came at all. I—"

"Hush."

Troy widened his eyes at the interruption. He wasn't accustomed to being treated as a servant.

"Rude."

Cleo glanced over her shoulder as a tall male nymph stepped out of the portal behind her. He was nearly as tall as Troy, with long golden hair and pale eyes. His uniform was black like the others, but it had a lot more gold splattered over the silken material, on the collar, on the cuffs, even on the hem of his pants.

Did that mean he was some sort of officer? Or did he just happen to have an abundance of gold thread hanging around he wanted to get rid of? The question was answered when Cleo waved an imperious hand toward him.

"Prepare the warriors, Llewen."

Llewen bent his head in a gesture of respect before silently jogging toward the back of the alley. He released a high-pitched whistle and in one motion, the gathered soldiers dropped from the rooftops. Next the male turned toward the wall and laid his hand against the worn bricks. There was a prickle of magic before a large portal opened. One by one, the uniformed servants darted through the opening and disappeared from view.

Troy glanced back at Cleo, who was watching him like a hawk eying its prey. A shiver raced through him. He was over six foot with the muscles of a linebacker, not to mention the fact he possessed powerful magic. He was usually the hawk, not the prey.

"Prepare the warriors for what?"

"We have a mission."

"What mission?"

Cleo smiled. The sight was more terrifying than her frown. "You're here to serve, not to ask questions."

Serve? Troy leaned forward. He was a prince, not one of her stooges. "I'll stop the questions when I get some answers, sweetness."

Cleo stepped forward, tapping the back of his hand. "Do you see this?"

Troy glanced down at the black crow etched into his flesh. Once he'd arrived in London the pain had eased, but he could still feel a faint throb, as if waiting to punish him for some misdeed.

"Hard to miss," he said, his tone tart. "It looks like I drank too much nectar and ended up in a cheap human tattoo shop. Couldn't you at least have made it a swan or an eagle?"

The sweet scent of figs filled the air. "This is your marker. It means that you are in debt to me."

"Yeah, I got that."

"Your debt includes obeying me." She brushed her fingers over the crow, sending sharp bursts of pain through Troy's arm. "Without question."

He gritted his teeth, refusing to back down. "No."

"Tread carefully imp." She intensified the painful jolts that moved up Troy's arm and into his chest, as if she was threatening to stop his heart.

"I might have unwittingly agreed to the debt, but that doesn't mean you own me body and soul," he grated through his clenched teeth.

"Mmm." The pain abruptly disappeared as she allowed her hand to wiggle through the opening of his cloak to touch his broad chest. "That provokes all sorts of delicious possibilities doesn't it, my prince? What do you suppose I would do with your body?"

A combination of lingering discomfort and erotic pleasure swirled through Troy. He didn't know if he liked it, but he readily hardened with anticipation.

"I have a few suggestions."

She used the tip of her finger to circle his flat nipple, sending delicious pleasure along the same path of the earlier pain.

"I bet you do."

Troy stepped back. He wasn't stupid. This female could easily become a destructive addiction if he wasn't careful.

"But my soul stays my own."

Something that might have been surprise darkened her eyes. Obviously she expected him to melt in a puddle of desire. Or maybe become another one of her devoted servants.

Never gonna happen.

With a sniff she turned to stroll toward the end of the alley. "Keep your soul. I only have need of your blood," she informed him, glancing over her shoulder. "And don't ever call me sweetness again."

Troy grimaced as the female disappeared through the portal.

"My blood?" he muttered, reluctantly following in her wake. "Shit, that can't be good."

Chapter 4

It took Locke nearly twenty minutes to escape the cell. The electrical currents he could draw from the air were capable of tremendous heat, but he could only use them in short bursts. Softening the metal around the lock took more time and energy than he wanted to exert, but eventually he managed to kick open the door.

He took a few more minutes to search the grove and to make several circles around the cottage before he slipped inside. He might not be able to detect magic, but he wanted to make sure there was no one lurking around.

When he was confident that the nymph was alone, he made his way through the small living room that was filled with the soft, cushy furniture and pretty doodads that females seemed to enjoy. Then he halted at the door leading to the kitchen.

He couldn't see Kyi, but he could smell her. Only now the rich scent of bougainvillea was laced with fresh herbs. Sage, thyme, and marjoram. It was an intensely compelling combination that lured him through the open door and into the shadowed darkness.

He had a vague impression of an open-beam ceiling and wooden cabinets that lined the edge of the room. His attention was focused on the female kneeling in the center of the flagstone floor.

She was wearing the same flowing sundress, but her hair had been pulled into a tight braid and her feet were bare. At the moment she was bent over a shallow ceramic dish that was filled with water.

Locke's fangs lengthened, throbbing with an insistent need. He told himself it was his fierce desire for revenge. He'd imagined ripping out her throat for the past century, hadn't he? But that didn't explain the hunger that jolted through him as his gaze lingered on the smooth curve of her exposed neck.

The image of grabbing that braid to tilt her head to the side so he could sink his fangs deep into her throat…

"Gotcha."

Kyi's low voice jerked him out of his distracted fantasy, and for a horrified second he feared that he'd once again been caught off guard. Twice in a row? He'd have to turn in his vampire card.

But thankfully, no cages fell on his head, and the floor didn't disappear from beneath his feet. Plus, the nymph never lifted her head from the bowl. He was guessing that she was speaking to herself.

Strolling forward, he waited until he was just inches away from her before he spoke.

"No, I got you."

With a loud gasp, Kyi jerked her head up, her eyes wide with fear. Obviously her concentration on the bowl had been so focused she had no idea she was no longer alone in the cottage. Once she realized who'd managed to sneak up on her, however, the fear was replaced with annoyance.

"You again?" she groused. "How did you get out of the cage?"

He arched a brow. Most fey would be screeching in terror to be alone with a vampire.

"You're not the only one with unexpected skills," he assured her, lunging forward with blinding speed as she lifted her arm to create a portal. "Not this time, female," he growled, kneeling next to her on the flagstones. "You're not going anywhere."

Frustration tightened her delicate features. "I told you the truth. What do you want from me?"

"As if I would ever trust a word coming out of your mouth."

"You want to be reunited with your mate?" she abruptly demanded. "I'll take you to her."

"She's dead." Locke braced himself for the pain at the mention of his mate. There was a faint twinge, but it was lost beneath the surge of anger.

Why wouldn't this female just admit the truth?

"Look." Kyi pointed toward the bowl.

Grudgingly, Locke turned his attention to the ceramic vessel, not surprised to discover an image shimmering on top of the water. Some fey creatures possessed the rare ability to scry. He didn't know much about the process beyond the fact they could magically spy on another demon. And that they always used a bowl of water.

He half expected to see the golden-haired nymph who'd been the center of his world for such a short time. Kyi was clearly attempting to trick him into believing his mate was still alive. Instead he caught sight of a moss sprite with ripples of bronze hair that cascaded down her back and the dewy freshness of youth. She was short and lushly curved beneath her green tunic and loose silk pants. When she smiled, deep dimples dinted her rosy cheeks. Even in the distorted image shimmering on top of the water she appeared unbearably innocent.

"Why does everyone assume I'm senile?" he snapped. "You could have at least tried to make her look like my mate."

"Why would I do that?" she sounded genuinely bewildered.

"So I don't rip out your throat."

He sensed her stiffen at his threat, but she didn't move away. Just the opposite. She leaned forward to touch the charm that he'd placed around his neck. He didn't know exactly why he'd done it, considering the trinket belonged to his enemy. It had been more instinct than rational thought.

"I could easily have taken this back and disappeared while you were in the cage. You would never have found me," she reminded him. Then, before he could assure her that there was nowhere in the world she could hide that he wouldn't find her, she once again pointed at the bowl. "She doesn't look like your mate because the nymph she'd infested is well and truly dead." She twisted her hand and the female in the water turned her head, almost as if being compelled by magic. "Look closer."

Locke frowned, but before he could insist she was lying, he noticed the pale, eerily white eyes.

Eyes that he'd only seen once before.

Baffled, his gaze slid down to her lush body, not sure what he was searching for until he caught sight of the distinctive tattoo that encircled her wrist. It looked like a series of small, interlocking circles with flames in the center.

Locke felt as if he'd just taken a physical blow. Was it true? Had he somehow been bewitched by a damned sorceress? It seemed impossible to believe, but there was no denying that those eyes were not just similar. They were exactly the same.

A growl rumbled in his chest. The thought was worse than believing his mate had been murdered, not to mention embarrassing as hell. Styx and the other Ravens would never let him live it down.

Locke squashed the stupid thought. He no longer had any interest in Styx or any other vampire. All that mattered was his driving need for revenge.

If Kyi was telling the truth, then he intended to hunt down the sorceress and destroy her.

"Fine." The word came out as a curse. "Tell me about Xuria. Or whoever the hell she is."

Kyi settled on the flagstones, the dress flowing around her like the petals of a flower.

"Xuria is her sorceress name," she explained. "I don't know what she used when she was a human."

"You keep referring to her as a sorceress. Is that different from a witch?"

"Yes." She didn't look surprised that he was clueless about human magic-users. Vampires avoided them like the plague. "Witches use spells that they create out of the natural magic that surrounds us." She waved her hand. "The earth, air, water, and fire."

Locke grimaced. "You make them sound harmless."

"Never," she denied in sharp tones. "Witches can be dangerously powerful. Especially when they gather as a coven. But whether they use magic for good or bad, it's at least untainted."

"And a sorceress?"

"A wizard or sorceress tap into powers from spirits. Usually evil spirits from the netherworld. They pervert the magic."

As far as Locke was concerned all magic was a perversion, but he wasn't there to debate the issue.

"What does she have to do with your mother?" he asked.

"She *is* my mother."

Locke stared at her in silent disbelief. He'd endured one shock after another. First the potential revelation that his mate wasn't dead. Next the horrifying possibility that she was a sorceress who'd enchanted him with her evil magic. And now this.

It was one shock too many. His brain simply refused to accept what she was telling him.

"Are you listening?" Kyi finally demanded.

"Xuria is your mother," he muttered, the words harsh enough to make her flinch.

"Humans aren't the only ones with dysfunctional families."

"No shit." Locke reached up to touch the star-shaped scar on the side of his neck. He could write the book on dysfunctional families. He'd been sired by Gunnar, a psychopathic vampire who tortured his children to relieve his boredom. The bastard would still be wreaking havoc if Locke hadn't stuck a silver dagger through his heart. "Obviously you aren't close to mommy dearest."

Her jaw tightened. "I spent my childhood with my father's tribe on Mount Olympus. All I knew about my mother was that she was a sorceress and that she was desperate for immortality."

"Not an uncommon desire for humans."

"According to my father, Xuria had acquired the power and wealth to extend her life, but that wasn't enough for her. She wanted more."

Locke recalled his brief time with the female. He sensed a smoldering hunger that burned deep inside her, like an unquenchable fire. He'd assumed it had to do with her desire for him. Despite his earlier taunting, he hadn't actually had sex with Xuria. She'd been too injured in the beginning and once he'd sensed that she was his mate, he'd wanted to wait until the formal mating ceremony.

At the time it'd been agonizing to leash his desire. Now sheer relief blasted through him. That was the only thing that would make this situation even more hideous.

"What did she do?"

"She made a bargain with my father."

Locke arched a brow. "Only a fool bargains with the fey."

She scowled, as if offended. Most fey took great pride in their ability to cheat, manipulate, and charm fortunes away from the unwary.

"My father was an honorable male," she said, her words more forceful than necessary. "Unlike my treacherous mother."

"What was the bargain?"

"My father desired a child."

"There's a simple solution for that." Locke deliberately allowed his gaze to lower to her slender body outlined by the light silk dress. "At least for fey creatures."

She glanced down at the bowl, using her thick fringe of lashes to hide her eyes from his gaze. Was she shy? No. It had to be an act. Like mother, like daughter.

"He wanted a baby with Xuria," she said.

Locke straightened, taking a step away from Kyi. Her warm, exotic scent was more distracting than he wanted to admit.

"Why taint his child with human blood?"

"The magic."

"Nymphs have magic."

Kyi rose to her feet as well, sending him a jaundiced glance. "Our tribe had been terrorized by a local clan of vampires. They raided our village, plundered our nectar, and terrorized our children. He hoped that a nymph capable of creating human spells would drive the leeches away."

Locke shrugged. Not that long ago his people had been savage creatures who slaughtered without mercy. Including each other. It'd been the former Anasso who'd set out to civilize the vampires.

He'd been semi-successful in his efforts.

"And what did your mother get out of the deal?" he asked.

"A starlyte crystal."

Locke searched his memory. After a couple thousand years of existence it was stuffed to the max with tidbits of information. At last he shook his head.

"I don't know what that is."

"A rare object that was given to my tribe by the Chatri," she told him.

Ah. Locke recognized the name of the pure-blooded ancestors of the fey. They'd disappeared from this world eons ago, although one of their females had returned to mate with Cyn, the clan chief of Ireland.

"What does it do?"

"For my people it was a symbol that they were favored by the Elders."

"That's it? No special magic?" She shook her head. "Not even fireworks?" he demanded.

"It was an honor bestowed on the tribe."

Locke rolled his eyes at her pious tones. Royalty made a habit of handing out worthless baubles and convincing their people it was some great prize.

"Sounds like a fancy doorstop to me."

"In some ways, I suppose," she grudgingly agreed. "But it also had the power to offer immortality to humans."

Locke considered her words. It made sense that her father was desperate to trade a ceremonial stone for the hope of ending the conflict with the vampires. And any human would be willing to sell their soul for immortality. His brows snapped together as he was struck by a sudden realization.

"Wait. I thought you said Xuria was a spirit."

"She is." Kyi's lips twisted. "The magic didn't protect her body, but it allowed her to preserve her soul inside."

"That sounds...inconvenient."

"I'm not sure my mother fully understood she would be incorporeal when she accepted the bargain." Kyi's lips twisted into a grim smile. Obviously she took pleasure in the idea that Xuria had come out the loser.

"Always read the fine details in a contract," Locke said dryly. "Especially with the fey."

Outside the cottage an owl hooted, as if a reminder that time was passing. Kyi glanced toward the dark window, suddenly looking impatient to be done with the conversation.

"To make a long story short, my mother gave birth to twins that she handed over to my father in exchange for the crystal."

"That's when you decided to kill her?"

She jerked her head back to send him a baffled glance. "Of course not. I was surrounded by my tribe; I didn't need a mother."

"Then what happened?"

"Xuria returned when I was still a small child." Kyi wrapped her arms around her waist, her eyes darkening with pain at the memory. "She destroyed our village with a powerful spell and we all fled. My father tried to take Cleo and me to the safety of the tunnels built deep in the mountain, but my mother cut us off in a thick grove."

Locke felt an odd pang of regret at forcing her to relive an obviously traumatic moment.

"I'm guessing she wasn't there for a family reunion?"

"I don't know why she came back. Maybe she'd discovered her body was still aging. Or maybe she's just a bitch." She shrugged. "But my father assumed that she was there to kill him. He hid me and my sister in a tree and tried to lead her away."

There was an aching loss in her voice that warned Locke what had happened. "She didn't follow?"

"No. She sent a deadly spell toward the tree. If my father hadn't leaped in the path of the magic we would have been dead."

"Your father?"

"The spell destroyed him." She bent her head, as if burdened by the full weight of her grief. Being immortal had endless benefits, but there were a few downsides. One of them was mourning loved ones for all eternity. "But he saved us."

"How?"

"The battle attracted the attention of the local dryads, who weren't happy that my mother nearly destroyed one of their beloved trees." Her hand lifted to her throat, instinctively searching for the tree-shaped charm that was currently hanging around his throat. She grimaced, allowing her hand to drop. "They managed to run my mother off and took me and Cleo into their tribe."

"What happened to your mother?"

"She disappeared and I forgot about her." Kyi paused, perhaps tucking away her ancient grief. Then, stiffening her spine, she met his gaze squarely. "Until she returned a hundred years ago. I was asleep in my cottage when she attacked. If I hadn't wakened at the last second she would have struck an iron dagger in my back." She shivered, perhaps from her near-death experience, but more likely from the icy tingles that swirled through the air. Locke didn't know why the thought of Kyi being attacked infuriated him, but he couldn't control his burst of anger. "That's when I decided to kill her," she at last continued, sending him a jaundiced glare. "But some annoying vampire interfered."

Chapter 5

Kyi studied Locke's bold Viking face. She told herself that she was searching for signs of remorse, but that didn't explain why her gaze traced each savagely perfect feature. The wide brow, the bold nose, the sharply chiseled cheekbones, and the unexpectedly full lips. It was a noble face, the sort that was carved out of wood and put on the helm of marauding ships. Even his eyes were captivating. The pale blue the color of a Nordic sky and rimmed with a shimmering gold.

Gorgeous. Lethally sensuous. But not a trace of remorse in sight.

Locke shrugged. "Why did she return?"

"I'm not sure," Kyi forced herself to respond. She hated talking about the female who'd given birth to her. The ruthless bitch had not only tried to kill Kyi more than once, but she'd also destroyed Kyi's father. A male that she'd adored with all her heart. "After she abandoned the nymph's body in the vampire lair, she disappeared again. I couldn't find any trace of her." Kyi deliberately reminded the vampire that he'd been beguiled by a sorceress. "I'm guessing she returned to her private dimension."

His lips flattened, but he didn't insist that she'd murdered his poor mate. Progress.

"Why do you suspect that she was back?"

"The trees warned me."

"The trees?"

A portion of her tension eased as she glanced toward the window that offered a view of towering cypresses. Her foster family had instilled a deep love for nature, and more importantly, trained her to tap into the magic of the trees. The woods that surrounded her cottage were connected to her in a way that went beyond a devoted gardener. They spoke to her as if they were old friends.

"I was raised by dryads." She pointedly glanced toward the charm that laid against his broad chest. "After the last attack I decided I needed better protection. I've been tending this grove for a century. Their magic keeps constant guard."

"Not to mention a hidden cage dangling midair." There was a tartness in his tone that warned he was still annoyed he'd been led into a trap.

She shrugged. "As I said, a female can't be too careful."

"Did the trees keep Xuria out?"

She shook her head. She'd once again been sleeping in her bed when her mother tried to attack. She would no doubt be dead if she hadn't created an early warning system.

"No, but they whispered she was trying to enter the grove," she told her companion. "She must have sensed that I'd been alerted to her presence because she fled. By the time I tried to follow, she'd disappeared again." At the time, she'd been caught between relief that she'd avoided an iron dagger in the back and smoldering frustration that Xuria had managed to escape. She'd been on the point of returning to the safety of her cottage when she'd caught sight of something wrapped around a nearby branch. "But she did leave behind a present," she continued.

"What?"

"A strand of hair."

He appeared less than impressed. "That's it?"

She clicked her tongue. Vampires were like ostriches when it came to magic. They couldn't use or sense it, so they stuck their heads in the sand and pretended that it didn't exist.

"I can use the hair to scry." She nodded toward the bowl on the floor. "Unfortunately I didn't have the supplies I needed. I had to travel away from my grove to collect them."

"That must have been when the necklace was triggered," he said.

Kyi felt a stab of self-disgust. Since Xuria was a spirit, Kyi could only scry the body that her mother was currently invading. That meant if she abandoned her current host, Kyi would once again lose track of her.

The knowledge had sent her rushing to the nearest nymph tribe to bargain for the magically enhanced bowl and a sprinkle of fairy dust to set the spell. Unlike some fey creatures, her talent for scrying was sketchy at best. She needed an extra *umph* to lock on her target.

In her haste, she hadn't bothered to wrap herself in the usual layers of magic that protected her from being detected. Sloppy.

In her defense, she'd only been worried about her mother finding her. It'd never occurred to her that Locke was hunting her after a hundred years. Stubborn leech. She sent him an accusing glare.

"Which means I am once again interrupted by an annoying vampire."

He flicked a golden brow upward, but once again he showed no guilt for having disturbing her. Taking a step toward the bowl, he studied the image floating on top of the water.

"Can you see where Xuria is?"

"Do you believe me?"

His features hardened. "I think it's possible the nymph lied to me." The air crackled with electricity. "It's even more possible you're the one lying to me. And until I discover the truth, I'm not letting you out of my sight."

Kyi trembled. It had to be irritation. How much precious time had she wasted trying to convince the stubborn leech that Xuria was his enemy? But there was a sizzling of excitement that had nothing to do with anger. And lots to do with his threat of not letting her out of his sight.

"You just can't admit you were wrong, can you?" she grumbled, not sure if she was more annoyed with him or herself.

"Because I'm never wrong."

"Leeches are—"

The insult died on her lips as Locke moved with blinding speed to stand directly in front of her. She sucked in a startled breath, drenched in his icy scent. Copper and lightning. Amazing.

"Careful, female," he growled. "Whether I allow you to live or die is still to be determined."

She should have been terrified. No nymph could survive a vampire attack. Not in a fair fight. But she'd learned from her mother. She was more than willing to use dirty sorceress tricks when necessary.

"Why do you continue to assume I'm helpless?" she asked in overly sweet tones, reaching into the pocket of her dress.

She always had a few ingredients hidden. Cloves, rosemary, thyme, and sea salt. They'd been combined to form a simple defensive spell that repelled an attacker, although it didn't cause any lasting damage. Even in her private grove there was the potential for danger. A wild animal, a stray human, or an unwelcomed vampire.

Grasping the linen sachet that contained the ingredients, she tossed it toward Locke. His eyes widened before he was flying backward to smack against the far wall. Kyi had precisely one second to appreciate the sight of him bouncing off the cabinets to land on his backside. In the blink of an eye he was once again in front of her, leaning down until they were nose to nose.

"I don't know if you're clueless or suicidal," he snarled.

Kyi hissed as his power danced over her bare skin. It felt like she was standing in the middle of a raging thunderstorm.

"What I am is busy," she forced herself to mutter. "You want to speak to Xuria, then stop wasting my time so I can follow her."

His eyes darkened with an undefinable emotion. "Definitely suicidal."

Parting her lips to order him to back off, Kyi was shocked into silence as his arm wrapped around her waist and she was hauled tight against his body. At the same time, he captured her lips in a kiss that stole her breath.

Electricity danced over her skin, lifting the hair on her nape and sending a thousand pinpricks of bliss darting through her body. The taste of him hit her tongue, a rich male nectar that stirred a hunger in the very depths of her being.

Damn her years of celibacy, she silently cursed. One kiss and she was ready to dissolve into a puddle of willing goo.

She lifted her hands to press against his chest, but along the way they forgot what they were supposed to do. Rather than pushing, they skimmed over the muscles that clenched and rippled at her touch.

Oh yum.

He was hard and chiseled and so damned sexy it made her ache. Leaning forward, she was about to slip her hands beneath Locke's leather jacket to expand her exploration when the press of his fangs against her lower lip jerked her out of her sensual haze.

It wasn't the small pain. That was insanely erotic. And it wasn't the warning that the male currently enflaming her passions was a leech. She didn't have any prejudices against vampires.

No, it was the reminder that she was melting beneath the touch of her enemy.

Muttering a swear word, she shoved him away. "Locke."

His eyes smoldered, his fangs shimmering with a snowy whiteness in the glow from the fairy lights. For a tense moment they simply stared at one another, the hunger between them pulsing through the air.

Then, with a sharp motion, he turned toward the bowl. "Find her," he commanded.

* * * *

Troy stepped out of the portal, surprised to find himself on a high cliff made of a pale golden limestone. The moonlight spilled over a crescent-shaped bay that shimmered in brilliant shades of green and turquoise. In the distance he could see the glow of a human town, and overhead the expansive sky was edged with the pastel promise of dawn.

As a hedonistic imp who adored bright lights and endless sources of entertainment, Troy rarely took the opportunity to appreciate the beauty of nature. Who wanted to stare at a bunch of trees or empty meadows? But this…

It was breathtaking.

Swiveling his head, he discovered Cleo standing at his side. Unlike him, she wasn't admiring the view. Her attention was focused on her warriors, who were forming a precise circle around them. Troy was briefly confused. Were they expecting to be attacked?

Then there was a pungent scent of figs before the warriors released a surge of power. Troy arched his brows as a protective shield settled around them like a shimmering dome. The magic would keep them concealed from any searching eyes.

"Where are we?" he demanded. "And why are we hiding?"

"Cyprus," her voice was clipped, as if she was on edge. "Near the gateway that Xuria uses to enter her private dimension."

Troy glanced around, unable to see any portal. "What's a Xuria?"

"An…acquaintance."

Troy sent the nymph a suspicious glance. "If Xuria's an acquaintance, then why are we hiding behind this barrier?"

"Because she will destroy us if she realizes we're here."

"Why?"

Cleo sent him a fierce glare. "Do you ever shut up? If I wanted a chatterbox with me I would have brought Levet."

"Yeesh, I thought my mom was a bitch," Troy muttered, although that wasn't entirely true.

His mother could be aloof and demanding and cunning. A typical imp. It was the fact that she was a queen that bothered him. She had an endless list of utterly unreasonable demands she expected of him. All of them more tedious than the last.

He was supposed to wear clothing that matched the royal house colors, a boring black and white. Bleh. He was supposed to attend formal dinners and be close at hand to tend to his mother's every need. He was supposed to charm diplomats from other tribes. He was supposed to train to become the leader of their army.

Above all, he was supposed to mate and produce a bevy of tiny Troys.

He shuddered, shoving aside the depressing thought as he concentrated on the female standing next to him.

"Why would your acquaintance try to kill us?"

"I don't know. She's been trying to murder me since I was a child." An unnervingly cruel smile curved her lips. "Thankfully I'm not very easy to kill."

Troy believed her. This female had maintained her territory in a city belonging to Victor, the vampire clan chief of London. She was not only ruthless, but a survivor.

"If she's so homicidal then why aren't we safely hidden in your lair?" Troy asked.

Cleo's gaze was locked on the beach below them. Troy didn't know what she was staring at. All he could see was golden sand and the opening to a cave etched into the limestone cliff.

"She has something I want."

"What?"

The nymph ignored his question as she tilted back her head and closed her eyes. She was obviously sensing something. But what?

"Llewen, be ready," she sharply commanded.

Troy leaned forward, studying the empty beach. At last a familiar tingle warned that a portal was about to open. Expecting the acquaintance to be another nymph, Troy was caught off guard when a moss sprite with a mane of bronze hair stepped onto the golden sand.

"That's Xuria?" he asked, his confusion only deepening at the unmistakable tang of human magic.

"Yes."

"I see a moss sprite, but I sense...sorceress."

"Xuria has the ability to invade host bodies and control them for a limited amount of time."

Troy grimaced. He'd had a few dealings with sorceresses. Once when he'd been captured in a magical net and had been forced to barter his favorite enchanted crystal to be released. And once when a sorceress had moved into the neighborhood where he'd opened a male strip club with Sophia, a pureblooded Were. They'd eventually handed over an obscene fortune to convince her to relocate. What choice did they have? None of their customers were willing to cross the path of a sorceress. That always ended badly. At least for the demon.

He stared down at the tiny female who had halted to turn back toward the portal.

"Host? Like inviting someone over for an afternoon tea party?" he asked.

"No, like crushing their mind and leaving them an empty husk."

"Charming." Troy's nose flared, his senses suddenly tingling with alarm. "Why do I smell salt?" His question was answered as a half dozen mer-folk appeared out of the portal. They were dressed as humans in jeans and sweaters, with their golden hair pulled into braids as if to disguise the blue tints. Nothing unusual in that. But he'd never seen such a blank expression on their delicate faces. As if they were asleep as they shuffled forward. "Why are the mer-folk with a sorceress?" he muttered his confusion out loud.

"When Xuria returns to this world she gathers fey creatures and herds them through the gateway."

"Why?"

"She uses them as slaves."

Her voice was deliberately vague, as if she wasn't revealing all she knew about the fate awaiting the poor mer-folk. Although, becoming slaves was bad enough as far as Troy was concerned.

"Seriously?" Troy hissed in horror. "Are you here to free them?"

"Absolutely not."

"But—"

Cleo's hand grabbed his arm with the speed of a striking snake. "We are here to enter the private dimension so I can get what I need from Xuria," she warned, her fingers tightening to dig painfully into Troy's flesh. "Nothing else."

He scowled, oddly disappointed. Did he actually expect the female to reveal a compassion hidden beneath her merciless exterior? Stupid of him. Still, he wasn't going to give in without a fight.

"You can't let them be enslaved," he insisted.

Her nails dug through the material of his cloak, stabbing into his skin until he could feel blood flowing down his arm.

"What do I care? They're not my people."

He clenched his teeth as she used the mark on the back of his hand to amp up the pain.

"Because it's indecent."

Cleo scowled, as if puzzled by his concern. Then, clearly sensing that her punishment wasn't working, she eased her grip and allowed her sumptuous fig scent to wrap around him.

"We're demons." She leaned forward, pressing the plush softness of her breasts against his arm. Heat swirled through Troy. "We're supposed to be indecent."

The sensual web she was weaving around him was a tangible force. It was as if she'd entered his mind, painting images of her luscious curves stretched on the sandy beach with him poised above her. Troy groaned. He wanted nothing more than to wrap his arms around her and drown in her sweet temptation. But another image thankfully refused to be dismissed.

The blank faces of the mer-folk who had no idea they were being led to their doom.

"We have to do something," he managed to insist in harsh tones.

The pain returned, slamming into Troy with enough force to send him to his knees. She grabbed his braid, yanking back his head to meet her malevolent glare.

"What we're going to do is remain hidden behind the shield until I give the command to enter the gateway," she informed him, the words slow and precise as if to ensure there were no misunderstandings. "If you attract attention to our position in any way I will make sure that you regret your decision for a very, very long time. Do you understand?"

"Yeah. I understand," Troy conceded defeat.

What else could he do? There was no doubt this female would destroy him if he didn't follow her orders.

Of course, that didn't mean that he couldn't find someone else to rescue the mer-folk.

Closing his eyes as if battling back the pain, Troy reached out to the one creature capable of hearing his silent voice.

Chapter 6

Levet was busy polishing the tip of his tail as he leaned against the dais. It didn't need the buffing. The appendage possessed a magnificent gloss beneath the glow of the chandeliers. But he'd grown bored with Inga and Rimm's conversation. Who knew that being a queen could be so tedious?

For the past hour the captain of the royal guards had been droning on about replenishing supplies, mapping the hidden tunnels that had recently been used by traitors in an attempt to steal the Tryshu from Inga, and expanding the layers of protection around the nursery. Or at least that was what he thought they were discussing. After the first couple of minutes it all became blah, blah, blah.

Why could they not be enjoying a nice meal in Inga's private chambers? Or better yet, tapping into the power of her mighty Tryshu to create a bubble they could use to float through the water? They did that once and it was glorious. Bounce, bounce, bounce along the bottom of the ocean.

Lost in his daydreams, Levet was distracted when the merman stepped onto the dais to stand next to Inga's throne. The male was wearing his usual uniform that was made from magically enhanced scales that molded to his lean body, and his blond hair with tints of blue was pulled into a long braid. On his side, he had a short trident in a holster.

"I have a list of uniform and weapon inventory as well as the guards' schedule for the next two weeks," he said, placing a stack of papers in Inga's unwilling hands. "Do you wish to review the revised treaties that arrived this morning or—"

"Fah," Levet interrupted. Inga was too polite to halt the pushy merman, but Levet could see in her tightly pinched expression that she was weary of the grindingly boring meeting. Or maybe she had a touch of gas. Either way, Levet was done. "No more, I beg of you, *ma belle*," he pleaded.

Rimm sent him a fierce glare. "These are important matters, gargoyle."

Levet wrinkled his snout. "They are dull matters."

The merman's eyes flashed with an unmistakable warning. "Dull?"

"Tiresome, monotonous, snore-festival," Levet explained.

Inga frowned before snapping her fingers. "Snore-fest," she corrected.

Rimm pinched his lips in a pucker, as if he swallowed something sour. "They might be dull, but they are duties that must be tended to on a regular basis. Unless you prefer to allow the castle to fall into chaos?"

Levet sniffed. "What I want is a royal feast with roasted pig and joyous entertainment, but seemingly that is…" He squiggled his fingers to indicate air quotes. "'Bad taste' at this time. As if those females would recognize good taste if it smacked them in the—"

"That will be all," Inga interrupted Levet's tirade just as he was hitting his stride, her gaze on a scowling Rimm. "We'll finish this later."

The male looked as if he wanted to insist that they continue the meeting, then, glancing toward Levet, he heaved a resigned sigh. Clearly he realized that Levet intended to continue interrupting until he succeeded in distracting Inga from her work.

"Very well."

With a stiff bow the male turned to march from the throne room, closing the door behind him with a restrained bang.

The merman was clearly in a snit.

"Are you going to be a grump forever?" Inga asked in weary tones.

Levet glanced toward her in disbelief. "I am not the grump. Did you not see how your captain shut the door? He was…" Levet's words trailed away as Inga arched a brow. "Perhaps there is a teeny tiny grumpishness," he conceded. "I do not comprehend why you allow yourself to be burdened with all the icky parts of being a queen and never get to enjoy the good parts."

Inga reached up to grab the crown that hung at a lopsided angle on her head. She tossed it carelessly on the ground.

"I'm not sure that there are any good parts."

Levet clicked his tongue. "Of course there are."

"What?"

"The parties."

"I hate parties." Inga shuddered, glancing toward the balcony across the room. It was attached to the ballroom on the upper floor where the formal events were traditionally hosted. "All those people gawking and staring."

Levet could sympathize. He often experienced people pointing and whispering behind his back. He assumed they were admiring his unique beauty. But Inga did not possess his confidence. She would naturally assume they were making fun of her.

"Your treasure trove," he instead suggested. "I have never seen so many priceless gems. Well, perhaps in a dragon's lair," he grudgingly conceded.

"I never go anywhere. And even if I did, the treasure belongs to the mer-folk, not to me," Inga reminded him. "What's the point of money if you can't spend it?"

Levet shrugged. "You can make people bow when you walk past them."

"And know that they would put a knife in my back if it wasn't for the Tryshu."

"What do you enjoy?" Levet demanded. He had a gift for pleasing the females, but Inga was not like the others.

No doubt that was why she fascinated him. But at the same time she made him a tad cray-cray.

"I like painting," Inga told him after she'd considered the question for a few seconds. "And bashing people over the head with my trident."

Levet's lips parted to respond, only to snap closed when a voice echoed through his skull.

"Oh," he breathed.

Inga jumped off the dais, standing next to him with her Tryshu clutched tightly in her hand.

"What's wrong?"

"Do you hear that?"

She frowned. "Hear what?"

Levet heaved a resigned sigh. "I was afraid of that."

"Levet."

He held up a silencing hand. "Troy is in my head." Closing his eyes, Levet concentrated on his connection to the imp. "Get out, you aggravating pest."

"Shut up and listen, gargoyle," Troy growled.

"Jerky jerk-face," Levet muttered.

Troy ignored the insult. "I'm being taken into some weird dimension with Cleo and her merry band of nymphs."

"Are you still complaining about that? I told you, the only way to follow the vampire was to—"

"Shut. Up." Troy rudely commanded. "I need you to get a message to Inga."

Levet grudgingly resisted the urge to slam shut the connection. There was a sharp edge in Troy's voice that warned Levet that this was serious.

Concentrating, he tried to peer into the imp's brain. He could sense urgency, and danger, and something that might have been disappointment. And there was something else. A scent of salt. As if he was standing close to the ocean. Or maybe the sea.

"What message?"

"There's a sorceress named Xuria who is enslaving mer-folk."

Levet sucked in a startled breath. That's why he could smell salt. "Mer-folk?"

"Levet." Inga grabbed the top of his wing. "Is Troy in trouble?"

Levet kept his eyes closed as he answered. "The imp is babbling about some sorceress enslaving mer-folk."

"My people are being enslaved?" Inga lifted Levet off the ground by his wing. "Where?"

Levet didn't struggle against her grasp. Obviously she was upset. "Where are you?" he demanded of Troy.

Troy sounded equally distressed. "Cyprus."

"He says he is at Cyprus." Levet passed along the information.

"Is he planning to rescue them?" Inga demanded.

"Are you—"

"I can't talk now. We're about to leave this dimension," Troy interrupted. "You'll have to deal with the mer-folk."

Levet scowled, but before he could insist that the imp deal with the sorceress, the connection was broken.

Opening his eyes, he sent Inga a regretful glance. "He is gone."

"What about the mer-folk?"

"He was doing nothing." Levet heaved a harsh sigh. "Once again, it is my duty to rescue them."

Inga lowered him to the marble floor, releasing his wing as she straightened with a determined expression.

"*Our* duty."

"How many times must we have this discussion?" Levet's tone was one of regret. Inga hated to be stuck at the castle when the action was happening out in the world. Unfortunately, she was the queen. That meant she had to stay protected behind the layers of magic. "Your place is here with your people."

"Not this time."

Without warning, the ogress turned to stomp toward the door. Her feet slammed so hard each step threatened to crush the marble floor and her neon purple muumuu with green stars billowed around her.

Levet scurried to match her long strides. "Inga, please listen."

"No." Stomp, stomp, stomp. "My warriors have no defense against human magic."

Levet studied the stubborn line of her profile. "And you do?"

"My ogre hide gives me some protection," she said, referring to her thick layer of skin that could deflect a war axe. "Plus I have this." She waved the massive trident. "Nothing can kill me as long as I hold the Tryshu in my hand."

Levet hesitated. "I suppose that's true."

"I'll tell Rimm where we're going and—"

"Wait." Levet flapped his wings to scurry toward a spot directly in front her.

Inga scowled, but thankfully didn't squash him with her impressively large foot.

"What now?" Coming to a halt, she contented herself with a fierce glare.

"Have you considered the fact that you're going to be recognized?" Levet asked.

"Recognized by who?"

Levet spread his arms. "Everyone."

"Why would I be recognized?" Inga appeared genuinely confused. "I spent my childhood as a slave, then five centuries hidden with Lilah in the wetlands of Florida, and the past months down here."

Levet deliberately allowed his gaze to roam from the massive trident to Inga's mighty form covered in the shockingly brilliant gown.

"You're a seven-foot ogress holding the Tryshu," he pointed out in gentle tones. "Who else could you be but the Queen of the Mer-folk?"

"Oh." She furrowed her brow. "I suppose I could leave the Tryshu—"

"*Non*." Levet shuddered at the mere thought of Inga roaming around without the powerful weapon. She had accumulated enemies at a remarkable rate since taking the throne. Not to mention the various mer-folk who refused to accept her as their ruler. They would do anything to kill her. Anything. "That weapon is never to leave your hands."

A growl rumbled in her chest, her eyes flashing crimson. "I'm going to rescue my people. No one is going to stop me. Not even you."

Levet held up his hand, even as he took a covert step to the side. He didn't think that Inga would smush him, but he wasn't willing to take the chance. "I have an idea."

The crimson faded from her eyes to reveal the stunning blue, but her expression was wary.

"No offense, Levet, but your ideas always end up in chaos and flames and occasionally bloodshed."

He made a sound of outrage, then, recalling one or two incidents that had included flames and mayhem, and splatters of blood, he shrugged.

"Fair enough," he conceded. "This one, however, should have only minimum chaos."

"What about the pain and bloodshed part?"

"You cannot deprive me of all my fun."

"Levet."

He held her gaze. "Trust me."

"I do," she said without hesitation.

Levet felt a warm tingle from the tips of his horns to his toes and all the yummy places in between. Now, however, was not the time to savor the sensations.

A shame, really. He would very much enjoy savoring many things with this female.

Swallowing a sigh, Levet led Inga out of the throne room and into the wide corridors covered in marble. It was thankfully early enough that only a handful of the mer-folk were up and about. Not that he was afraid that Inga would be sidetracked by her friends. She frankly didn't have any. But he didn't want to attract the attention of the guards who might tattle to Rimm. The captain had never developed a fondness for Levet. Peculiar. Levet assumed it was a personality defect. In any case, he often interrupted when Levet tried to get Inga alone.

They wound their way down a long staircase and through more hallways until they reached the lower floors where the marble and chandeliers were replaced with barren walls and thick doors.

Avoiding the guardroom and the entrance to the dungeons, Levet chose a rarely used passage to reach the vast armory at last. Once in front of the heavy wooden doors, Levet stepped aside, waiting for Inga. The silver lock needed a key. Or the magic of the Tryshu.

With a frown, Inga pushed open the door. "Are you searching for a weapon? I have several swords and daggers in my private collection."

Levet shook his head, waddling into the center of the cavernous room. Overhead the fairy lights stirred to life. The delicate globes danced and bobbed through the air, spilling light on the countless weapons that were hung along the walls. Swords, pikes, shields, bow and arrows, and the peculiar tridents used by the majority of mer-folk warriors.

"I am searching for Riven's magical artifacts," he told his companion.

Inga arched her brows. "The lethal artifacts that are so dangerous you insisted that I keep them protected with the power of my Tryshu?"

"*Oui.* Those artifacts," Levet readily agreed, confused by the question. Did she have other magical artifacts? If so, he wished to see them AARP. Wait, that wasn't right, was it? ABBA? ASAP?

His rambling thoughts were interrupted by Inga.

"Why do you want Riven's collection of awful things?" she demanded.

Levet crossed the floor that was carved from the seabed, heading toward the narrow opening that was blocked by layers of magic that shimmered in the fairy light.

"There is a ring that will allow us to move through the world unnoticed," he assured his companion.

In two long steps, Inga was standing next to him. "Does it make us invisible?"

"Not exactly."

Inga frowned. "Then *exactly* what does it do?"

"You will see." Levet waved an impatient hand toward the barrier. Inga hesitated, as if debating whether or not to agree to a wild scheme that might end in disaster. Then with a wave of the Tryshu, she stepped into the vault. This was where the most dangerous weapons were stored, which was why only the king or queen had full access to the space.

Levet hurried toward the glass case that surrounded the items collected by the previous King of the Mer-folk. Riven had been pure evil, but he had possessed a talent for gathering powerful artifacts.

Pressing a claw against the glass, he glanced up at Inga. "There it is. The golden ring with the opal."

Inga licked her lips, obviously nervous as she opened the case. "Can I touch it?"

"*Oui*, but do not put it on until we are out of the castle," Levet warned.

"Why?" Inga reached into the case and cautiously plucked the ring off a shelf.

"If Rimm realizes you intend to leave the castle without him there will be hell to purchase."

"Oh. You're right," she conceded, wrinkling her nose. No doubt she was imagining Rimm's furious outrage if she confessed she was off to rescue her people. The Captain of the Royal Guards took his role as her protector very, very seriously. "Maybe I'll leave a note," she suggested.

"Good choice," Levet assured her in dry tones.

Chapter 7

Kyi stepped out of the portal, trying to ignore the vampire who stood directly behind her. She might as well have tried to ignore the nearby waves that crashed against the cliffs, or the stars that were splattered across the velvet sky.

Locke was a force of nature that charged the air with an icy electricity that pulsed around her like a living force. Was it deliberate? A warning? A reminder that he still didn't trust her?

Kyi shivered. Not out of fear, but with a relentless awareness that she couldn't control.

"Is this the spot?" he demanded, glancing around.

They were in the middle of an isolated bay that was framed by turquoise water and golden sand. Behind them were towering limestone cliffs with caves that had been hollowed out by a millennium of salty sea air.

"Approximately." Kyi shrugged. "It's as close as I can get." She turned her head to see his skeptical expression. It made her feel oddly defensive. "Scrying isn't my finest talent."

"No?" He stepped closer, towering over her as a mysterious smile played about his lips. "What is your finest talent?"

The awareness intensified, sending sizzling jolts of pleasure through her. Kyi didn't try to disguise her response to his proximity. How could she? The very air was drenched in her scent of awareness. But she could maintain a veneer of dignity.

"Not being distracted by annoying vampires," she informed him in tart tones.

His smile widened to give a hint of fangs. "You think I'm distracting?"

Trust Locke to take an insult and turn it into a compliment. She narrowed her eyes. "I think you're a pain in the—"

He swooped his head down, cutting off her words by the simple means of a kiss. Not that there was anything simple about the kiss. His lips were cool to the touch, but a heat combusted as soon as their mouths met. Kyi gasped as the sparks danced over her skin, intensifying the pleasure until her toes curled and her hands reached up to grasp his arms.

His fingers skimmed down her back as he spoke against her mouth. "If you can't say anything nice, then you shouldn't say anything at all."

"Fine, if you want me to be silent, I can do that."

He lifted his head, studying her upturned face with a brooding gaze. "I thought I knew exactly what I wanted."

"What's that?"

"Revenge."

Her lips twisted. It was a common reaction to any creature who had the misfortune to cross paths with her mother. The female used, abused, and discarded both humans and demons.

"And now?" she asked.

He cradled her butt in his hands, pulling her close enough to feel the hard thrust of his erection.

"I'm losing track," he murmured.

Her hands started to slide up his arms, relishing the hard muscles as she reached his shoulders. But as she started to press against the solid strength of his body, there was an eerie wail as the wind swirling through the bay echoed through the various caves.

"Let me help." Pressing her hands against his chest, she stepped back. "We're supposed to be searching for Xuria."

Electric pinpricks crawled over her skin, but with a rueful smile, Locke slowly turned to glance around.

"It doesn't take much searching to realize she isn't here."

"She was." Kyi walked toward the burnt spot she could see in the sand. "This is where a portal opened," she said.

Locke tilted his head, as if testing the air. "Moss sprite," he murmured, then he frowned. "And salt?"

It took Kyi a second to recognize what they were smelling. "Mer-folk," she said in surprise. The creatures rarely left the protection of their castle.

Locke appeared equally startled. "Are they helping her?"

"Doubtful. My guess is that she comes to this world to capture fey creatures to use as slaves." She pointed toward the largest opening in the center of the cliffs. "Their trail goes that way."

He narrowed his eyes. "Conveniently located in a cave."

She sent him a puzzled glance. "What's convenient about it?"

"It's perfect for an ambush."

"Stay here if you're afraid." With a shrug, she started walking across the sand.

Predictably, Locke was quickly catching up to her. Males were males, no matter if they were leeches, orcs, or humans.

"No one has doubted my courage. At least no one who's still living." He sent her a dry glance, then tossed her own words back in her face. "But a vampire can't be too careful."

Reaching the cliffs, she waved a hand toward the opening. "Do you want me to go first?"

"I insist on it."

She rolled her eyes, entering the cave. The walls and ceiling were jagged limestone and the floor was packed sand. It no doubt looked exactly the same as any other cave along this coastline. But Kyi didn't miss the scorched line in the sand. She walked to the center of the cave and squatted down.

"This must be the gateway." She forced herself to touch the mark. There was a taint of…evil. That was the only way she could describe the oily imprint left by her mother.

Locke joined her, his nose wrinkling in disgust. "It smells like sulfur."

"My mother's magic." She slowly straightened.

"I didn't smell it near the portal."

"Xuria used the sprite's magic to create the portal," she murmured, turning in a slow circle.

She'd assumed that her mother had used the entrance to return to the protection of her hidden lair. But now that she was standing next to the gateway, she wasn't so sure.

"She can use the power of her…" Locke made a sound of disgust. "Christ, I don't even know what to call them."

"Victims," she suggested, her words distracted.

"She can use the power of her victims?"

Kyi shrugged. It was a question she'd spent centuries pondering, ever since she realized the sorceress could hijack other creature's bodies.

"She seems to be able to manipulate their magic, although I'm not sure how well she can control it," she admitted. "And I suspect that it drains her own powers. When I finally managed to confront her in the vampire's lair, she didn't try to kill me. Obviously, she was too weak to do anything but flee."

He nodded once, no doubt tucking away the information. Like any successful predator, he would want to know as much about his prey as possible.

"What's the difference between a portal and a gateway?"

"A portal is like parting a curtain and stepping through. It leaves no trace of the passage."

"And a gateway?"

She glanced down at the scorched earth in revulsion. Humans weren't intended to travel through the veils. The only way they could do it was to pervert the natural order of the world. "It's a permanent rip between dimensions. It creates a…sort of scar tissue. The damage is never fully healed, which means the gateway is always open."

"Can you follow her?"

It was a question she couldn't answer, mainly because she'd never really considered the possibility of entering Xuria's private lair. Not when she had no idea what magical snares the woman might have waiting for intruders. The thought was enough to make her stomach clench with dread.

No, she'd followed her mother in the hopes she could catch her before she disappeared through the gateway.

A hope she was still clinging to. "I don't need to," she murmured.

"Why not?" In the dim shadows of the cave, his eyes glowed like brilliant sapphires, surrounded by a halo of shimmering gold.

Kyi turned away, refusing to be captivated. She was on the hunt for her mother. Nothing was more important, no matter what her body was trying to tell her.

"The mer-folk went through the opening, but Xuria didn't." She headed toward the entrance of the cave.

"Are you saying that she's still here?"

"It's likely she opened another portal. Probably close to the first one."

He followed behind her, the air sizzling as if he was annoyed by her distraction. "Why would the mer-folk go through the gateway but not her?" He cursed as she came to an abrupt halt and he was forced to leap to the side to avoid tumbling over her. "Kyi?"

"Figs."

Kyi closed her eyes, absorbing the air. She didn't have the acute senses of a Were, or even a leech, but she'd honed her skill at self-preservation. A useful talent considering her mother had been trying to kill her since she was a young child.

"Excuse me?"

"My sister was here." She opened her eyes, unease vibrating through her at the realization that Cleo and a large band of her warriors had passed through here. How had she missed their scent when they first arrived in the bay? They had to have been shielded by some sort of magic. Her thoughts were distracted as she caught the rich scent of fruit. Her brow furrowed. "Along with an imp."

"A regular family reunion," Locke drawled.

A humorless laugh was wrenched from Kyi's lips. "That's the stuff of nightmares."

He studied her for a long moment. "Your mother or your sister?"

"Both." She took another deep breath, doubling back to the scorched spot on the ground. "Cleo went through the gateway with the mer-folk."

"Perhaps she's working with Xuria?" Locke suggested.

"Never." Kyi shook her head in sharp motion. "The only creature who hates my mother more than me is my sister."

"Then maybe your mother captured her and forced her to go through with the mer-folk."

"It's possible," she agreed, although it still didn't feel right. Her mother had the power to capture Cleo, but could she have overpowered the guards as well? It seemed unlikely. She swallowed a frustrated sigh. "A question for later. Right now we need to discover where my mother created the portal she used to leave."

Locke pointed toward the far corner of the cave. "Over there."

Kyi blinked, caught off guard by his ready response. "I thought vampires couldn't sense magic?"

"I can't, but I can smell moss sprite. It's stronger over there, which means she used her magic."

Okay. That made sense. Kyi moved across the packed sand to discover the spot he was pointing to.

"Yes." She could feel the tingle of magic that lingered in the air. It was fresh, as if they'd missed her mother by a few minutes. "Right here."

"Can you follow her?"

"Not through her portal," Kyi conceded, reaching into the pocket of her sundress. "But I have her hair. It will allow me to get in the general area."

He moved to stand beside her. "You say that a lot."

She sent him a sour glare. "You don't have to come with me."

"I told you, Kyi." Without warning Locke was at her side, his arm wrapping around her waist to pull her tight against his body. "I'm not letting you out of my sight."

She tilted back her head, telling herself to be annoyed. He didn't have the right to manhandle her. If she desired a male to touch her then she would ask him.

"Is that a promise or a warning?"

He lowered his head until they were nose to nose. "What do you want it to be?"

What she wanted was to throw him on the ground and strip off his clothes. She knew it. He probably knew it. But she wasn't going to admit the truth. Not until she was ready.

Which might be never.

He was, after all, threatening to kill her, she reminded herself.

"Do you seduce every nymph who crosses your path?" she demanded.

"Jealous?"

"Discerning."

He used the tip of his fang to outline her lips. "Discerning?"

The sensation of the sharp tip pressing against her skin was oddly erotic. Almost as erotic as the jolts of pleasure that darted through her.

"I'm not going to have sex with whatever creature happens to be handy," she said. It was more a reminder to herself than a warning for him.

He lifted his head, studying her wary expression. "Do you have sex with *any* creature?"

Kyi hissed. Enough was enough. Locke had just hit her last nerve. Pressing her hands against his chest, she stepped away.

"None of your business," she snapped.

He folded his arms over his chest, his eyes glowing with a sensual invitation. "What if I decide I want to make it my business?"

Kyi's heart slammed against her ribs, anticipation surging through her. She spun away, clenching her teeth. It was one thing to have her body respond to the male. He was a vampire. They were irresistible to every creature. But she couldn't allow her heart to get involved.

Reaching into her pocket, she pulled out the hair. "I'm going to find my mother. Are you coming?"

He paused, no doubt assessing whether this was a trap. Then, obviously noticing the faint glow on the edge of the horizon, he stepped toward her.

"Let's go."

Chapter 8

Inga stepped through the portal she'd created and hastily glanced around the isolated sanctuary. It was a perfect hideout for renegade demons. Dingy? Check. Grimy? Check. Decaying? Check. Hidden behind a raging waterfall that ensured everything was constantly coated in mold? Check.

She'd deliberately chosen to enter through the attic despite the fact that it was stuffed with broken weapons, busted furniture, old treasure chests, and dust. Lots and lots of dust. On the plus side, it was usually empty and it would give them the opportunity to prepare for the inevitable encounter with Harrat.

Levet stepped beside her, his gaze wide as he spun in a slow circle. "What is this place?" he breathed. "It is *très* interesting. Are those treasure chests?"

Inga smiled with a fond resignation. That was what she loved about the tiny gargoyle. Any other creature would have bitched and moaned to realize she'd led them to a filthy attic that smelled like mold. Levet could only see the best of any situation.

"When I was a slave to the goblins they would occasionally hide out here," she told him.

Levet tilted his head to the side. "Hide from who? Or is it whom? I can never remember."

"They were marauders and smugglers and thieves," she said, ignoring the question about "whom." No one knew when it was supposed to be used. "The goblins were always on the run from someone who wanted them dead."

"So this is their secret lair?"

"Not really secret. But it's tucked behind a waterfall and wrapped in several magical layers of protection. Only demons with invitation are allowed to enter."

Levet turned to study her with a curious gaze. "How did you open a portal here?"

She held out her arm, revealing the tattoo that had been engraved into the skin of her inner wrist. "With this."

Levet wrinkled his snout. She didn't have to explain that the mark had been inflicted by her former master, like she was a dog being microchipped. The gargoyle had endured his own troubles with slavers.

"Ah."

Inga nodded toward the window that was heavily shuttered. "It's daylight outside. We can wait here until nightfall."

"Is it safe?"

"No."

Levet's wings drooped. "I do not know why I bother to ask."

"Neither do I," Inga agreed. They were, after all, currently standing in a hideaway reserved for the dredges of demon society.

Levet swiveled toward the narrow door across the warped wooden floor. "I smell imp."

Inga sniffed, catching the scent of rotting peaches. "Harrat."

"You know him?"

"He owns this place."

Inga stepped forward, feeling an odd tingle of anticipation. It was crazy. She'd spent months cringing each time the throne room doors opened to reveal an elegant, perfectly charming visitor. And now, when she was about to face a foul-mouthed ruffian who would happily slice her throat and steal her valuables, she felt nothing but eagerness. Probably because she was used to foul-mouthed ruffians. They might be crude, but you knew exactly what to expect from them. The sophisticated mer-folk who filled the castle, and even the various diplomats who traveled to negotiate treaties, would pretend to be her friend and then betray her at the first opportunity.

"Let me handle him," she told Levet.

"Your ring," the gargoyle reminded her.

Inga reluctantly pulled it out of the pocket of her muumuu. The delicate piece of jewelry looked way too small and fragile to fit on her finger.

"Is it necessary?"

"You don't want to be recognized, do you?"

Inga shrugged. In the castle she was a freak. Out here in the real world, her appearance was an advantage. Only a fool would willingly tangle with an ogress.

"Actually it wouldn't be a bad thing. They don't like strangers at this hideout."

Levet clicked his tongue. "And if they discover that you are a queen?"

Inga frowned. She had no idea where Levet was going with the conversation.

"They don't care about royalty."

"They would if they thought they could use you to blackmail the mer-folk."

"How could they blackmail them?"

Levet sent her an impatient glare, as if he suspected she was being deliberately obtuse. Which was totally unfair. There was nothing deliberate about her obtuseness. It came naturally.

"They could take you hostage and demand payment to get you back," he explained.

Inga snorted. "As if my people would pay to have me back."

Levet pointed toward the massive trident clutched in her hand. "What would they pay to have the Tryshu back?"

"Crap." She heaved a gusty sigh. The mer-folk would burn the world to the ground to regain control of their precious symbol of authority. "You're right."

Levet reached up to grab the ring. "Allow me," he murmured.

Inga reluctantly held out her hand. She didn't like the thought of using some unknown magic. Especially when Levet was in charge. He had many fabulous qualities, but he did tend to cause mass destruction.

"If this turns me into a frog I will never forgive you."

"If you turn into a frog I will kiss you and turn you back into a queen." Levet grabbed her hand, pressing his lips to her fingers. "I promise."

She released a nervous twitter, heat flooding her cheeks. Dear goddess, was she blushing?

"Maybe I'll just stay a frog," she tried to tease.

Levet slowly shoved the ring on one thick finger, the magical item easily stretching to fit. Inga stared down at the opal that began to shimmer with an inner fire. Yellows, oranges, purples, even red. Mesmerized by the beauty of the gem, she wasn't prepared for the blast of power.

Grunting in pain, Inga fell to her knees, the magic cascading through her with a ruthless intensity. It was like being battered by a thousand fists, all at once. Had Levet made a mistake? This didn't feel like a disguise spell. Bowing her head, Inga clenched her teeth to keep from passing out.

"Inga." Levet patted her face. "Inga are you hurt?"

Inga winced as he continued to pat, harder and harder.

"I'm fine," she rasped, forcing open her eyes. Immediately the room spun in a dizzying circle and a dull ache throbbed at the base of her neck. "The magic hit me harder than I expected."

Levet smoothed his hand down her shoulder in a gesture of comfort. "It's a powerful spell. I should have warned you."

She carefully turned her head, afraid any movement might bring back the pain. Levet was standing next to her, his expression troubled.

"Have you used the ring before?" she asked.

"*Non*, but I was once transformed. I was seven foot tall. It was glorious." His eyes twinkled at the memory, then he reached up to rub between his stunted horns, with a rueful smile. "And occasionally painful."

Inga studied her companion. He seemed…bigger. As if discussing his transformation had somehow expanded him. Inga frowned. That was ridiculous, of course. She was the one who was supposed to have changed.

"Do I look different?"

Levet studied her from head to toe, his expression impossible to read. At last he stepped back and waved his hand toward the broken mirror that was leaning against a far wall.

"See for yourself."

Cautiously, Inga rose to her feet and crossed the crowded space. She had to climb over a pile of barrels and clay pots, but at last she was standing in front of the mirror. The dust was too thick to make out more than a vague outline, and with an inpatient curse, she waved the Tryshu in front of it. A surge of power instantly cleared away the layers of filth. It even repaired the shattered glass. Inga's lips twisted. She would never get used to the immense power of her weapon.

Holding her breath, she leaned forward to peer into the mirror. She wasn't sure what she expected. Maybe different-colored hair. Or skin. She might be taller. Or shorter.

What she hadn't expected was an utter makeover.

"Oh." She lifted a hand to touch her face, which was now a perfect oval with smooth skin the shade of rich honey. Her features no longer looked as if they'd been chiseled out of granite by a drunken sculptor; they were delicately carved with a narrow nose and high cheekbones. Her lips had the plush softness of a ripe fruit and were tinted pink. Even her teeth were now white and straight without the sharp points.

Only her eyes remained the same. A bright, mermaid blue.

"Inga?" Levet tugged on her gown, as if reminding her that she wasn't alone.

Her hand lifted to sweep through the glorious mane of satin gold hair. "That's…me?" she demanded in disbelief.

Levet patted her arm. "Do not fear, *mon ami*. It is only temporary."

She barely heard the words. She was too busy feeling…actually, she didn't know how she felt. Amazed, scared, faintly nauseous.

"I'm beautiful," she whispered, her gaze lowering to take in the flimsy gown that clung to her soft, slender curves. It looked like a piece of tissue paper that might tear if she took too deep a breath. And more shocking, it dipped down at the neckline to showcase the upper mounds of her breasts. "I've never been beautiful before."

"What do you mean?" Levet sounded genuinely perplexed. "You have always been *magnifique*."

She glanced down at the gargoyle regarding her with a somber expression. A bittersweet smile tugged at her lips.

"Levet, not even you can deny that I'm usually big and ugly and awkward." She waved her hands down her graceful body. "Look at me now."

"Fah." His voice was uncharacteristically harsh. "You cannot judge a book by its quilt."

"Cover," she absently corrected.

The gargoyle touched the bare skin of her arm. "This means nothing." He went on his tiptoes to touch the center of her chest. Directly over her heart. "This means everything."

"You don't understand."

"Who could understand better, *ma belle*?" he asked in dry tones.

Inga grimaced as regret sliced through her. No matter what her feelings for Levet, there was no doubting that most demons considered him a freak. Just like her.

"I'm sorry." She started to bend down to…what? Kiss him? No, no. Now wasn't the time for such foolishness.

As if to emphasize her panicked reminder, the sound of approaching footsteps echoed through the attic.

"You need to do something with that," Levet warned, pointing toward her hand.

"What?" Inga glanced to the side, belatedly noticing the large trident. She'd been so focused on her transformation she'd forgotten about the Tryshu. "Oh. It's not something I can hide."

"Use the ring's magic to disguise it."

"Disguise it into what?"

The door abruptly flew open, revealing two heavily armored trolls carrying cudgels.

"Something pointy," Levet suggested.

The trolls stepped to each side of the door, allowing a tall, slender imp to enter the attic.

Harrat was less refined than most imps. His reddish blond hair was shaved into a mohawk and he wore leather rather than silk. His face was thin, with a perpetual sneer on his lips. And his eyes were a pale green and gleamed with a menacing warning.

"I don't know who's stupid enough to trespass into my private establishment," he drawled, lifting a large iron dagger over his head. "But you're about to die."

Inga rolled her eyes even as she concentrated on the magic flowing through her to disguise her trident behind an illusion of a slender rapier. The imp had always had a flare for the dramatic, as if he was an actor on a stage, and not the owner of a sleazy refuge for the dregs of the demon world.

"Hello, Harrat," she said.

The imp halted, his expression suddenly puzzled as he allowed his gaze to drift over her. "Who are you?"

"Inga—" Her words were cut short as Levet stomped on her foot. "Oof," she grunted, astonished at the pain that radiated up her leg. Obviously she was a lot more fragile than she used to be. "Ingala," she finished lamely.

"Ingala?" Harrat remained puzzled, but there wasn't the wary aggression she usually encountered. Was it because he didn't see her as a potential threat? Inga blinked. She'd never been underestimated before. Not even when she was a slave. She wasn't sure whether to be happy or scared. "How did you get in here?" the imp demanded.

"Blectchen sent me." She held out her wrist, revealing the tattoo that was still visible despite the transformation. Some things never changed.

"Blectchen?" The imp shook his head. "I thought he was dead."

Inga shrugged. "He pissed off a clan of vampires a few centuries ago and he's been laying low ever since," she smoothly retorted.

It wasn't a lie. Her former master had crossed paths with Styx in South America and ended up with his body parts spread across the jungle. It'd been a spectacular death, with lots of spurting blood and screams for mercy. Until she'd met Levet, Inga had always considered that the greatest night of her life.

"Smart," Harrat readily accepted her explanation. "So where is he?"

"Waiting until daylight to make his escape," she said. "I'm here to prepare his rooms."

"Prepare them how?"

Inga blinked. She hadn't been expecting that question.

"We have a magical spell created by a coven of witches that will allow him to remain shrouded from demons." Levet came to the rescue. "He cannot be too careful."

The imp glanced toward Levet, his brow furrowing as he took in the sight of the three-foot gargoyle with fairy wings. Obviously, he didn't like what he saw.

"I don't remember being asked if I have rooms available," he snapped.

Inga hastily regained control of the encounter. Levet had many fine qualities, but he did tend to piss off males. No matter what their species.

"No problem," she drawled, lifting her hand as if she intended to create a portal. "I'll return to Blectchen and tell him that—"

"Now, now." Harrat smoothly moved to stand directly in front of her, the obnoxious odor of rotted peaches assaulting her nose. "No need to be hasty," he drawled. "I'm sure something can be arranged. It will cost, of course."

Inga reached down, relieved to discover that the large money pouch she'd placed in her pocket was still there. Pulling out several coins, she handed them to the imp.

"Here."

Tossing the gold toward one of his guards, Harrat stepped closer. Was he trying to intimidate her?

"That's a nice down payment." He reached out to wrap his arms around her waist, jerking her hard against his body. Nope, he wasn't trying to intimidate her, she realized with a stab of shock, feeling his erection poke into her stomach. "Why don't we go to my private quarters and we can negotiate a payment plan?"

"Let go," Inga snapped.

"Don't be that way." Harrat lowered a hand to cup her ass, squeezing hard enough to leave bruises.

"I said," Inga pressed one hand against his chest, "let go."

The idiot chuckled, as if they were playing some sort of game. "Do you want rooms here or not?"

"I've paid for our room."

"You're going to have to come up with more than gold." Harrat leaned down, licking his tongue over her cheek like a dog. "We can start with you sucking my…argh."

The imp reeled backward, his eyes wide as he gazed down at the rapier that was now sticking out of his stomach. An explosive silence filled the attic, and then, without warning Levet fell to the ground, his laugher echoing through the air.

Chapter 9

Locke couldn't detect the portal that Kyi created, but he did realize something was wrong the second he stepped through it. Instinctively leaping to the side, Locke pulled a hidden dagger from his boot and glanced around.

He had a vague impression of wind whistling through a vast expanse of towering pine trees and a canopy of endless black sky. As if they were at the top of the world. Maybe the Canadian Rockies? But before he could determine an exact location, his searching gaze landed on Kyi, who was lying on the ground, blood pouring from a wound on her head.

What the hell had happened?

Fear slammed into Locke. Not for himself, but for the female who he'd once been determined to kill. How was that for irony? Dropping to his knees next to her unconscious body, Locke gently touched her cheek. He could feel the brush of her breath and hear the unsteady beat of her heart. She was alive, but she was gravely wounded.

Glancing around, he searched for whatever or whoever had hurt her. If the attack had been magical, he was screwed. He had no ability to detect a spell.

There was a sound like a grunt from behind them, and Locke turned his head to see a mongrel demon watching him with a blank expression.

Locke slowly straightened, placing himself between Kyi and the creature, which looked like a cross between a troll and a fairy. He was as tall as Locke and thicker through the body. He was wearing rough clothes that might or might not have been made from human skin and his features looked as if they'd been flattened by a shovel. His head was egg-shaped and completely bald. To add insult to injury, it appeared too big for his body, making him hunch over as he started to shuffle forward.

Locke blinked, oddly hypnotized as he inanely wondered whether gravity would win and the creature would tip over. Lost in his strange thoughts, Locke nearly missed the weapon that was launched with a flick of the male's massive hand.

Ducking at the last minute, he watched a heavy object fly inches from his face before it did a U-turn and headed back to the creature's waiting hand.

Was that a silver hammer? Really? Locke straightened with a roll of his eyes. Thor-wannabe.

"Who are you?"

The male continued to shuffle forward. This time he maintained his hold on the hammer as he swung it in a killing arc.

Locke leaped back, angling away from Kyi. The air was brutally cold and the rocky ground was coated with ice. And worse, they were on a steep incline. His years living in Iceland had taught him several important lessons. One was that he was a vampire, not a billy goat. He tried his best to avoid the slippery stuff.

Swerving to the side, he released a bolt of electricity. The mongrel was tossed backward, the skin flayed from the side of his face and down his neck.

"I asked you a question," Locke growled, trying to keep the creature distracted as he struggled to maintain his balance.

The male stared at him with his blank eyes. Locke didn't know if he couldn't hear what he was saying or if he was just ignoring him. Or maybe the lights were on but nobody was home. Being a demon didn't mean you had any brains.

Seemingly indifferent to his burned flesh, the male gripped the weapon tight in his hand and swung it at Locke's head. A mistake. Anyone who knew Locke could have warned the creature his skull was as thick as a brick wall. Waiting until the last possible second, Locke bent low and charged forward.

He intended to pin the attacker to the ground and cut off his head with his dagger. But with his current streak of bad luck intact, Locke's foot slipped on the ice and he only managed a glancing blow.

The mongrel spun away, his boots giving him enough traction to keep his balance. He swung the heavy hammer in a semicircle, catching Locke on the side. The sound of cracking ribs echoed through the nearby trees.

Locke flew through the air, landing awkwardly on the icy ground. He grunted in pain, but with a fierce determination he was rolling to the side to avoid the hammer that shattered a rock in the precise spot his head had been.

Muttering a curse, Locke flowed to his feet. He was going to get pummeled if he didn't get off the damned ice. Locke waited for the male to take another swing with his hammer. Ducking low, Locke stabbed upward with the dagger he held in his hand.

He felt the blade slice through the male's arm. The weapon wasn't magically enhanced, but it was razor sharp and the creature wasn't a pureblood. His skin wasn't nearly as thick as most trolls. A thick, greenish blood flowed down his hand to drip from his fingers.

The demon didn't appear to notice the wound. In fact, he didn't even appear to notice Locke as he shambled past him, heading directly toward Kyi.

Shit.

"Hey, shovel-face," he called out. "Where are you going?"

Nothing. Locke hit him with another jolt of his power. The creature grunted, but he didn't turn around.

"Dammit. Over here," he shouted.

"Locke." Kyi's voice was little more than a whisper. "He can't hear you."

His gaze snapped toward the female still lying on the ground. She'd turned her pale face in his direction. His heart twisted in the strangest way at the sight of the blood that was smeared over her cheek.

"Why not?" he demanded in harsh tones.

"He's already dead. It's my mother's magic that's keeping him moving."

With blinding speed, Locke was moving to stand between the mongrel and Kyi. He didn't know why he was compelled to protect her, and right now it didn't matter. If the mongrel was being driven by magic then they were in serious trouble.

He held out his dagger, his gaze focused on the silver hammer. "Xuria's inside him?"

"No, she cast a spell," Kyi told him, moaning softly as she forced herself to a seated position.

"Like a compulsion?"

"Yes."

Locke eyed the creature with a grimace. If he was under compulsion then he wouldn't comprehend fear or pain. There would be no way to scare him off.

"Can I kill him?" he asked. A stupid question considering he already knew the answer.

"No," Kyi confirmed. "The spell will eventually wear off."

Locke hissed, leaning back as the hammer swung toward his face. It brushed the end of his nose, the silver searing his skin.

Glancing down, he released a burst of power to shatter the ice beneath the creature's feet. On cue, the mongrel fell onto its back, sliding a few feet down the pathway.

It didn't kill the thing, but it gave Locke a second to gather his thoughts.

"Eventually is a little vague for a timeframe," he pointed out. "Can't you be more specific?"

"I don't know when she cast it," Kyi told him, her voice not entirely steady. He sensed that she was struggling to stay conscious. "They usually fade in ten or fifteen minutes."

"Great." Locke watched the mongrel struggle to his feet. "How can I lead him away?"

"You can't. Mother no doubt commanded him to kill the first nymph who stepped out of the portal. He won't stop until he completes his goal. Or..." Her words faded as the creature took one step forward and then abruptly halted. A full minute passed, then without warning, the demon tumbled forward, landing flat on his already flat face. "Or if the magic runs out," Kyi completed her thought.

Locke frowned, moving toward the male. His steps were slow and cautious, not only because he had to make certain the creature wasn't playing possum, but there was a very real danger of falling on his ass. Thankfully, he didn't have to reach the demon splayed over the pathway to discover all he needed to know. The odor was wafting through the frigid air.

"He's dead," he announced in firm tones.

"Hopefully for the last time," Kyi added.

Locke turned back, staring down at the nymph. "How badly are you hurt?"

With a strained smile, she held out her hand, allowing him to help her to her feet.

"The hammer caught me with a glancing blow. My ego is more wounded than my head," she assured him. "I should have been prepared for an attack."

Locke frowned, reaching to wipe the blood from her cheek. He wasn't convinced that she was okay. The wound was healing, but her skin was still pale and her scent of bougainvillea was muted. Her expression, however, was set in stubborn lines, as if daring him to point out the obvious.

"How could she know that we were following her?" he instead asked.

Kyi made a sound of disgust. "She has some way of tracking me. I don't know how, but it's annoying. I've tried dozens of protective spells, charms, and illusions. Whenever I get close she either runs or she sets a trap."

"Motherly instincts?" he asked dryly.

She sent him a speculative glance, as if considering his words. "Xuria has the mothering instincts of a rattlesnake, but it's possible she has a connection to me because of our blood ties."

He glanced around. The frigid temperature didn't bother him, but Kyi was wearing nothing more than a sundress with soft slippers. Hardly suitable attire for a winter night in the mountains.

"We need to find somewhere for you to rest," he muttered.

"Not yet." She glanced toward the icy pathway. "We're close."

Locke arched his brows. "Xuria is still here?"

"Yes."

"Why can't I smell her?"

Kyi pointed toward the faint outline of footprints that led into the nearby trees.

"Those are her tracks."

He reached to grab her arm, but Kyi was already following the footprints with light steps that made it appear she was floating over the icy ground. Locke grimaced, plodding behind her. At least there was a thin layer of snow as they walked between the thick tree trunks. It offered a minimal amount of traction.

Concentrating on his footing, Locke was forced to skid to a halt as Kyi rounded a large bush and abruptly jumped backward.

"Oh."

He stepped to stand at her side, his dagger clutched in his hand. "What is it?"

Kyi pointed at the dead moss sprite that was sprawled across the snow. "She's taken another body."

Bending low, Locke circled the dead creature. There were dozens of smells laced through the air. The traditional wildlife. Wolverine, bighorn sheep, grizzly bears. Along with several demons. Sprites, werewolves, sylphs, and a goblin.

"There's too many scents to determine which demon she's hijacked," he muttered in frustration.

"I might have a way," Kyi told him, hurrying back toward the pathway.

With a curse, Locke followed at a speed that made him feel every bit of his three thousand years. Perhaps it was time for him to consider giving up his lair in Iceland and head to a tropical island. Then he grimaced. He might have been transformed into a vampire, but at heart he would always be a Viking.

At last catching up to Kyi, Locke found her standing next to a towering aspen tree. She had her palm flat against the trunk and her head tilted back with her eyes closed.

"What are you doing?" he asked.

"I was raised by dryads," she murmured.

It took him a second to realize what she meant. "You can speak to the trees?"

"Not in the same way as a true dryad, but I can communicate simple ideas."

Locke folded his arms over his chest. He'd been a part of the Ravens for centuries. It taught him to play well with his fellow warriors and to trust them to watch his back. He hadn't, however, expected to depend on this female and her ever increasing list of skills.

He didn't know whether to be pleased or annoyed.

He shrugged. For now he would accept her assistance. "What ideas are you communicating?"

"I'm asking them to reveal which direction the sorceress went," she at last explained.

"They can recognize her even in someone else's body?" Locke asked in surprise.

"Trees don't have eyes. They sense the world around them. They feel the vibrations in the ground, the scents on a breeze, the cool presence of a vampire or the heat of a werewolf." Her lips twisted in a hard smile. "My mother can disguise her physical appearance, but her foul magic stays the same."

A silence descended as Kyi became lost in her connection to the tree. Locke tried to concentrate on their surroundings. He didn't doubt for a second that Xuria had more than one nasty surprise waiting for them. And even if she didn't, there were dangers in the frosty darkness. In the past twenty-four hours he'd been led into a trap by Kyi, and nearly had his head removed by a silver hammer. He'd be damned if he'd get blindsided again.

His stern determination, unfortunately, was swiftly undermined as his gaze was captured by the sight of Kyi. Her head was still tilted back, allowing her raven hair to spill down her back and her pale features to be bathed in a pool of silver moonlight. She looked like a rare orchid.

One that he itched to pluck.

Grimly, he forced his attention back to the surrounding forest. The female was distraction-worthy. On an epic scale. But he wasn't going to get them both killed because he was too busy gawking like a moonstruck dew fairy.

A few minutes later, Kyi turned from the tree and motioned toward the top of the mountain.

"She traveled that way."

"Alone?" Locke asked as they began to climb the steep pathway.

Kyi shrugged. "That's all they can tell me."

"She's going to have more surprises, isn't she?" Locke muttered.

"Without a doubt."

Locke glared at the ice beneath his feet. "Perfect."

* * * *

Kyi kept a brisk pace despite the fact her legs felt as if they were as heavy as lead and each step was jarring her aching head. She told herself it was an urgency to track down her mother. She would claw her way up the mountain on her hands and knees for the opportunity to destroy Xuria. But there was a tiny part of her that was willing to admit that she didn't want to look weak in front of Locke.

Not because she feared he would take advantage of her vulnerability, but because she wanted him to…what? Admire her?

How stupid was that?

Seriously, seriously stupid, she answered her own question.

A shiver raced through her and instantly Locke was walking next to her, his astonishing eyes glowing in the moonlight.

"Are you cold?" he asked.

Kyi nodded. It was a better explanation than the truth. And the frigid breeze was beginning to layer frost on her bare skin.

"A little."

"Here." He started to remove his heavy leather jacket, but she held up a hand.

The jacket was too large and heavy for her slender frame. It would not only hamper her movements but make it impossible to reach her pockets where she kept her magical spells.

"No, thanks." She released a small burst of magic to heat the air around her.

She winced as the effort intensified the pounding in her head. Just how hard had the creature hit her with that stupid hammer?

They walked in silence, both intently studying the thick layer of trees that lined the paths. There was no doubt her mother had left behind a snare. It was just a question of how many. And if they would survive…

"I don't know much about dryads," Locke said abruptly, as if hoping to ease her snowballing anxiety.

She slowed her pace, sending him a grateful glance. "Few creatures do. They're not only rare, but they prefer to remain isolated in their groves."

"Were they good to you?"

Kyi smiled. The dryads had arrived just seconds after her mother had tried to kill her and Cleo, whisking them away from the sight of her father's broken body and the murderous determination of Xuria. At the time Kyi had been in shock, unable to fully understand what was happening. But eventually, the gentle care of the dryads had allowed her to heal and become a part of their tribe.

"They treated me as one of their own," she told her companion. "Dryads have only one mating season and many are never blessed with a baby. It makes children precious to them." She felt a swell of gratitude at the memory of the tiny creatures fussing over her as if she was some remarkable treasure. It was their kindness that kept her from drowning in bitterness. "They passed me from home to home so each one could have an opportunity to raise me."

An odd expression settled on his face. Not precisely wistful, but something close.

"You were lucky," he murmured.

"Yes," she agreed without hesitation. "The only decent thing my mother ever did was to try and kill me in a dryad grove."

They slowed as the pathway sharply angled around a jagged outcropping of boulders. She felt a chill tingle over her that had nothing to do with the icy air. Locke was using his powers to seek out any potential enemies.

"What about your sister?" he asked, obviously able to multi-task.

Kyi instinctively stiffened. She didn't like discussing Cleo. "What about her?"

"You said the dryads took her in as well."

"They did. For a time."

She grimaced. At first they'd kept Kyi and Cleo together, but eventually it became obvious that Cleo had no desire to become a part of the dryad tribe. She'd refused to join in the daily activities or even the tribal celebrations. She had no desire to learn any special skills, and instead spent endless hours by herself at the edge of the grove, simply waiting until she was convinced she could fend for herself.

"And then?" he prompted when she fell silent.

"Cleo was bitter."

"Not surprising."

"No," she agreed with a sigh. "But she couldn't find peace in the grove. She was obsessed with Xuria and revenging the death of our father. As soon as she was capable of taking care of herself she left the grove and disappeared."

"Disappeared literally or figuratively?"

"Both." She'd felt the moment that Cleo had left the grove. It had been as if a piece of herself was suddenly lost. She'd cried for days, even though their sisterly bond had been broken the moment Xuria had tried to kill them. "A few years later she appeared in London with her own tribe of nymphs. I visited her a couple of times. I foolishly thought she might be happy to see me."

"I'm assuming she wasn't pleased?"

Kyi shuddered. She'd heard vague rumors of a powerful young nymph who had established a lair in the center of a small Roman outpost called Londinium. It could have been any nymph, but Kyi had known deep in her heart that it was Cleo. Packing a bag, she'd rushed to be reunited with her only remaining family. She wasn't sure what she'd expected. Certainly not overwhelming joy. Cleo, after all, had known where Kyi was the entire time. She could easily have reached out if she wanted to see her sister.

But she hadn't expected open hostility. Or being run out of Britain by Cleo's personal guards.

"She accused me of being a spy for Xuria," she finally admitted.

"A little paranoid."

Kyi frowned. "It was more than just paranoia. She was plotting something." She made a sound of frustration. Over the long centuries, Kyi had tried to figure out what her sister was up to, but she was no closer to the truth than in the beginning. "I don't know what, but she obviously feared my mother would discover her plans. I pleaded for her to work with me. Together we could have destroyed Xuria, but she refused to trust me."

"It might not have been about trust."

She sent him a suspicious glance. "What do you mean?"

"You said that she was obsessed with her need for revenge."

"Yes."

"Then it's possible she didn't want to share the satisfaction of killing your mother," he explained. "Not even with her sister."

It was a likely theory, she had to admit. Cleo had always been self-centered. Even when they were very young children. She never shared the toys their father lovingly carved for them and preferred to spend time with herself rather than join in the games with the other nymph children. Still, Kyi was convinced that there was more than just selfishness. Cleo was driven by a need to accomplish a goal. Kyi just didn't know what that goal might be.

On the other hand, she wouldn't doubt that the male walking next to her would be fiercely determined to be the one to strike the killing blow.

"Are you speaking from experience?" she asked.

He turned his head to reveal his grim expression. "I didn't want anyone interfering in my quest to kill you."

Kyi flinched, hurt by his stark admission. "I'm glad I didn't know," she muttered. "It was bad enough thinking my mother wanted me dead."

* * * *

Troy reluctantly stepped through the gateway. He'd never traveled this way before and unlike the nymphs that surrounded him, he didn't assume it would be like a portal. This wasn't created by a demon. It was human magic. Which meant that anything could happen.

Cleo, however, moved forward with her audacious style, her head held high. Troy admired her courage. She was a hell of a female. Bold, determined, unafraid to reach out and grasp whatever she wanted.

A shame she was also ruthless, immoral, and utterly focused on her mysterious plans.

Already on edge, Troy stepped through the gateway and was immediately forced to leap to the side when he nearly stumbled over Cleo, who'd halted directly in his path. A quick glance around revealed they were standing in the middle of a vineyard, the scent of plump grapes and the sweet perfume of roses wafting through the air. The sunlight poured from a brilliant blue sky, blanketing them in an unexpected warmth.

Cleo snapped her fingers, her expression impossible to read. "Llewen, search for the trail of the mer-folk," she commanded. Instantly the warriors spread out, silently moving through the vineyard. Once they were out of earshot, she turned to glare at Troy. "This isn't a different dimension."

Troy blinked, belatedly realizing she was right. There was a specific "feel" to every dimension, as if each place had its own unique atmosphere. And they were definitely in the same world they'd just left.

Turning in a slow circle, Troy studied the nearby hills. Each had clusters of stone buildings and paved roads that bustled with humans.

"This is Rome," he announced, his voice edged with surprise. "Or at least it's the Rome I remember from two thousand years ago," he corrected himself.

Cleo released her breath on a low hiss. "Damn. We didn't travel through the veils, we traveled through time."

Troy studied her tense expression. She looked like she wanted to kill something. Probably several somethings.

"I'm guessing that's not what you expected?"

Her hands clenched, but even as Troy braced himself for the inevitable punishment, Cleo gave a sharp shake of her head.

"No. I spent countless years and an enormous amount of money to discover the means to locate the gateway." She muttered a low curse. "I never considered that Xuria would hide in the past."

Troy glanced over his shoulder. He could still make out the shimmering outline of the gateway.

"How did you locate it?"

"The last time Xuria was in our world…" Cleo stopped, making a sound of disgust. "Or rather our time, I managed to place a tracing spell on her."

"Pricey." Troy whistled softly. He'd heard of tracing spells, of course. He had a distant cousin who specialized in creating them. That's how he knew that only a few demons in the world could afford to buy one.

"Outrageous. And worse, I had to wait for Xuria to return to this world before it would trigger." She glanced around in frustration. "I've waited decades for this moment."

"Mistress," a voice called out.

They turned to watch Llewen jog up the slope to join them.

"Nothing's changed," Cleo muttered to herself, squaring her shoulders as the uniformed soldier halted directly in front of them. "Did you find the trail of the mer-folk?" she demanded. "They should lead us to Xuria's lair."

Llewen hesitated. As if he was reluctant to share bad news. Troy didn't blame him. Cleo was no doubt the type of leader who enjoyed blaming the messenger, not the message.

"We haven't been able to find them."

An ominous fury darkened Cleo's cognac eyes. "They must be here."

"We searched…argh." Llewen's words were choked off as Cleo reached out to wrap her fingers around his throat, squeezing hard enough to turn his face blue.

Troy watched in silence. A part of him considered the bonus of having one fewer warrior to worry about if he decided to try and escape this madness. On the other hand, they didn't yet know what they might encounter. If the mysterious Xuria decided to stay in this place, they might need every soldier with them to keep from being slaughtered.

Hmm. Decisions, decisions.

At last he heaved a resigned sigh. Llewen was making weird, gagging noises that were grating on Troy's nerves.

"Have you considered the time factor?" he asked.

Cleo turned, stabbing him with a fierce glare. "Explain."

"You didn't travel from dimension to dimension," he reminded her. "You traveled through time."

"I'm aware of that."

"Then you must know that since we didn't step through the gateway at the precise moment as the mer-folk, we wouldn't arrive at the same instance."

She scowled, suspecting that he was trying to confuse her. "We were only minutes behind them."

"Minutes could translate into hours, days, or even weeks."

"Weeks?"

Troy shrugged. "That would explain why there's no sign of them."

Cleo glanced around the vineyard, her jaw tight. "Unless we came to the wrong place."

"I suppose that's possible," Troy readily agreed. "Maybe we should just go home—"

"Llewen, gather the soldiers," Cleo interrupted his very fine suggestion, releasing her chokehold on the male.

The warrior offered an elegant bow, as if being throttled was a regular occurrence, before he turned to sprint toward the other guards.

Troy swallowed a resigned sigh. The female wasn't going to listen to reason.

"Where are we going?" he asked.

Cleo headed down the slope. "On a treasure hunt."

Chapter 10

Inga glared at the tiny gargoyle who had collapsed on the sagging cot shoved in one corner. He hadn't stopped laughing since she'd stabbed Harrat in the belly.

"It wasn't that funny," she muttered, heat crawling beneath the skin of her face.

It'd been at least ten minutes since one of Harrat's servants had led them to this cramped room. It was nothing more than barren stone walls carved out of the side of the cliff, with no windows and mold coating the flagstone floor. Even by Harrat's standards it was nasty.

"Of course it was, *mon ami*," Levet protested, perched on the edge of the cot. "His expression when you stuck the sword into his belly was priceless."

"You wouldn't be laughing if Harrat had tossed us out the window," she said tartly.

"*Non*. I would now be a lump of stone, which would be no fun at all." The twinkle remained in his gray eyes. "But well worth the sound of Harrat squealing like a porky."

"Piggy," Inga corrected, heaving a soul-deep sigh. "The idiot shouldn't have put his hands on me."

"I believe he has learned his lessons."

Inga wrinkled her nose. She'd overreacted. There was no doubt about it. But in her defense, she hadn't been expecting the idiot to maul her. Why would she? It wasn't like she'd ever had any male slobbering over her like an animal.

"It's stupid," she muttered, speaking more to herself than her companion.

Levet jumped off the cot and waddled toward her. "What is?"

"I always wanted to be tiny and delicate. Like a flower," she admitted. How many nights had she spent fantasizing about waking to discover she was a beautiful princess? Now that she'd experienced it first-hand, she wasn't as impressed as she expected to be. "I didn't consider being pestered by creeps like Harrat."

Levet clicked his tongue. "You took your magnificence for granted."

"Magnificence." Inga snorted, but she couldn't halt the flood of warm pleasure. Only this gargoyle had ever considered her oversized bulk and raw strength a source of admiration.

And if she was being honest, there'd been a few minutes when Harrat was manhandling her that she'd regretted her lack of muscles. She had never considered that ogre blood gave her more than a hulking body. It gave her strength, and courage. Other creatures might snicker behind her back, but they wouldn't dare do it to her face.

She gave a small shake of her head. "We should get some rest. As soon as the sun sets I want to rescue my people."

Levet waved a hand toward the cot before moving to stand next to the wooden door.

"You rest. I will keep guard."

"But—"

"I have no need for sleep," he reminded her.

She grudgingly nodded, moving to lie on the cot, her rapier clutched in her hand. Harrat had given them the room because he feared Blectchen arriving and being furious that his servants weren't there waiting for him. That didn't mean she trusted him any further than she could throw him. And in this body, that wasn't very damned far.

"Wake me if something happens," she muttered, closing her eyes.

"You do not trust me to protect you?" Levet demanded, a hint of reprimand in his voice.

"Of course I do. I just don't want to miss the fun."

* * * *

Locke ignored the tiny prick of guilt at Kyi's wounded expression. He hadn't been trying to hurt her, but then again, he wasn't going to lie. He had plotted her death for years.

Now, however, he was willing to give her the benefit of the doubt. At least until she proved she was untrustworthy.

On full alert, Locke came to a halt as they rounded a large outcropping of rock, and he caught the unmistakable scent of honey.

"There's a tribe of pixies just ahead," he said in a low voice.

Kyi sniffed the air, then sent him a warning glance. "Let me go first."

"Why?"

"Because you're a vampire."

"Yeah, I noticed," he told her dryly. "What does that have to do with you going first?"

She moved to stand directly in front of him. "We need information, but they'll flee if they get spooked. Let me reassure them you're not looking for a late-night snack."

The warm scent of bougainvillea teased at his nose, stirring a hunger that was becoming increasingly difficult to ignore.

"I'm not opposed to a late-night snack," he assured her, his gaze lowering to the slender curve of her neck.

She stepped back, as if she could hide the desire that suddenly spiked the air between them.

"You can ask one of the pixies after I find out if they've seen my mother," she told him tartly.

His fangs lengthened, aching with a brutal need. And not just for blood. "I'm not hungry for pixie," he informed her.

She abruptly turned away. With long strides he was walking beside her. "Aren't you going to ask?"

She kept her gaze firmly locked on the pathway. "Ask what?"

"What I'm hungry for?" He reached to trace a finger down the length of her bare throat.

Her head jerked to the side to send him a frustrated glare. "You are…"

"What?"

She paused, as if searching for the right word. "Relentless."

Locke arched a brow. Was that supposed to be an insult or a compliment? "I've been called worse."

"Shocker."

They came to a side trail that led into the thick woods. Kyi held up her hand.

"Wait here."

She started to turn away, but Locke swiftly reached out to grab her arm. "Kyi."

With obvious impatience, she glared over her shoulder. "Now what?"

Locke tilted back his head, absorbing his surroundings. The sharp air. The rich resin of the trees. Frozen moss. And the scent of honey that was too faint for any pixies to be nearby.

"The village is empty," he said.

With a frown, she hurried forward, ignoring his protests. Locke growled with frustration before following her into the small glade that was dotted with mounds that provided homes for the pixies. Kyi was already in the center of the opening where a fire had been reduced to smoldering coals.

"They were here." She held out her hands to absorb the lingering warmth. "Recently."

"Yes."

Locke moved from mound to mound. There was no sign of struggle. No blood had been shed, and inside the dens nothing had been disturbed. In fact, in several of them there was food on the tables, as if they'd just set down to dinner. Had the entire tribe suddenly decided to walk away? It didn't make any sense.

"Did we frighten them off?" Kyi asked the obvious question.

Locke turned his attention to the perimeter of the village. Moving in a slow circle, he at last found the spot where dozens of footsteps led deeper into the trees. At the same time, he caught the unmistakable stench of sulfur.

"I think someone else did," he muttered.

Kyi rushed to his side, her breath hissing between her clenched teeth. "Xuria."

Locke resumed his searching. It was possible that Xuria was currently disguised as a pixie, but he sensed another creature who'd been lurking in the shadows.

At last he came to a halt and bent down.

"Here," he murmured, touching the trail of footprints that had entered the village from the opposite direction.

Kyi wrinkled her nose at the pungent odor. "She's taken the body of a goblin."

Locke straightened. "Of course it's a goblin. Why couldn't it be a dew fairy?"

"Xuria enjoys being unpredictable."

"At least we have a trail to follow," Locke muttered, returning to the spot the pixies had left the village.

Together they weaved their way through the trees. "Why pixies?"

Kyi sent him a puzzled glance. "What?"

"First she was traveling with mer-folk," he reminded her. "And now pixies. Why?"

"Either she's using them as protection, or she's enslaved them."

Locke considered her words. It couldn't be protection, he quickly decided. You wouldn't choose mer-folk or pixies if you wanted muscle. Not when you could have orcs or trolls or goblins. Or even vampires.

"Slaves to do what?" he asked, speaking his thoughts out loud.

"I don't know."

They walked in silence, both of them hyperaware of the slightest sound and scent that might warn them of danger. The trail led them up the mountain and then along a steep ridge. They left behind the trees, allowing them an unobstructed view of their surroundings. It also allowed the wind to whip against them with brutal force.

Locke grimaced. There was a layer of snow over the ice that provided an illusion of traction, but he wasn't eager to pick up their speed. The path was narrow and there was a sheer drop just inches away. He'd preferred not to slip and tumble down the razor-sharp rocks.

It wouldn't kill him, but it would hurt like a bitch.

The thought had just passed through his mind when Kyi abruptly pulled him backward.

"Look out," she rasped, holding her palm toward the path directly in front of them.

There was the faint sound of something popping and suddenly the path in front of him disappeared. No, it didn't disappear, he silently corrected himself. The illusion that had been woven over the path disappeared. Suddenly he could clearly see the gaping hole where the path had eroded away. One more step and he would have plummeted down to the rocks he'd been so anxious to avoid.

"That was close," he muttered. "Too close."

Kyi leaned forward, studying the two-foot span of empty space. "Hmm."

"What?"

She glanced around, as if searching for something. "It was too easy to avoid."

"For you," he said dryly. He would never have been able to see through the illusion.

"This was a ploy." Kyi glanced back at him, her expression tense as the wind whipped her hair around her shoulders. "She wants us to think this is the trap, but it's not the real one."

He eyed her in confusion. "Is that supposed to make sense?"

She made a sound of impatience. "If your opponent is expecting an ambush, then how do you lead them into it?"

He didn't have to consider the question. He'd been in enough battles to know exactly what he would do.

"Allow them to believe they managed to avoid the ambush with a diversion."

She pointed toward the opening. "Exactly."

Locke was about to ask if she could sense any more illusions in the area when he was distracted by the scent of honey.

"Pixies," he growled in warning, watching the two approach from above at the same time he could sense three more coming from behind.

Kyi was suddenly holding her black dagger. Locke blinked. Where the hell had that come from?

"They're being compelled by magic," Kyi warned.

Locke swore. The pixies were delicate creatures with gossamer wings and skin that sparkled as if dusted with diamonds. Their eyes were a pale blue and their white hair was short enough to reveal their pointed ears. They were no match for a vampire, but he'd already seen what happened when Xuria coerced a creature to fight for her. They wouldn't stop until her magic ran out.

As if his dark thoughts had conjured the sorceress, he caught the scent of goblin. Locke frowned, realizing that it was coming from below them. Peering over the edge of the cliff, he searched the woods they'd just left.

He caught a flicker of movement. A goblin scuttling through the trees.

"There." He pointed toward the fleeing figure. "She's using the pixies as a diversion, while she doubles back." He watched the creature's lumbering movements. What was she doing? Trying to lure them away? No, that didn't make sense. Had she realized that she was being followed? Yes, that seemed more likely. "She's trying to escape," he warned.

Kyi squared her shoulders. "I'll stop her."

He moved to stand directly in front of her. "No."

A dangerous expression settled on her face. "What do you mean, no?"

"She must have sensed that she was being followed," he pointed out. "She'll be expecting you to try and stop her." A cold smile of anticipation curved his lips. "She won't be expecting a vampire."

Her jaw tightened. "She's my mother."

He deliberately glanced over her shoulder at the approaching pixies before returning his gaze to her stubborn expression.

"We both have a thirst for revenge. Does it matter who strikes the killing blow?" he demanded.

Her eyes shimmered like molten gold as she struggled against her intense desire to be the one to punish her mother. Not only for trying to kill her, but for destroying her father and scattering the nymphs who'd been her family. Kyi had even lost her sister because of Xuria.

Of course she wanted to be the one to stick a dagger in the evil bitch.

But she was smart enough to know he was right. Xuria was expecting her. And no doubt had more nasty surprises ready to spring.

Their best chance to stop her was to catch her off guard.

"Go," she muttered at last, turning toward the approaching pixies.

"Be careful," he growled.

She glanced back with a startled expression, but before she could say anything he turned to step off the edge of the cliff. Landing on one of the frost-coated boulders, he leaped to the next, using the slick surface to send him flying in a zigzag pattern down the side of the mountain. He was aware that he was risking an injury. One slip and he'd be skewered on a sharp peak, or his skull bashed open. But he had Xuria in his sight. Nothing was going to stop him from confronting the sorceress.

Dropping the last ten feet onto the frozen ground, Locke absorbed the impact that shuddered up his spine. Then, sniffing the air, he weaved his way through the trees, moving at a blinding speed. It was imperative that he have the element of surprise against the sorceress.

Once he judged that he was far enough ahead, Locke halted at the edge of the narrow path, careful to remain hidden in the darkest shadows as he waited for the goblin to approach. He wasn't too proud to run away if she started tossing around magic. What was that saying? Something about living to fight another day?

The stench of the demon polluted the crisp air and with a focused burst of power, Locke knocked down a nearby tree to block the narrow path. A few seconds later the goblin rounded the corner and halted with a growl of frustration. Hidden in the trees, he could make out the goblin's harshly carved features and her eyes that were glowing with a distinctive white fire.

The same white fire that he'd seen in his mate's eyes. The white fire he'd been certain that he would never, ever see again. There was no mistake. This was the creature he'd mourned for decades. The one he'd spent enormous amounts of time and energy and wealth to revenge.

He waited for the fury to hit him. The utter sense of betrayal. Oddly, all he felt was…satisfaction.

As if he'd already accepted that Kyi was telling him the truth, even without the proof he'd been silently telling himself that he needed. Which was ridiculous. He'd already been fooled once. It was suicidal to allow himself to be once again blinded by a pretty face and pretense of innocence.

Shrugging away his disturbing thoughts, Locke concentrated on Xuria. Any creature capable of magic was a dire threat to vampires. And it didn't help that she'd played body snatcher with a goblin. They were notoriously difficult to kill.

"So it's true," Locke drawled, hoping to shock her into making a lethal mistake. "My mate is not only alive and well, but she's managed to transform herself into a goblin."

There was a hissing sound as the goblin whirled to the side, the white gaze searching through the shadows. Locke could tell the second the sorceress caught sight of him. Her hulking body stiffened, the thick fingers curling into tight fists. Locke prepared for the creature's attack, but instead Xuria forced herself to relax her tense muscles.

She even managed a smile. Or at least Locke assumed it was supposed to be a smile. It looked more like rigor mortis was setting in.

"Hello, Locke," she retorted, her voice oddly smooth. Goblin-speak was usually so garbled it was impossible to interpret. "Did you miss me?"

"Not really. I did, however, waste an inordinate amount of time plotting revenge on your killer."

Xuria appeared genuinely baffled by his words. "My killer? What killer?" Her eyes widened. "Oh. You thought…?" Harsh laughter splintered the night air.

The already frosty air dropped several degrees as an electric pulse made the ground tremble.

"You know the old saying," Locke said in ominous tones, moving along the edge of the pathway. He didn't want the fallen tree between them. "Fool me once, and I rip out your throat and eat your heart."

The amusement was wiped from the goblin's face. "There's no need to be hasty, Locke. It was a tragic misunderstanding."

"Yes," he readily agreed. Although it wasn't a misunderstanding. It had been a ruthless deception that had made him look like a fool. An unforgivable crime as far as he was concerned. "But it's about to be corrected."

"You don't want to do this." Lifting a hand, Xuria took a step back. "We were created to be together. Don't you remember?"

Locke felt a strange tingle. Like a feather being skimmed over his skin. It was a familiar sensation. One he'd experienced a century ago. Just before he'd scooped an injured nymph off the ground and carried her into Leonidas's lair.

It wasn't the actual spell; he couldn't detect magic. This was his physical reaction to the compulsion she was casting.

Locke's fangs lengthened. He'd hoped to get some answers but had to kill her before she could cloud his mind. Preparing to leap forward, he was abruptly distracted by a warmth at the base of his throat.

What the hell? Warily lifting his hand, he touched the spot. For a second he was puzzled by the feel of hot bronze beneath his fingertips. Then he realized that it was the amulet that he'd taken from Kyi.

Why was it so hot? A reaction to being near Xuria? Like an early warning system? Or did it have something to do with the spell she'd cast?

Hmm. Locke studied the goblin, who was regarding him with a smug expression of anticipation. The sorceress obviously assumed that he was caught in her web of compulsion. Maybe the amulet was protecting him from the magic.

Only one way to find out.

Locke furrowed his brow, as if having difficulty forming his thoughts. "I remember..." He shook his head. "You lied."

She took a cautious step forward. "Only because I had to," her voice was a low purr, no doubt trying to deepen her compulsion. "My life was in danger."

"I was protecting you."

"You're right. I should have trusted you." Another step closer. "I promise to do better. Can you forgive me?"

The amulet seared against Locke's skin, but his mind remained clear. Thank the goddess.

"Why are you in these mountains?" he asked, keeping his tone deliberately light, as if it was nothing more than vague curiosity that prompted the question.

"Just passing through."

"Passing through to where?"

She took another step forward, raising her arm. "Take my hand and I'll show you."

No way in hell. Locke shook his head, as if attempting to battle against her spell.

"Kyi," he muttered.

The goblin's face pinched with annoyance. Then the white gaze moved to the amulet around his neck.

"Ah. Of course." The faint tang of sulfur curled around Locke with a physical force. He shuddered. The sensation was unnerving. "That's how you found me. You're traveling with her." The goblin glanced nervously toward the trees. "How did the two of you get together?"

"I intended to kill her."

"Why didn't you?" Xuria asked. "You would have solved half my problems."

"She told me that you were still alive." He didn't have to lie. "And she promised she would lead me to you."

"What else did she say to you?"

"That you were using me."

"And you believed her?"

"I…" He allowed his words to fade away, as if confused. But the truth was, he hadn't been confused. He'd accepted Kyi's words with a shocking readiness, despite his efforts to pretend he didn't trust her.

Xuria kept her hand outstretched, as if intensifying her spell. "Listen to me, Locke. You can't trust Kyi. She's trying to manipulate you into destroying me."

"Why?"

"It's her destiny."

"Destiny?" That was an odd choice of words.

The goblin made a rasping sound, as if aggravated by the realization she'd given away more than she intended.

"You said that you wanted to protect me."

"Yes."

"Then you must return and end Kyi's threat," Xuria commanded.

Locke studied the creature. He'd been expecting the sorceress to demand that he help her complete whatever mysterious goal had brought her to this dimension. Why was she so obsessed with her daughter? Did it have something to do with the destiny comment?

"You want me to kill Kyi?" he pressed.

"Yes." She waved an impatient hand. "You can easily destroy her. She's just a nymph."

"Okay." He took a step back before halting to send her a puzzled gaze. "Aren't you coming with me?"

"No, I need to…" The goblin licked her lips, as if struggling to think of a convincing lie.

"What?"

"I have an important task to take care of."

The answer was vague, but there was nothing vague about the tension humming around Xuria. She was desperate to get away.

Was she on some sort of timetable? Did she have somewhere she needed to be? Or somewhere to go?

Or was she just scared of Kyi?

Questions without answers.

"What task could be more important than the two of us being together?" He forced a smile to his stiff lips. "I don't want to be separated again."

"Go."

"But—"

The goblin stomped one large foot. "I command you."

Locke grimaced. There was an edge in the creature's voice that warned Xuria was done with the conversation.

Time for her to die.

Stepping forward, Locke dropped his pretense of confusion. "Yeah, I don't think so."

Xuria scowled, the eyes flashing with white fire. "Hear my words."

"Oh, I hear them." Locke smiled to reveal his fully extended fangs. "I just don't give a shit."

With a low growl, Locke leaped forward, slamming his shoulder into the chest of the goblin. His momentum and superior weight sent the creature flying backward and they landed on the pathway with enough force to knock the air from the goblin's lungs.

He angled his head, his fangs fully extended as he prepared to rip out the goblin's throat. Before he could strike, however, he realized the demon wasn't moving. It wasn't the immobility of fear. Or even of being knocked unconscious. It was the flaccid stillness of death.

Damn.

Chapter 11

Kyi wasn't helpless. She not only had the abilities of her nymph father, but she could manipulate magic. Not as well as her mother, but enough to protect herself when necessary. And of course, the dryads had given her a share of their gentle talents. But even under normal circumstances she would have a hard time fighting off five pixies.

And these weren't normal circumstances.

They were fighting on a narrow ledge coated in ice. The pixies were under a compulsion spell that meant they didn't feel any pain, and until the magic was gone, they couldn't die. And she was still recovering from the hammer blow to the head that had sapped her energy.

All in all, not her best night.

Gripping the dagger tight in her fist, she kept the two pixies in front of her from attacking while she used a spell to create a barrier behind her. But with each passing second the attackers were creeping closer, and the barrier was starting to thin. She wasn't going to last much longer.

Too tired to keep herself warm, Kyi shivered as the frigid wind ripped and battered against her, her feet already numb. Perhaps sensing that she was weakening, the pixies moved even closer, the scent of honey thick in the air.

"Where are you, Locke?" she muttered, her breath creating tiny puffs of fog.

She didn't question her confidence that the vampire would manage to survive a battle with her mother. Or that once his goal was accomplished, he would return to help her. It was just an unshakable conviction.

Swinging the knife in a weak motion, Kyi braced herself for the inevitable blow from the approaching pixies. She had to try and keep them from knocking her off the slick path. But even as she spread her feet, the fey creatures froze in place, as if someone had turned off their battery. And in a sense, that's exactly what had happened, she acknowledged. It was her mother's magic that was animating them, and once it was removed there was nothing but an empty shell left.

They stared at her with blank eyes and then, swaying in the wind, they slowly toppled to the side and plummeted over the edge of the cliff. Cautiously, Kyi glanced over her shoulder, finding the pathway empty. The three behind her had disappeared.

Either Locke had managed to disrupt her mother's magic, or it had run out of juice.

Releasing a shaky sigh of relief, Kyi was attempting to sheath her dagger when the scent of copper and raw male power swirled around her. Locke.

"Kyi." There was a blur of motion before the vampire was standing at her side, his expression concerned. "Are you okay?"

"I'm fine."

The lie barely managed to leave her frozen lips when a darkness rolled over her and she fainted like some ridiculous female from a fairy tale. The ones she hated because they were always waiting for some incompetent hero to ride to their rescue.

* * * *

Kyi had no idea how much time passed when she at last managed to open her eyes. It was still dark, but she was no longer standing on an icy cliff. In fact, she was lying next to a blazing fire that provided a delicious warmth.

Carefully rolling onto her back, she stared at the open-beamed ceiling above her head. She was in some sort of shelter. And by the smell that clung to the leather furniture that surrounded her, it belonged to a human. And a dog. Not a Were. A Labrador who liked to lie on the rug where she was currently stretched out. She wrinkled her nose. She liked dogs, but she didn't want to be covered in fur.

Slowly she sat up and glanced around the small room. Beyond the sofa and chair there wasn't much to see. The floors and walls were rough wooden planks. There were two windows without curtains and a pile of logs and newspapers in one corner. The only thing of interest was the large stone fireplace that had been built with polished rocks that shimmered with flecks of silver.

No vampire.

"Locke?"

There was the sound of a door opening, and she glanced over her shoulder to watch the tall male step into the room. His dark gold hair had been pulled from his face and tied with a leather strap. It emphasized the chiseled perfection of his features and the stubborn line of his jaw. Closing the door behind him, his astonishing eyes shimmered with sapphire fire in the glow from the flames.

She watched him stride toward her, looking like a conquering Viking despite the modern leather jacket and heavy boots. All hard muscle and sizzling determination.

It was sexy as hell.

He was sexy as hell.

"I'm here," he murmured, crouching down beside her.

A delicious shiver raced through her. "Where's here?"

"A human hunting cabin." He confirmed her theory.

She paused, sorting through her fuzzy memories. They'd been on a mountain. And then the pixies had attacked. What happened next?

Oh, yeah.

"My mother?" she demanded.

He grimaced. "Gone."

"Dead gone or gone gone?"

"Gone gone."

It wasn't really a surprise. Xuria had survived for several millennium because she was a cunning, ruthless bitch. Still, she wasn't going to miss such a perfect opportunity.

"You let her escape?" She arched her brows. "I thought vampires were supposed to be some sort of superior species? You know, top of the food chain and all that."

"I didn't *let* her do anything."

"Then what happened?"

"The usual." He shrugged. "We chatted, she cast a weird love spell that I assume was supposed to convince me that we were eternal mates, and then she ordered me to kill you."

Her lips twitched. His teasing helped ease the sting of his words. "How did she escape?"

"I had the goblin pinned to the ground and then…poof. The goblin was dead and Xuria was gone."

Kyi wrinkled her nose. "She became incorporeal."

"What does that mean?"

"She's in her spirit form," Kyi clarified.

She wasn't entirely sure exactly what happened to her mother when she was invisible. She assumed she floated around, looking for another demon to infect.

"Can you follow her?" Locke demanded.

Kyi shook her head. "There's nothing to follow until she takes a new body."

He muttered a savage curse. "I was afraid you were going to say that."

Kyi sympathized with his frustration. The knowledge that Xuria was out there plotting her death was twisting her gut into a tight ball.

"Another wasted opportunity," she muttered.

There was a short pause, as if Locke was battling to regain control of his temper. Then he slowly shook his head.

"Not entirely wasted."

Kyi blinked in confusion. "You do you mean?"

She mentioned destiny when she talked about you."

"Destiny?" Kyi remained confused. "What's that mean?"

"I don't know, but it usually refers to some preordained event," he said, his voice confident as if he'd been considering his encounter with Xuria while Kyi was unconscious. "I think she fears that you're fated to interfere with her plans."

"That's not destiny, it's a promise," she informed him, although she couldn't deny a prick of satisfaction. She wanted her mother afraid. The bitch had terrorized her for centuries. Fair was fair. "Did you figure out what her plans happen to be?"

"No." His features hardened with self-disgust.

She sighed. "So I'm no closer than I was before."

He reached out to lay a hand on her shoulder. "You'll never be able to capture her, Kyi. Not as long as she can change into her spirit form."

She sent him a frown. If he was trying to comfort her, he sucked at it. "I'm not going to wait around for her to try and kill me again."

His fingers lightly traced the curve of her throat, sending zigzags of pleasure shooting through her.

"I'm not suggesting you wait."

She cleared her throat, struggling to concentrate on his words. "You have a plan?"

He answered her question with a question. "Do you know what happened to your father's tribe after your mother's attack?"

She hesitated. It still pained her to speak of her family that had been scattered by her mother's brutal attack.

"I lost track after the dryads took me in."

He looked surprised. "You never tried to find them?"

She hunched her shoulders. "To be honest I was afraid they might not want to see me," she confessed, her voice husky.

"Why not?"

"I thought they might blame me."

"You?" His tone was sharp. "You were just a child."

"Xuria was my mother," she insisted. "If it hadn't been for me and Cleo, she would never have attacked them."

His jaw tightened, as if he wanted to argue with her, but he seemed to recognize that she wasn't going to change her mind.

No doubt it was her stubborn expression that gave it away.

"You have no idea where they might be?" he asked instead.

"There were rumors that the ones who survived fled to Alimia."

"Where's that?"

"A small uninhabited island off the coast of Greece."

He nodded. "That makes sense. Nymphs prefer to remain close to their homeland." His fingers moved to cup her cheek. "Can you take me there?"

His fingers were cool against her skin, but the electric tingles that sizzled through her were as hot as the nearby flames.

She cleared her throat. There was a strange lump that refused to budge. "Why?" she managed to ask.

"If we can discover what Xuria is doing in this dimension it will help us track her down."

Kyi agreed with the theory. If they actually knew what her mother was trying to accomplish, they might get ahead of her rather than constantly being two steps behind. But she was puzzled by his interest in the nymphs.

"Xuria was never a part of our tribe," she reminded him.

"No, but she still has a connection."

"Me?"

"The starlyte crystal."

She waited for him to continue. When he didn't, she shook her head. "There was no need to attack the tribe for the crystal. She already had it. That's what keeps her immortal."

His fingers traced the line of her jaw. "Yes, but she's not fey."

She instinctively tilted back her head, silently encouraging his touch. A mistake, no doubt. This male had sought her out to kill her. And even though he now seemingly believed her, there were still a hundred reasons he was dangerous. But there was a part of her that was starved for his caress. As if she'd been waiting centuries for him to appear and awaken her lust.

Like Rapunzel, she wryly conceded. Complete with an evil mother.

"I'm painfully aware of that," she finally managed to say.

"So how does she fuel the crystal?"

"Fuel it?" Kyi wasn't sure she heard him right.

"Any power takes fuel," he pointed out. "And to keep your mother immortal it would have to consume an enormous amount of power."

Oh. She considered his words. She'd never thought about magical artifacts demanding fuel, but there was no denying that they had to have some source of energy. Either taking power directly from the user or through potions and incantations.

"So how is my mother using an artifact that should need the magic of a fey?" she murmured softly.

"Exactly." He used the tip of his finger to trace her lips. "Perhaps one of your tribesmen can answer the question."

"True." She leaned back. It was impossible to think when his fingers were creating internal chaos. "Do you want to go now?"

He closed his eyes, as if searching for something beyond the cabin. At last he shook his head.

"The sun hasn't fully set on that side of the world." He settled on the rug and shrugged out of his jacket. Then, with a gentle care that trapped the air in her lungs, he wrapped the leather around her before pulling her into his arms. "Besides, you need to regain your strength."

Ignoring the voice of warning that whispered in the back of her mind, she snuggled against his broad chest. She was weary. Not only from her recent injury and the battle with the pixies, but from scrying for her mother, and creating a portal large enough for herself and Locke.

Besides, it felt nice.

She couldn't remember the last time anyone had held her in their arms. "What about you?"

"What about me?" he asked.

"Are you going to rest?"

"I'll keep watch."

She tilted back her head to discover his gaze was locked on her face, the gold circling his eyes seeming to shimmer in the firelight.

"Keep a watch on what?"

He smiled, deliberately revealing the razor-sharp points of his fangs. "A dangerous question."

"It wasn't meant to be," she whispered.

"Are you afraid?"

"Should I be?"

As if able to sense her deepest fantasies, Locke scraped the tip of his fangs down the side of her neck.

"No," he murmured.

Her heart skipped and skidded, refusing to find a steady rhythm as the image of those fangs sliding deep into her flesh seared through her mind. But even as pleasure jolted through her, a disturbing memory made her arch back to study his pale features.

"I assume that meeting my mother has convinced you I'm telling the truth?" she demanded.

"I'm willing to accept Xuria used magic to convince me she was my mate," he conceded.

"And that I didn't kill her?"

"And that you didn't kill her."

She paused, telling herself to close her eyes and get some rest. Locke had admitted that he was convinced that Xuria was the villain, not her. That's all that mattered. Right?

She released a slow breath, willing her muscles to relax. They refused. Not when her mind was still focused on the past. Screw it. She was going to ask the question gnawing at her.

"Are you sorry?"

He lifted his head to study her with a curious expression. "About what?"

"That Xuria wasn't your mate?"

He flinched, as if she'd hit a raw nerve. "Hell, no."

She frowned at his fervent denial. "You spent a century plotting revenge for her death."

"But not mourning her loss," he said in harsh tones, his fury at being fooled into believing Xuria was his mate sending sparks of electricity through the air. "Which should have warned me that something wasn't right."

She lifted her arm to place her hand over his unbeating heart. "You were bewitched when you were together," she reminded him in comforting tones. "You had no power to resist her charms."

A wry smile curved his lips. "Actually there was more resisting than I allowed you to believe."

"Resisting of what?" she asked in confusion.

"Charms."

She studied his clenched jaw, not sure she understood what he was implying. "You never…?"

"Never." His nose flared, his eyes smoldering with suppressed emotions.

A hard knot that had been lodged in the pit of her stomach slowly eased at his words. She hadn't realized until this moment just how bothered she was by the thought this male had been intimate with her mother.

She narrowed her eyes. "Why did you make me believe you'd been lovers?"

"The truth?"

"Yes."

He cupped her cheek in his palm, the cool touch strangely addictive. "To keep you at a distance."

She smoothed her hand over the hard muscles of his chest. "Why did you want to keep me at a distance?"

He lowered his head until a mere inch separated them. "Because you tempted me from the moment I caught sight of you."

"And that was a bad thing?"

"You were supposed to be my enemy," he reminded her in low tones.

"And now?"

His fingers skimmed over her cheek before tangling in her hair. "And now I'm ready and willing to embrace temptation."

She heard the words "embrace" and "temptation" before her thoughts shattered into a thousand pieces. Arching against his hard body, she tilted back her head to offer full access to her neck.

"Locke."

He lowered his head, placing a light, all-too-brief kiss on her lips. "But for now you need to rest."

A pang of frustration made her scowl, but she wasn't truly angry. Her head still ached and she was weary enough that even the smallest movement took an enormous effort.

"Tease," she chided, snuggling her head against his chest and promptly falling asleep.

Chapter 12

Entering the ancient city, Troy glanced around until he spotted a familiar landmark. Ah, perfect. He knew exactly where they were, and more importantly, *when* they were in Rome.

Turning toward the center of town, he hurried up the wide road that was recently paved and lined with shallow gutters. The flowing water not only kept the area clean, but cooled the terracotta containers that were buried below the ground in the nearby buildings to preserve foodstuff and wine. Around them humans strolled past in linen robes and soft leather slippers. Occasionally they stopped to stare at Troy and the nymphs, but with a shrug they hurried on. Rome was filled with foreign visitors who dressed in odd clothing. Or perhaps they assumed they were actors in a farce.

"Where are you going?" Cleo appeared at his side, clearly annoyed that he had taken off without her.

"I have a cousin who runs a bathhouse," he said, his quick pace never slowing. He wanted to be done with their task and back home.

She clicked her tongue. "I didn't bring you here for a family reunion."

He turned a corner, the scent of fried fish and boiled pork assaulting him from a nearby vender.

"Do you want to find the mer-folk or not?" he demanded.

"How can your cousin help?"

"At this point in time she's the leader of demon society," he told her. He, on the other hand, had just left his father's palace and his position as prince. He hadn't actually realized how hard it would be to fend for himself. Out of desperation, he'd sought out the one family member who might be willing to offer assistance. A mistake, of course. Imps were notoriously tight-fisted when it came to money. "If there have been mer-folk in the area, she'll know."

Cleo frowned, but she allowed herself to be led through the bustling crowd. "How can you tell what date this is?"

He pointed toward the towering amphitheater that dominated the center of the city. Even from a distance it was easy to see the humans who were working to complete the limestone and brick structure.

"Do you see that?"

"The Colosseum?" she asked in confusion.

"Yes, it was being constructed the last time I was here to visit my cousin."

They turned again, this time onto a street that was even wider and lined with elegant buildings and walled gardens.

"What happened to him?" Cleo demanded, her gaze darting from side to side as if she was expecting an ambush.

"Her," Troy corrected. "In our time she lives in Las Vegas and runs an online dating site."

Troy halted as they reached the large structure built out of brick and covered in a pale stucco, with large, arched windows that allowed the sun to fill the inner chambers with light. The roof was tiled and lined with chimneys for the fires that warmed the water that was piped in beneath the building. The surrounding grounds were beautifully manicured with marble benches for patrons to sit and relax.

"Llewen." Cleo pointed toward the street as her guard hurried to stand at her side. "Do a quick sweep of the neighborhood. I don't want any unpleasant surprises."

The male frowned. "I can send the soldiers. I should stay with you."

Cleo arched a brow. "Are you now in charge?"

"No, but I don't trust the imp."

Troy blew a kiss toward the glowering captain. "The feeling is entirely mutual, sweetie."

Cleo muttered something under her breath. Troy caught the words "balls" and "pea-sized," so she couldn't be talking about him. His balls were anything but pea-sized.

"I can take care of myself," she snapped, flicking her hand. Llewen flinched, as if he'd been hit with an unseen burst of magic, then with a last glare at Troy he turned to lead his soldiers around the corner of the bathhouse. Turning back, she sent Troy an annoyed frown. "What are you looking at?"

Troy shrugged. He didn't feel sorry for Llewen. The male had no doubt known what he was getting into when he agreed to become Cleo's captain, but it pissed him off to see any fey creature treated like dirt. Especially when they weren't in a position to fight back.

It was one of the reasons he'd left his parents' castle.

"Have you ever heard the old adage that you get more flies with honey?" he demanded as they stepped through the open door and into the baths.

Cleo sent him a sour glare. "You expect women to be sweet? Preferably spineless?"

Troy snorted. The woman he admired most in the world was an ill-tempered ogress who wore outrageous muumuus and possessed the artistic skills of an angel. She had more spine than any other creature he'd ever known.

"I don't expect women to be anything." He shrugged, halting in the center of the vast rotunda. "But I have discovered loyalty is a better means to lead people than fear."

Something flared through her eyes. Not regret, but maybe a yearning that things could be different. Then, she sniffed and turned away.

"What people do you lead?" she mocked.

"*Touché*." Troy acknowledged the hit with a dip of his head. There was no denying that he'd walked away from his duties. "Do what you want. It's none of my business."

"Take me to your cousin," she snapped.

Troy strolled across the mosaic tiled floor to enter the inner chamber. This was the area where the bathers removed their clothes and left them on marble benches. Heading through the arched door, he entered the circular room that was occupied by a dozen naked humans who sprawled in a shallow bath in the center of the room. The steam swirled through the air, the scent of myrrh nearly overpowering. They passed into another chamber, this one larger with another bath. This time the water was several degrees cooler and a series of benches were set on a riser. The next room would be larger with even cooler water until a patron reached the center of the establishment, where the water was cold enough to make them shiver and the sun poured through an oculus in the middle of a domed roof.

Troy, however, turned toward a door that was hidden behind the fluted columns. Stepping into the demon section, he glanced around the small reception area. It was just as elegant as the human side, but without the windows. Several demon species tended to be sun-challenged. The floor was tiled with precious gems and long tables were arranged against the walls. They held bowls of fruit and ambrosia along with a pitcher filled with nectar.

An imp wearing a knee-length silk toga and leather sandals appeared from a portal, tossing his golden curls as he moved to block their path.

"These are private baths," he drawled in ancient fey.

The scent of figs swirled through the air and Troy hastily stepped in front of the nymph. They wouldn't get any information if Cleo started killing off the servants.

"Inform Astra that Troy is here to see her," he commanded.

The male ran a disdainful glance over Troy's flamboyant attire. "I don't care if you're the emperor. Astra doesn't meet with strays who wander off the street—"

"Now." Troy released a burst of power, rattling the heavy chandelier above the imp's head.

The male pinched his lips, but turning on his heel, he marched across the floor and disappeared through an arched opening. A few seconds later the essence of roses filled the air, and Astra appeared.

She was stunning, of course. All fey creatures possessed a surface beauty. But Astra took it to a different level.

Tall and slender, she was wearing a white toga that hooked over one shoulder while leaving the other one bare. He'd heard men exclaim that her face would make angels weep in envy. Troy wouldn't go that far, but there was no denying that her features were elegantly carved with a slender nose, full lips and eyes that looked as if they were made from polished jade. Her skin was smooth as silk and kissed with a hint of copper, while her hair was highlighted with the brilliant hues of autumn leaves and pulled into elaborate twists on top of her head.

It wasn't her beauty that captured Troy's attention. It was her golden tiara studded with rubies that flashed in the light from the chandelier.

Troy's fingers itched. It was a fabulous tiara, but without bragging, he could safely say that he would wear it with far more style than his cousin.

As if capable of sensing his burst of envy, Astra lifted a slender hand to touch the jewelry.

"If you've returned to beg for money..."

"Not on this occasion," he interrupted with a wry smile. Obviously he'd just missed meeting himself at the bathhouse. The first of the many problems when traveling through time.

The second problem became obvious when Astra narrowed her eyes to take in his cloak that was meant for a far cooler climate.

"What on earth are you wearing?"

Troy ran his hands down the leopard print. "Don't you adore it?"

Astra waved a dismissive hand. "You look like a fool."

Troy sniffed. "You never did have a sense of style."

"At least I'm not a flighty butterfly who refuses to settle down and build a life."

"So? I love butterflies."

Cleo made a sound of impatience at the family squabble, stepping forward to take command of the situation.

"We're here for information," she announced.

Astra slowly turned her head to take in the nymph. The two females had similarities. Both were strong-willed, ruthless, and ambitious. But while Cleo hid her passionate nature behind a façade of cool control, Astra truly was cold-blooded. Not in a bad way. She was like a snake. Pure survival instincts.

"Who are you?" Astra demanded.

"This is Cleo. A…" Troy searched for the right word. He couldn't find it. "Friend," he finally muttered.

Astra turned back to Troy, less than subtly snubbing the nymph. "What information?"

Cleo hissed, but Troy kept his cousin's attention focused on him. "We're looking for mer-folk."

There was a short pause, as if Astra was waiting for the punchline. Then she snorted. "Have you been dipping into the nectar?"

"Not yet." Troy cast a longing glance toward the pitcher on the table. Really, the least his cousin could do was offer them a glass. "Unfortunately."

Ignoring the blatant hint, Astra lifted a hand to her lips, as if hiding a yawn. "The mer-folk disappeared a long time ago. Something to do with dragons. So, if that's all…"

"I knew this was a waste of time," Cleo muttered.

Troy scowled. He didn't think she was lying, but it was possible the mer-folk managed to pass through the streets without attracting notice.

"Have there been any strange clusters of demons moving through the city?" he expanded the scope of his question.

Astra looked impatient. "There's always strange demons around here. I heard there's a new fighting pit beneath the Pantheon that's importing combatants from around the world."

Troy waved a hand to indicate their elegant surroundings. "Demons who bypassed your very fine bathhouse, along with the other demon establishments in the area. As if they're in a daze?"

Astra's eyes widened. "Ah."

Troy step toward her. "You know something?"

"It'll cost you."

Of course it would. There'd never been an imp born who didn't grasp the opportunity to make some easy money.

"How much?" Troy asked, bracing himself. The demand would be outrageous. This was Astra, after all.

Clearly not wanting to disappoint him, Astra pointed at Cleo. "That emerald."

Troy rolled his eyes, even as Cleo released a low growl, the smell of figs thick in the air.

"Let's negotiate," he urged.

"I did." Astra's finger continued to point at Cleo. "The emerald for the information."

"My turn to negotiate," Cleo snarled, charging toward the female imp.

"Cleo…" Troy made a futile attempt to stop the nymph. "I wouldn't."

Ignoring his warning, Cleo wrapped her fingers around Astra's neck and started squeezing.

"Give me the information or I'll rip out your throat."

Arching a brow, Astra glanced toward Troy. "Where did you find her?"

Troy sighed. "The future."

"Really?" Astra returned her attention to the female attempting to choke her. "It explains so much."

The scent of figs was abruptly drowned by the thick perfume of roses before Astra released a burst of power that sent Cleo flying back to slam against the marble wall.

"You." Cleo regained her balance, her face flushed with fury.

Swearing beneath his breath, Troy rushed to stand directly in front of the nymph. He grabbed her shoulders, feeling her trembling with outrage. She'd been a dictator of her tribe for so long she didn't remember how to compromise.

"Give her the gem."

"Have you lost your mind?" she hissed.

He parted his lips to inform her that Astra had only revealed a small portion of her powers. She could have crushed Cleo if she wanted. One of the benefits of having a mother who was an Elemental and capable of manipulating air. Wisely, however, he bit back the warning. Cleo was alpha enough to prove she was the more powerful fey. And while he enjoyed watching a spontaneous throwdown as much as the next dude, he was in a hurry.

"Did you have it when you were in this time?" he asked, barely capable of keeping Cleo from wiggling from his grasp.

She paused, clearly puzzled by his question. "No."

"Then it will come to you in the future," he said.

She furrowed her brow, her expression suspicious. "You're sure?"

Troy shrugged. He didn't have a clue. No one understood what happened when you screwed with timelines. Yet another reason not to do it.

"We need the information," he reminded her.

Cleo hesitated, no doubt weighing the cost of succeeding in her mission against the loss of the priceless stone. At last she reached up to grasp the emerald, giving a sharp tug to break the chain that was looped around her neck.

Troy gently took it from her stiff fingers before turning to his cousin. Astra held out a slender hand, her expression impossible to read.

"First the information," Troy said, keeping the gem clenched in his hand.

A taunting smile curved his cousin's lips. "You don't trust me?"

"Astra."

"Fine." Her slender fingers touched the amber broach that held her toga together. "I've seen several groups of demons huddled together over the past few years."

"What demons?" Troy asked.

"Mostly fey," Astra told him. "Sprites, nymphs, and pixies." She paused, as if thinking back. "Sometimes there have been brownies and goblins," she added.

Troy nodded. It was impossible to know for certain they'd been brought through the gateway, but it was the most promising lead they had.

"Where did you see them?"

"They travel down the main avenue." She paused, grimacing at the memory. "They're strange."

"Strange?"

"They never look around or acknowledge the people who crowd the city. They just ram them out of their path. As if they're in a trance." She shrugged. "And they often are wearing odd clothing."

Triumph flared through Troy. Yes. That's exactly what the mer-folk had looked like before disappearing through the gateway.

"Where do they go?"

Astra stretched out her arm. "Give me your hand."

Troy hesitated. He didn't think his cousin would hurt him, but then again, she hadn't risen from being an outcast to a wealthy businesswoman without a ruthless determination to succeed. If she thought she could gain an advantage, she would sacrifice him without hesitation.

Then, when both females glared at him, he grudgingly held out his hand. Grabbing it, Astra used the tip of her finger to draw an invisible pattern on his palm.

Once done, Astra stepped back, admiring the emerald she now held in her hand. Troy ignored her smug smile, keeping his attention on his palm. There was a tingling sensation that was just on the right side of pain before a thin, black line began etching a map on his skin.

It was easy to see the path they needed to take through Rome and into the nearby hills. There was even an X to mark the spot where he assumed the tranced demons were headed.

"So if that's all," Astra murmured, obviously anxious to get rid of them.

"One more thing," Troy said, lifting his head.

Astra looked impatient. "What now?"

Troy pointed toward her head. "About that tiara…"

Astra reached up to grab the circlet of gold, shoving it in his hand. "Here."

"Always a pleasure, cousin," he murmured.

She ignored him, instead blowing a kiss toward the seething Cleo. "Pleasure doing business with you, nymph."

Cleo's hands clenched, but before she could do something stupid, Astra formed a portal around them and in the blink of an eye, they were standing in the street outside the bathhouse.

Troy turned away, holding his palm up to study the map. "We need to go north."

"Not until I teach that bitch a lesson in manners," Cleo snapped, her gaze locked on the front entrance of the nearby building.

"Knock yourself out," Troy drawled, not about to argue with the furious female. He wasn't stupid. "One question before you go. After you die will I be stuck in this timeline?"

Cleo's face twisted, as if she'd just taken a bite of something foul. Then, as if realizing that she was no match for Astra, she squared her shoulders and tilted her chin to a proud angle.

"Lead the way."

Chapter 13

Locke could sense the moment that Kyi woke. It was in the way her breathing changed, and the beat of her heart. An unexpected pang of disappointment raced through him. Holding her in his arms as she'd slept had been shockingly pleasurable. Not just the warm press of her body, but he'd spent the past hours studying her face in the firelight, almost as if he was trying to memorize each curve and sweep.

The thought of having to let her go was more painful than he wanted to admit.

Slowly her lashes fluttered up, revealing her sleep-dazed eyes. She stiffened, as if she wasn't quite sure where she was, or why she was lying in the lap of a vampire, but even as he prepared for her to wiggle out of his arms, she reached up to lightly touch the star-shaped scar on the side of his neck.

"Tell me about this," she murmured.

He flinched. The wound had healed centuries ago, but it still caused him pain. Not physical pain, but the mental torment that would never be eased.

"You're supposed to be resting." Reaching up, he pressed her fingers against the side of his neck, hiding the scar. As if he could block out the unwelcomed memories.

"I am," she murmured, her gaze searching his tense face. "Does it bother you to talk about it?"

Locke conceded defeat. She wasn't going to let this go. "It's not a pretty story," he warned.

"Was it a battle?"

"Nothing so glorious."

"Battle wounds are glorious?" There was no missing the hint of reproach in her tone.

He turned his head to glance toward the fire. He didn't want her to see his shame. Not because he was abused. It'd started when he was too vulnerable to fight back. But because it had taken him so long to find the means of escaping his tormentor.

"Better than being brutalized by my sire."

She jerked, as if horrified by his words. "Your sire wounded you?"

Locke's lips twitched. The fact she could be shocked by his sire when her own mother was determined to kill her revealed the essential purity of her heart. She obviously wanted to believe in the goodness of others. Locke, on the other hand, had allowed himself to become jaded. He expected the worst and he was rarely disappointed. Except for Kyi. She'd been a complete and utter surprise. In the best way.

"He enjoyed tormenting his children," he forced himself to confess. She needed to understand his past if—Locke cut off the thought. Now wasn't the time to think about the future. Not until Xuria was dead and Kyi was safe. "His favorite pastime was tying us to the floor in a special room he had built in his lair," he continued, his gaze still locked on the dancing flames.

"What was special about it?"

"There were small holes drilled into the roof."

"Why would he want holes? I'd think that would defeat the purpose of the roof."

Locke clenched his fangs, unable to halt the memory of his earliest years from forming in his mind. He had no recollection of being a human, of course. His current life had started when he woke as a vampire in the northern reaches of what was now Norway. He'd been trapped in a massive castle surrounded by ice. The cold, barren setting was a reflection of his cold, barren existence behind the high stone walls.

"He wanted beams of sunlight to reach us."

Kyi gasped. "Why?"

Locke's lips twisted. He could still hear Gunnar's laugh as he stood in the shadowed doorway, his ice-blue eyes glittering with malicious amusement.

"It was a game. The first to flinch or cry out in pain would have their head chopped off."

The words came out clipped, almost detached. As if it'd happened to some other vampire. The only way for Locke to survive during that time was to cut off all emotion.

Fear, grief, compassion. The only thing in his heart was a burning, relentless hatred.

"Why?"

Locke glanced down, meeting her sympathetic gaze. "He was evil. His only enjoyment was watching others suffer."

"His own children," Kyi breathed.

"Vampires have a different perspective on offspring. Very few sires bother to discover if they've created a child or not," Locke reminded her, not bothering to mention that most vampires perished within the first week of being created. "A shame that Gunnar wasn't so indifferent."

Kyi paused, then seemingly sensing he didn't want to discuss the intimate details of the various tortures he'd endured for centuries, she turned the conversation to a happier subject.

"What happened to your sire?"

A genuine smile curved Locke's lips. This was a memory he enjoyed dredging up.

"Gunnar locked us in a dungeon once night fell to keep us from escaping." Locke shuddered. There'd been a dozen of them crammed in one small cell, barely able to move. "But to keep us alive, he had to occasionally feed us. Usually that meant shoving a fey creature into the cell and having us fight over the meal." He grimaced at her hiss of disgust. He'd warned her that it wasn't a pretty story. "Thankfully he was sloppy one evening. He brought a sprite to the cell that he hadn't thoroughly checked."

"Checked?"

"To make sure he didn't have hidden weapons."

"Did he?"

His smile widened. "No, but he did have a plodo crystal hidden in his braid."

She frowned, as if trying to identify the rare stone. "Aren't those for creating fire?"

"This one specifically created small explosions," he said. "The sprite was smart enough to negotiate with me. He would use the crystal to open the cell door and I would let him live."

"I assume you took the bargain?"

"Yep." At the time he'd had to fight several of his siblings who were too hungry to believe that freedom was more important than dinner. Eventually, however, he managed to beat them into compliance.

"And your sire?"

"I tracked him down and stuck a silver dagger in the center of his black heart."

She didn't look surprised by his grim retribution; no doubt that was exactly what she'd been expecting him to say.

"Did it help?"

Locke considered the question. There'd been no denying the sheer elation that had filled him as he'd watched the disbelief change to horror on his sire's face. The bastard had been so smugly confident that he'd never have to pay for his sins. Claiming retribution with his own hand had been glorious.

"At the time."

"But?"

Locke shrugged. Even as he'd watched Gunnar's body turn to ash, he'd realized it hadn't been enough. Maybe nothing would ever be.

"But it didn't erase the pain he'd inflicted." He squeezed her fingers that still cupped the side of his neck. "Or heal my scars."

"It stopped him from continuing his madness. Who knows how many vampires you saved," she said, as if trying to reassure him that destroying his sire was the honorable choice.

Warmth swirled through him. Lowering his head, he brushed his lips over her wide brow. "A nice thought."

She trembled, her sweet passion scenting the air. But even as he skimmed his lips down the soft skin of her cheek, she was tilting back her head to study him with a curious expression.

"What happened after you killed your sire?"

"Not all of my siblings were delighted to be freed from Gunnar's insanity." Locke had been shocked when he returned to the dungeon to release his siblings, only to discover they were in a full-blown panic. They had no idea how to survive without Gunnar, and they blamed him for leaving them without a master to protect them. "They condemned me as a traitor."

"Did they drive you away?"

"Worse. I was staked to the ground to meet the sun." Locke grimaced. The silver stakes they'd driven through his wrists and ankles had been agonizing. But not as painful as the sense of betrayal.

She blinked. "Seriously?"

Locke stared down at her beautiful face, abruptly realizing how similar their lives had been. They'd both been cursed with a monster for a parent, and both had been abandoned by their siblings when they needed them the most.

Perhaps that's why he'd felt an instant connection. Or maybe it was just destiny.

Probably both.

"It's the nature of vampires to bite the hand that feeds us. Figuratively and literally."

She shook her head, her brow furrowed. "They wanted to be tortured?"

"No, but they had never experienced the world beyond Gunnar's lair. They were terrified of trying to survive on their own."

Her confusion slowly cleared as she heaved a sad sigh. "Better the devil you know?"

"Exactly."

"How did you escape?"

His fingers absently threaded through her hair, savoring the soft texture. "A vampire happened to be passing the area, and he released me."

Her eyes widened. "That was lucky."

"At the time I thought it was more than lucky. I thought it was destiny. Especially when my savior asked me to join him on his mission to civilize the vampires. It seemed like a glorious stroke of fate that he would pass by on the particular night to rescue me. I didn't hesitate to join his quest."

"Civilize the vampires?" She widened her eyes in faux incredulity. "That sounds like a futile task."

He gently tugged her hair. "In some ways," he admitted. "In others, the Anasso was remarkably effective. He managed to create peace between most clans." A sorrow that he'd refused to acknowledge after the death of the previous Anasso pierced his heart. He'd known from the beginning that Gunnar was a ruthless bully who took joy in hurting others, but he'd trusted the Anasso, which meant his treachery had been a hundred times worse. "At the end, however, he proved unable to battle his own demons."

Easily sensing his pain, Kyi moved her hand from his neck to gently brush his cheek in a comforting gesture.

"I'm sorry."

He nodded, allowing himself a rare moment of introspection. "I think his death was one of the reasons I became so obsessed with revenge for the murder of my supposed mate," he confessed. "It gave me something to concentrate on besides my sense of betrayal."

Her fingers drifted down the line of his jaw, the light caress sending sparks of desire shooting through his body.

"And now?"

He smiled as a wicked heat sizzled in the air between them, as if their desire had become a tangible force.

"Now I have other distractions."

She blushed, but she tried to pretend she didn't notice. "Killing Xuria?"

"Killing Xuria," he agreed, using the tip of his fang to trace her lower lip. "Indulging in temptation." He kissed her softly, speaking against her mouth. "Eventually returning to the new Anasso to resume my role as a Raven."

"Raven?" Her fingers returned to stroke over the scar on his neck. Locke didn't flinch this time. In fact, her touch was deeply soothing. "I assume that's some sort of warrior?"

"It is." Locke quickly diverted the conversation. He'd shocked himself when he admitted he was considering returning to his position as a Raven. And while it had felt right when the words left his lips, he wasn't prepared to commit his loyalty to Styx. Besides, he had better things to concentrate on. "Aren't you more interested in the temptation I mentioned?"

Her eyes darkened with invitation. "Very interested." Desire surged through Locke as he lowered his head, but with a teasing smile, she reached up to place her hand over his lips. "But first we need to find my father's tribe."

His anticipation shattered, leaving an aching hunger in its wake. Still, his lips curved in rueful amusement as he accepted she'd managed to get revenge for his earlier refusal to indulge their mutual need.

"Tease," he murmured.

* * * *

Inga stood in the center of the cave and scratched her nose. Somewhere nearby there was an olive grove. They always made her sneeze, even when they weren't in bloom. She barely noticed. Her gaze was locked on the spot where the footsteps abruptly disappeared.

She bent down to brush away the thin layer of sand that covered the stone floor. "This is where they stepped through the portal."

"*Non.*" Levet moved to squat next to her, his claw tapping at the faint scorch marks. "Not a portal. A gateway."

Inga sent her companion a puzzled glance. "What's the difference?"

"Human magic doesn't create portals. They make gateways."

"Oh."

She shrugged. She'd spent most of her early years as a slave to a variety of demons. She'd been forced to mine rubies in the deepest bowels of the earth; she'd hauled massive boulders from the tops of mountains to build lairs for her masters; she'd rowed goblin ships around the world, more than once. She rarely had the opportunity to spend time with humans. Not until Riven, the former King of the Mer-folk, had convinced her to spy on a human witch named Lilah.

Unfortunately, that didn't help her now. A witch and a sorceress were both human, but that's where the similarities ended.

Levet straightened. "Can we follow?"

She glanced toward the rapier she held in her hand. "Perhaps with the Tryshu." The truth was she had no idea what the mighty trident could or couldn't do. She was learning on the job. Never a good thing. Her thoughts were shattered by the distinct sound of a footstep outside the cave. Surging upright, she turned to face the opening. "Someone's coming."

Levet sniffed the air. "Mer-folk."

The word had barely left his lips when two males and a female stepped into view. They were dressed in the familiar armor made out of scale-shaped plates with helmets that covered their heads.

"Don't move." It was the female who raised her trident to point it at Inga and Levet, nodding toward the two males. "Take their weapons," she commanded.

Levet sent her a raspberry. "I do not think so."

The female's brows snapped together as she stared at Levet with an expression of wary confusion.

"What are you?"

"Are you blind?" Levet spread his fairy wings. "I am a gargoyle, of course."

The female shook her head, whether in disgust or disbelief was hard to say. "Kill him," she commanded.

Inga swallowed a sigh. She'd wanted to avoid attracting attention to herself, but it was obvious she had to take control of the situation.

"Stand down," she said in sharp tones, dropping the illusion around the rapier to reveal the Tryshu.

With audible gasps of shock, the mer-folk stared at the weapon. "How did you get that?" the female demanded.

Inga shrugged. "It chose me." She kept the "unfortunately" to herself.

The mer-folk exchanged baffled glances before they fell to their knees. "Your Majesty," the female breathed. "We had no idea a new queen had been chosen."

It took Inga a second to realize that she was still hidden behind the façade of magic. Her lips parted, but before she could speak one of the males pressed a hand over his heart.

"Thank the goddess," he muttered.

The second merman nodded in agreement. "I told you that Inga creature had to be the work of some evil magic. An ogress." He turned his head to spit on the ground, as if just the mention of her name had left a bad taste.

The female surged to her feet, holding her trident over her head. "Long live the new queen."

The two males followed her lead, shouting with unnecessary force. "Long live the queen!"

Levet stomped his foot, his tiny face hard with anger. "Stop this at once."

"Levet." Inga shook her head.

She wasn't going to pretend that the mer-folk jubilation at her supposed dethroning didn't hurt. But it was nothing that she hadn't heard whispered behind her back. And right now her wounded feelings weren't important. Finding her people and bringing them home was the only thing that mattered.

Tilting her chin, she forced herself to meet the mermaid's gaze. "I need information."

The female swiftly nodded. "Of course, how can we be of service?"

"I received word that mer-folk were being kidnapped. I've come to rescue them."

One of the males released a shaky sigh, as if he was about to cry in relief. "Bless you."

Inga kept her attention on the mermaid. She was obviously in charge of the small group. "Tell me what happened."

"We were traveling to meet with the Queen of the Sylphs to negotiate safe passage through the Alps when we were approached by a moss sprite," she explained in crisp tones.

Inga nodded. Her mother had been busy attempting to forge a variety of new treaties now that the mer-folk were moving through the world again. She hadn't understood every detail about the various negotiations, but she trusted her mother's judgment.

The first rule as a queen was to delegate duties to the best qualified, and most loyal subjects. So far she depended on her mother, her aunt, and her Captain of the Royal Guards. Not nearly a large enough circle.

"Did you recognize the moss sprite?" Inga asked.

"No." The mermaid shook her head. "None of us had ever seen her before."

"She was strange," one of the males added.

Inga turned toward him, surprised to discover that he was studying her with a blatant male appreciation. She waited to feel the surge of pleasure at his gawking. Nothing. Not unless you counted the urge to thump him on the head with her trident.

"Why do you say that?" she forced herself to ask in a calm voice.

"Her eyes were white, and they glowed."

"Sorceress," Levet murmured.

The merman shrugged. "I don't know what she was, but as soon as she was close to us she started speaking in a language I've never heard before. The next thing I knew we were following the stranger to this cave."

"How did you escape?" Inga asked.

The mermaid took over the story, firmly reclaiming her role as leader. "We were the last to step out of the portal. It was already starting to close and I suspect it must have disrupted the spell." She waved her hand toward the opening of the cave. "The three of us fled across the beach and hid in the water."

Inga nodded. That made sense. "And the others?"

"They never came out of the cave." The mermaid shuddered. Inga suspected she wasn't as composed as she wanted them to believe. The disappearance of her friends had clearly rattled her. "We don't know what happened to them."

Inga turned back to study the spot where the mer-folk had disappeared. "The sorceress must have taken them to another dimension," she murmured.

"*Non.*" Levet firmly shook his head. "Another time."

Chapter 14

Kyi hid a smile as Locke stood on the far side of the cabin while she put out the fire with a burst of magic. As a highly flammable demon, he clearly tried to avoid open flames whenever possible. Which made the fact he'd overcome his aversion to keep her warm as she slept all the more remarkable.

A melty sensation swirled through her as she crossed the floor to grab his hand. "Ready?"

"I go first." He sent her a warning frown, clearly expecting an argument.

Kyi shrugged. "Fine. You can get thumped on the head this time."

His frown deepened as he reached up to lightly touch the healing wound on her forehead. It was barely visible now, but it'd done far more damage than she'd been willing to admit.

"No one's going to thump me," he growled. "And they most certainly aren't going to thump you."

"Famous last words," she said tartly, although she couldn't disguise her pleasure.

She didn't need his protection, but it was nice to have someone watching her back. Since leaving the dryads she hadn't had anyone who cared whether she lived or died. She hadn't realized just how much she'd missed having a companion.

Maintaining her grip on his hand, she lifted her other one and swirled it in a large circle, creating a portal. There was a tingle of soft fey magic before the opening appeared.

Locke stiffened. He wasn't able to see the portal, but he would have felt the warm breeze and caught the scent of clover that rushed into the cabin.

Not giving him time to lecture her on who was supposed to go first, Kyi tugged them through the portal.

Abruptly they were standing on a beach with the sea behind them and moonlight spilling from a vast sky above. Kyi sucked in a deep breath, catching the faint scent of approaching nymphs. On the point of warning Locke they weren't alone, she watched as he was lifted off the ground by glittering bands of magic.

"Wait," she cried, moving to stand in front of the vampire, who was cursing as he fought to free himself.

"Leech!" A voice cried from the line of trees that guarded the inner center of the small island. "Gather the warriors."

Things were spiraling out of control. Quickly. If she didn't take action there was a good chance someone was going to get hurt. Including herself. Clearing her mind, Kyi chanted low words, conjuring a human spell as she reached into her pocket. Grabbing the small bag she'd prepared before leaving her grove, she pulled it out and tossed it in the air.

At first there was nothing but strange sparkles that twirled above her head. She could see the approaching nymphs pause as if wondering if it was supposed to be some sort of distraction. The answer came a second later when a massive cyclone of sand and small pebbles swirled through the air and headed directly toward them.

Kyi closed her eyes, waiting until the projectiles stopped whipping around her. Then hearing a loud thump, she turned to see Locke climbing to his feet. Her spell had thankfully disrupted the fey magic to release him from the bands. Not that he looked particularly appreciative to be released. His fangs were extended and the air was tingling with electric current.

Rage zaps, she silently dubbed them. And something she would no doubt have to become accustomed to if she intended to spend time with this particular vampire.

His lips parted, as if to share his opinion of being dropped like a sack of potatoes, but the words never left his lips. Instead his gaze locked on something behind her. Whirling around, Kyi expected to discover one of the warriors sneaking up on them. Instead she realized that he was gaping at the damage she'd created with her spell.

It was impressive, she silently admitted. The sand had gouged deep groves into the ground and turned over boulders. She'd deliberately avoided the trees. Not just because she didn't want to hurt the nymphs, but her dryad training was too deeply ingrained to be dismissed easily.

"Remind me not to piss you off," Locke murmured.

She snorted, moving forward. "Too late."

"You are very easy to underestimate."

"That's my superpower."

He glanced to the side, deliberately allowing his gaze to run down the length of her body.

"*One* of your superpowers," he murmured.

She ignored his words, scaling the rocks that formed a natural barrier between the main island and the beach. Ahead of them a dozen warriors scrambled to climb the trees for a better shot.

Like most nymphs, they were slender creatures with golden hair pulled into long braids. Most of them were wearing form-fitting clothes that allowed them to fade into the shadows of the branches. With lethal expertise they pointed their wooden arrows directly at Locke's heart.

"I don't think we're welcomed," he murmured.

"How would you react if strange demons intruded into your private lair?" Kyi asked, her nerves on edge. Each step was taking them closer and closer to potential death.

Locke didn't have to answer. They both knew he would destroy anyone he considered a threat without hesitation.

Reaching the tree line, Kyi sent him a warning glance. "Let me talk to them." She stepped forward, spreading her hands in a gesture of peace. "Hold your fire. We're not here to cause trouble."

"Then why are you here?" A male stepped out of the trees.

He was tall for a nymph, with hair that had faded to a pale shade of honey, and a lean face that had been honed to sharp angles by time. His body, however, remained unbent by age and his eyes were as clear and hard as emeralds. In contrast to the other nymphs, he was wearing a long robe that shimmered like silver in the moonlight and there was a crown of bronze leaves in his hair.

Kyi froze, her brow furrowing as she stared at the male. It'd been centuries, and he'd obviously aged, but she was certain she recognized the male.

"Quell?" she at last asked in a hesitant voice.

The male froze in confusion at the sound of his name. "Who are you?"

"Kyi."

"That's..." The male blinked, his nose flaring as if trying to capture Kyi's scent. Then, with a shaky cry, he was rushing forward. "You're alive."

Locke smoothly moved to block the male from reaching Kyi. With a click of her tongue, Kyi stepped to the side so she could see the nymph.

When she was just a baby this male had carved toys for her out of driftwood and would sneak her extra sips of nectar when her father wasn't looking.

"Yes, I'm Kyi."

Quell studied her with a frantic gaze, as if struggling to accept that she was truly there and not a figment of his imagination.

"What happened to you?" he finally demanded. "We returned to search for you and Cleo, but we couldn't find any trace."

"We were taken in by the dryads," Kyi answered.

Quell's eyes snapped with sparks of emerald, as if he was outraged by her explanation. "You were kidnapped?"

"No, no. We were treated as cherished guests," Kyi hastily reassured the older male.

There was a short pause, as if Quell was determining whether she was telling the truth before he glanced over her shoulder toward the beach.

"Where is Cleo?"

"London." Kyi's voice was clipped enough to warn Quell she didn't want to discuss her sister. That was a conversation for a later date. "At least that's where she was the last time I spoke with her."

"Both alive," Quell breathed, wisely not pressing for more information. "It's a miracle from the goddess."

Kyi glanced toward the trees where the warriors continued to point arrows in their direction.

"How many of the tribe survived?"

"Thirty who traveled to our new homeland," Quell told her. "There may be others who scattered to join other tribes."

Kyi flinched. There'd been over fifty tribesmen before the attack. A tragic loss. "I'm sorry."

Quell tilted his head to the side. "For what?"

"That you were attacked." Kyi waved a hand toward the nearby beach. "That you were driven from your lairs and forced to hide on this remote island."

Quell reached out to grab her hand, giving her fingers a gentle squeeze. "We are quite happy here, and it certainly wasn't your fault that your mother attacked us."

"But—"

"No one is responsible except Xuria," he firmly overrode her objection. "Just Xuria."

Something that she thought eternally broken slowly knit back together as Quell pulled her hand to place it over the steady beat of his heart. It wasn't healed, but it was…mended.

"I thought you might not want to see me again."

"Oh my love." He appeared horrified by the unsteady words. "The fear that you and Cleo were lost to us has been an endless source of grief. Now we can celebrate your return."

Without warning, Locke reached to grab her arm, firmly tugging her hand away from Quell as if he was jealous. She glanced at him in surprise, but his attention was focused on Quell.

"First we have some questions."

"This is your mate?" Quell asked Kyi, his gaze on the tree-shaped amulet that Locke wore around his throat. *Her* amulet.

Kyi was oddly flustered by the question. "This is Locke."

"We're here to find a means to destroy Xuria," Locke smoothly added, as if sensing her unease.

His distraction worked. Quell's face hardened with an unmistakable hatred. "She still exists?"

Kyi nodded. "Yes."

"We will postpone the celebrations." With one wary glance toward Locke, the older fey turned to walk back toward the trees. "Follow me."

Kyi readily trailed the male she'd known all her life, acutely aware of Locke stalking beside her. She appreciated his determination to be vigilant. It would be foolish to drop their guard just because they were surrounded by her old family. Not only had it been centuries since she'd been a part of this tribe, but they had every reason to blame her for the deaths of their loved ones. And there might be any number of hidden dangers lurking around the island.

Kyi, however, found it impossible to remain wary as they entered the trees and the warriors jumped out of the branches to circle them as they headed toward the center of the island. There was nothing threatening in their behavior. In fact, most of them were staring at her with blatant joy, as if they truly were delighted she was there.

A few minutes later they stepped out of the trees into a clearing. In the middle a large fire crackled, tossing out sparks that drifted on the soft breeze. Beyond that there was nothing to see but a dozen or so small mounds that were covered with wildflowers.

During the day nymphs preferred to live in the open, savoring the tapestry of nature no matter what the weather. At night, however, they usually slept in underground burrows that were connected by a spiderweb of tunnels. It not only offered protection, but a measure of privacy.

Quell led them to a burrow on the far edge of the clearing, parting the wildflowers to expose a narrow opening in the ground. With fluid grace the male dropped out of sight. Kyi followed quickly behind him, swallowing a chuckle as Locke muttered a curse.

She didn't know if he was annoyed because she hadn't waited for him to make sure this wasn't a trap, or because he was in constant danger of whacking his head as they moved through the cramped tunnel.

Probably both.

Thankfully they didn't have far to travel before Quell entered a large space dug into the hard ground.

Kyi stepped in and glanced around. It was obviously Quell's private quarters. The dirt floors were covered with brightly striped rugs that had been handwoven and several fluffy pillows that were tossed in a circle in the center of the space, as if he used this area as a meeting place. In the far corner were a wooden bookcase and cubbies chiseled into the walls to hold his clothing and few possessions.

Quell gestured toward the cushions and Kyi moved to take a seat. Locke settled beside her while the elder fey sat across from them. The scent of clover swirled through the air, settling around Kyi like a familiar blanket.

"It smells like home," she murmured.

Quell smiled with pleasure. "This will always be your home, Kyi. We're your family."

A bittersweet emotion tugged at Kyi's heart. The horror of her mother's brutal attack had marred her memories. She couldn't think of her childhood without it being tarnished by regret and guilt and a burning need for revenge.

Now there was something wonderful about being in the company of Quell, as if he offered a promise that someday she could look back and recall the good parts of the past.

Easily sensing the turmoil inside her, Locke wrapped an arm around her shoulders and pulled her tight against his side. The gesture only added to her sense of belonging.

"Can we ask you a few questions?" he asked Quell.

The nymph nodded. "Of course, although I'll warn you that I didn't know much about Xuria. I'm not sure how much help I can be."

"For the moment we're more interested in the starlyte crystal," Locke assured him.

Quell stilled, obviously surprised by the direction of the conversation. "We no longer have it."

"Do you know the history of the crystal?" Locke pressed.

"It once belonged to the Chatri," Quell said, referring to the original fey purebloods. "They fled from this world eons ago."

Locke nodded. "What was the purpose of the crystal?"

There was a short pause before Quell answered. "It was a vessel for power."

Kyi studied the male. He seemed…cagey. As if he didn't want to reveal the truth of the crystal.

"I don't understand. What do you mean by vessel?"

There was another pause before Quell heaved a sigh of resignation. Clearly he realized that she wasn't going to be satisfied until she had every scrap of information.

"For the original fey it was a means to store their own power to use during a battle," he explained.

"Like a backup battery?" Locke asked.

"If a battery could destroy an entire tribe with one blast," Quell said dryly.

Kyi made a startled sound. She'd known the crystal somehow gave her mother immortality, but she hadn't realized its destructive force.

"Where did the tribe get it?"

"From your father." Quell glanced down at his hands that were folded in his lap. Was he avoiding her gaze? "I asked Kahn when he first brought it to the village where it'd come from. He claimed that it'd been given to him for doing a favor for some mysterious stranger."

"You didn't believe him." Her words were a statement, not a question.

"I think it's more likely the crystal was forgotten when the Chatri left this world and Kahn stumbled across it in one of their abandoned lairs."

Kyi was puzzled. "Why would he lie?"

"He used his supposed blessing by the Chatri to take command when our previous leader was murdered by a rival tribe."

"Oh." A strange foreboding inched down Kyi's spine.

Locke tugged her closer. "Could Kahn control the crystal?"

"No." Quell shook his head. Emphatically. "It took the special powers of the pureblooded fey."

"Or human magic?" Kyi added.

"Yes. That's why he went in search of a sorceress."

"And found my mother." Kyi shivered. How did a nymph go about finding a sorceress? It wasn't like he could have put an ad in the paper. Or posted an opening in social media. Quell nodded, his expression grim. Kyi shivered again. "But why have children with her?" she demanded. "And why give away the crystal?"

"Kyi." A worried expression settled on Quell's lean face. "Kahn was a good male in many ways. He cared for his tribe and he adored his children. Leave it at that."

The warning solidified from the vague premonition into a physical dread. It felt as if she had a ball of hot lead in the pit of her stomach.

"I can't." Her voice was hoarse, but insistent. "My mother will never stop trying to destroy me. My only hope is to kill her first."

Quell blinked, as if puzzled by her words.

Chapter 15

Locke struggled against the urge to slam his hand over Quell's mouth. He could feel the tension and pain that was humming through Kyi as she was forced to accept her father wasn't a paragon of virtue. Since his heroic death she'd no doubt put him on a pedestal. The last thing he wanted was for her to endure more disappointment.

But she'd spoken the truth when she said there was only one way to stop Xuria's determination to kill her.

"We need the truth," he forced himself to say between clenched fangs.

Quell turned his head to meet Locke's fierce glare. With obvious reluctance he nodded his head.

"Very well." Quell took a second to gather his thoughts. Or maybe it was his courage he was gathering. Eventually he sucked in a deep breath and returned his attention to Kyi. "Kahn never trusted the sorceress despite the arrangement they made. He knew that once she had her hands on the starlyte crystal she would eventually betray him. What he needed was someone trustworthy who would also have the magic he needed to fuel the crystal."

"A daughter," Kyi rasped.

"Yes. And two daughters doubled his chance for success," Quell continued. "Both you and Cleo had the magic of a sorceress running through your veins, but you would be raised to be loyal to your fey family."

Locke could see Kyi flinch as the revelation she was no more than a convenient tool slammed into her. Her resolution, however, never faltered. At least not on the surface.

"What was the point of children if he gave away the crystal to create them?" she asked.

Quell grimaced. "Once he had the daughters he needed, he intended to steal it back."

"Steal it?" Locke arched a brow. He wasn't shocked Kahn would be willing to lie, cheat, or pilfer to gain power. It was a fine demon tradition. But he couldn't imagine anyone being stupid enough to piss off a sorceress.

"In his mind, it belonged to the fey," Quell said.

Locke glanced toward Kyi, noting the tight line of her jaw.

"What happened?" he asked Quell, taking command of the conversation. Kyi was struggling to accept this new image of her father.

"Kahn sent a dozen warriors to Cyprus to retrieve the crystal from Xuria." The scent of scorched clover blasted through the air. Obviously it was a memory that still pissed off the male. "Only one returned."

"They were killed?" Locke asked in surprise. Just how powerful was Kyi's mother?

"Yes, we discovered that as long as Xuria was actively using the crystal it was impossible to take it away from her." His gaze darted toward the silent Kyi before returning to Locke. "Worse, she followed the returning warrior and attacked."

Locke tucked away the information that the sorceress had managed to destroy eleven nymph warriors and instead concentrated on the question that was nagging at the back of his mind.

"If Xuria was mad at Kahn, why try to kill her own daughters?"

Quell slowly shook his head. "I wasn't aware that she did," he said, and Locke was reminded of the male's puzzled glance when Kyi had mentioned her mother's attack. "We assumed they were innocent casualties when Xuria killed Kahn."

"No." Kyi visibly shook away her distraction. "She was aiming her spell at Cleo and me. There was no mistaking that she wanted us dead. It was Dad..." She was forced to halt and clear her throat before she could continue. "He sacrificed himself to protect us."

Quell nodded, not seeming to be surprised that Kahn would go to such lengths to save his daughters.

"Perhaps she realized you would eventually be able to control the crystal," the older fey suggested, his brow furrowed as he tried to rationalize Xuria's filicidal tendencies. "If she got rid of the competition there would be no need for Kahn to try to steal it back."

Locke wasn't satisfied with the answer. Xuria had used the word "destiny." That made it sound like she'd decided to kill her daughters before the fey warriors bungled their attempt to snatch the crystal.

"Exactly how does she harness the power?" Locke moved to his next question. Time was ticking and he wanted to be done with this family reunion so they could move on to the "killing Xuria" part of his plan.

"Magic."

Locke narrowed his eyes. Quell was being deliberately evasive. "What sort of magic?"

The older male's jaws tightened. He didn't want to answer. "Fey magic," he eventually ground out.

Kyi made a sound of disbelief. "That's impossible. She doesn't have fey blood."

Quell glanced toward her, struggling to hide his revulsion as he spoke of the sorceress. "The crystal drains the strength from demons and Xuria uses that power to keep herself immortal."

Kyi released a shocked gasp, her gaze turning toward Locke. "That's why she captured the mer-folk. She's not using them as slaves, she's using them as fuel."

"And the pixies," Locke added.

"I don't understand," Quell glanced at them in confusion.

Locke shook his head. He didn't have the time to explain that Xuria had been corralling fey creatures and herding them through a mysterious gateway.

"How did Kahn expect his daughters to use the crystal?" he instead asked.

Quell lowered his gaze. "By tapping into the power of our enemies."

"What enemies?" she rasped.

Quell hunched his shoulders. "Rival tribes."

Locke felt Kyi shudder, her eyes wide with horror. They all knew what "tapping into the power" meant. A slow, probably painful death.

"He told me he needed human magic to protect our tribe from the vampires," she whispered.

Quell reached over to lightly touch her hand. "I'm sure that was part of his plan, but Kahn was ambitious. He wasn't content with being leader of a small obscure tribe. He wanted to create an empire."

She shook her head, her expression unbearably sad. "I never knew."

"How do we destroy the crystal?" Locke asked, anxious to veer the conversation away from Kahn. Eventually Kyi would have to deal with her father's complicated legacy. But now they needed to concentrate on stopping Xuria.

Quell settled back in his cushion, his expression hard. "You can't."

Locke refused to accept the older male's warning. "There is always a way."

"Not as long as Xuria has it under her control," Quell stubbornly insisted. "The sorceress would have to die. Or willingly surrender it."

Locke ignored Kyi's snort of derision. Everyone knew Xuria would never willingly surrender the crystal.

"So no one can touch it as long as she's using it? Not even Kyi?"

Quell shook his head. "One of the Chatri could obviously manipulate the crystal." He stopped to consider his answer, then he shrugged. "Or perhaps a fey with royal blood."

"And Kyi?" Locke pressed.

"Not as long as Xuria is using it."

Locke ground his fangs together. That wasn't what he wanted to hear. If they couldn't forcibly gain command of the crystal, then how the hell could they stop Xuria?

Unless…

Locke leaned forward, stuck by a sudden inspiration.

"Would Xuria have to physically hold onto the crystal to use it?"

Quell slowly shook his head, his brow furrowed as he considered the question. "No. In fact, the crystal would need to be close to the fuel source."

Kyi made a choked sound. The "fuel source" was poor fey creatures imprisoned by her mother.

Locke tucked her even closer to his side as he considered his next question. "What if she was cut off from the crystal?"

There was a long silence, as if Quell was caught off guard by the question. Obviously he'd never considered the possibility. Probably because the older fey didn't realize that Xuria had created a gateway to travel to another dimension.

"I suppose it's possible," Quell agreed, his tone dubious. "But it would take a massive amount of magic."

Or the closing of a gateway, Locke silently added.

With an abrupt need to get on with the hunt, Locke surged to his feet. During his long years in Gunnar's less than tender care, he'd learned the value of patience. It was the only way to remain sane while he waited for his opportunity to kill the bastard.

But that patience was nonexistent when it came to keeping Kyi safe. He had to take action.

Now.

"We have what we need," he announced.

"We do?" Clearly confused, Kyi slowly rose to her feet.

"Yes."

Quell moved to join them, a disappointed expression on his lean face. "You're leaving?"

Kyi reached out to lightly touch his shoulder. "I'll return." Her lips twisted in a wry smile. "Assuming I find a way to stop my mother from killing me."

"You'll always have a home here," the nymph assured her.

"Thank you," she whispered, her voice not quite steady.

Locke felt an unexpected flare of fury, as if the thought that Kyi might accept Quell's offer was…a betrayal. Grimly, he leashed his temper that threatened to send jolts of electricity through the air.

Kyi had spent centuries terrified her family blamed her for the horrific attack on their village. She needed to know that she was still a welcomed member of her tribe.

Not that he intended to allow her to spend her eternity hidden away on this island.

The absolute certainty that Kyi's future was bound to his own barely created a ripple of unease as Locke led her out of the cramped burrow, as if he was ready, even eager, to accept the webs of fate binding them together.

Once they were back in the clearing, Locke stepped aside so the other nymphs could gather around Kyi, their soft chatter filling the air as they touched her with gentle hands. At last she turned, managing to escape the eager nymphs so she could move to join him.

In silence they returned to the beach. Locke sensed she was struggling to wade through a tidal wave of emotions. Joy that her tribe still loved her, swiftly followed by betrayal at the knowledge her father had intended to use her and the crystal to enslave rival fey. But as they reached the spot of her portal, Kyi turned to face him.

"Why did you say we have what we need?" she asked.

"We know why she's in this dimension," he pointed out.

"To collect fey creatures to power the crystal."

"Yes."

She made a sound of impatience. "We won't be able to track her down."

"We don't need to."

"Why not?"

Locke smiled. "We know where she's headed."

She looked puzzled. "You mean her gateway?"

"Yes."

Kyi frowned, no doubt wondering if he'd lost his mind. "We have no idea when she'll return there. She's had to jump from body to body, which saps her strength. She'll have to rest before she can find a new demon to infect. And she still needs to capture more prisoners to fuel the crystal. It might be days or months before she decides to return to her dimension."

"Good." Locke's smile widened. "Can you open a portal to Cyprus?"

She planted her hands on her hips. "Not until you tell me what you're plotting."

"I'm plotting to destroy the gateway. That should cut off her connection to the crystal."

Her eyes widened, something that might be hope easing her tense expression. Then the frown returned.

"How can we destroy the gateway? It's not like a portal that's meant to be temporary. It would take an enormous amount of magic to close it, let alone damage it enough Xuria couldn't get it open again."

Locke shrugged. "Jagr."

She waited for him to continue. "I don't know what a Jagr is," she finally said in exasperation.

"A fellow Raven," Locke told her. Locke had always been closer to the massive goth warrior than most of the other vampires. Like him, Jagr had endured a torturous past that had left him scarred and wary. They also shared a love for knowledge. It was a power that could overcome any weapon or magical spell. Hopefully it could also overcome a demented sorceress. "He has the largest library since Alexandria sank into the sea."

Something sparked in her eyes at the thought of such a vast collection. Clearly she was a fellow bibliophile. Locke silently promised to take her to Jagr's lair so she could browse to her heart's content. Her expression, however, remained confused.

"It sounds impressive, but how will that help us?"

"In one of those thousands and thousands of books, there has to be a way to destroy a gateway."

She stared at him with a wary hope. "Do you really think so?"

Leaning down, he placed a soft kiss on her lips. "We're about to find out."

Chapter 16

Levet glared at the mer-folk. He had several very nasty spells he wanted to lob at their smug, too-pretty faces. Fireballs were always a favorite. They usually didn't cause excessive damage, but they would make the mer-folk screech in terror. Or he had a lovely hex that could cause massive boils that never healed. And another one that would steal a demon's voice. Perhaps that would teach the fools to keep their lips shut.

Unfortunately, he knew that Inga wouldn't be pleased. No matter how cruelly her people treated her, the ogress refused to retaliate. And worse, she refused to allow him to teach them a lesson.

It was all *très* unfair.

Muttering beneath his breath, Levet slowly turned. He was standing next to Inga as she lifted her Tryshu and pointed it toward the gateway.

"Ready?" she asked.

"*Oui.*"

She shot him a warning glance. "There's no guarantee I can get us back."

Levet shrugged. He'd been trapped in hell-dimensions, and in the crypts beneath Notre Dame, and for one terrifying day in the rafters of a mannequin factory. Nothing could scare him now.

"What does it matter?" He reached to touch her arm. "We will be together."

"Together. Yes," Inga breathed, her features softening.

Did she wish they could get stuck someplace together? A place where she didn't have to be a queen and he wasn't the official Knight in Shining Armor? It was a tempting vision.

Levet sighed at the fantasy of a warm, tropical island with him and Inga lying beneath a star-studded sky. There would be fruity drinks with tiny umbrellas and the scent of…

His snout twitched and the fantasy shattered. "I smell olive trees," he murmured.

"And humans," Inga added.

"The gateway is open," Levet pointed out the obvious.

"Yes."

They shared a rueful glance, then together they stepped forward. At first Levet felt nothing. It was like stepping through an open doorway. Then a ripple of magic shimmered around them, like waves lifting them off the beach and washing them to open water.

The sensation lasted only a few seconds before the magic disappeared and they were left standing in the middle of an olive grove. Inga slowly glanced around, holding her Tryshu in front of them as protection.

Anyone stupid enough to attack would be very, very sorry.

A minute ticked by. And then another. There was no attack. In fact, there was nothing but the distant cricking of crickets. Is that what they did? Levet silently pondered. Crick? Croak?

"Where are we?"

Levet allowed his gaze to skim over the landscape. They were surrounded by hills. Seven hills. Each with clusters of buildings and homes constructed out of stone and covered with plaster.

"Rome," Levet answered, nodding toward the Palatine Hill, the location where Romulus and Remus had been discovered by the she-wolf. Levet hadn't actually met the wolf, but he'd heard she was a charming female. At least as charming as a werewolf could be.

Inga wrinkled her nose as the scent of burning fish oil and a nearby latrine wafted on the breeze.

"Ancient Rome," she added.

Levet nodded. "It makes sense. In this time Rome would have been one of the human centers of power. An ambitious sorceress could control the course of history from here." He glanced toward his companion. "Are you familiar with the city during this time?"

Inga shook her head. "No. I was never allowed near human settlements while I was a slave. What about you?"

Levet pursed his lips. He's spent a number of centuries roaming the world after his mother had put a bounty on his head. Which meant he tried to avoid most large towns where word of him might be whispered back to Paris. But there'd been a period when he'd lived in Rome among the gladiators beneath the Colosseum. Not the human gladiators, since the building hadn't been finished, but the demon ones that fought deep underground. He'd made a tidy fortune betting on the battles.

"I spent a few years in the area," he admitted.

"Did you hear about a sorceress?"

"*Non.*" Levet started to shake his head, only to suck in a sharp breath. "Wait."

"What is it?"

"A memory. Give me a moment." He turned to study the city that was dotted across the hilltops before spilling into the valley. He'd been alive for a very, very long time. He had a lot of memories stuffed into his brain and it wasn't always easy to pluck out the one he needed.

He could vividly recall his nights at the fighting pits, and visits to the elegant bathhouse where a demon could purchase anything they desired, including a brewed grog that could set a demon on fire. It'd taken him three weeks to grow back his wings, but it'd totally been worth it. And of course there'd been endless orgies. Or at least he had heard there were orgies. His own invitation had obviously been lost in the mail.

He'd also spent numerous evenings at a small, sleazy demon club where the local misfits could gather in peace to drink ale and share gossip.

"There were rumors of a mysterious witch," he finally said in triumphant tones. His vast knowledge amazed him at times.

Inga didn't look nearly as impressed. "We're not searching for a witch."

Levet shrugged. "Demons rarely understand the difference between witch and sorceress."

Inga considered his explanation before nodding. "What did they say about her?"

"That she performed foul magic."

Inga snorted. "Demons think all human magic is foul."

"True. But when they spoke of her it was always in whispers."

"Ah." Few demons would be scared of a lone witch, although anyone would fear an entire coven. But a sorceress didn't need others to amplify her powers. Which made them far more dangerous. "Do you remember where her lair was?"

Levet pursed his lips, his attention turning toward the distant hills. "It was not in the city. The local vampire clan chief had banned all magic-users."

"Typical," Inga muttered. "Vampires are big babies when it comes to magic."

"It is the only thing they fear," Levet said, then wrinkled his snout. "Well, beyond the sun. And wooden stakes. And the wrath of their mates.

Do you know I once witnessed Styx turn a weird pasty shade of gray when Darcy—"

"Perhaps we can discuss the vampire mating habits later?" Inga interrupted, her tone tart. Levet frowned. She sounded as if she was envious. But why? Because he mentioned mates? Hmm. Inga frowned. "I think dawn is about to make an appearance."

"*Oui*," Levet agreed, although his senses told him that they still had over an hour before the sun peeked over the horizon.

Inga glanced around. "Where would a sorceress hide?"

Levet didn't have to consider the question. He pointed toward a vast marble structure that was perched on a peak above their heads.

"In the largest villa on the highest spot so she can look down on the demons who cast her out of the city."

Inga sent him a wry glance. "Machiavellian."

"Precisely."

Inga hefted the Tryshu over her shoulder, a considerable feat considering the massive weapon was nearly as large as her new body.

"It is as good as any place to start," she agreed, heading up the narrow path that wound its way through the olive grove.

Levet effortlessly kept pace with her shorter strides. It was also easier to glance up to study her delicate profile, but Levet wasn't pleased. He missed his Inga. He liked when she towered over him in her ridiculous muumuus and her short tufts of red hair sticking out. He liked her speckled in paint and her expression dreamy as she created one of her exquisite murals. He liked seeing creatures cower in fear when she was in a full-blown fury.

Heaving a sigh, he asked the question that had been on his lips since they stepped through the gateway.

"Do you wish to discuss what occurred with the mer-folk?"

Her eyes flashed crimson. "No."

"I do."

"Of course you do," she muttered, picking up the pace, as if hoping to outrun the unwelcomed conversation.

"It is not good to hold in your emotions. They stew and fester until bang." Levet fluttered his wings in a dramatic fashion. Plus, it allowed Inga an opportunity to admire their sparkly beauty. "They explode."

Inga scowled, clearly not in the mood to admire anything. No matter how sparkly.

"Stewing and festering is better than dragging them out and digging through them," she growled. "They should stay properly buried. Like rotting fish."

"Yeesh." Levet grimaced. "This conversation is making me queasy."

"Me too," Inga readily agreed. "Let's change the subject."

They stepped out of the grove onto a neat, stone paved pathway that led up the hill. The Romans could always be counted on to provide a decent road.

"Not until we discuss your reaction to the mer-folk," Levet stubbornly insisted.

Inga heaved a harsh sigh, turning her head to glare at him. "What do you want me to say? Did it hurt my feelings when they cheered the end of my rein as queen? Or when they revealed that they were ready and eager to worship anyone on the throne as long as it wasn't Inga the Ogress? Of course it did." She returned her attention to the road, her profile as hard as the stones beneath their feet. "But yammering about it doesn't change anything."

Levet absorbed her fierce words, his heart sinking. He understood. He truly did. How many times had he been driven from a demon community because he looked different? *Sacrebleu*, his own mother tried to kill him. But the one thing he'd learned was that he couldn't allow bitterness to taint his soul.

That was the only way the haters won.

"They only see the surface," he reminded her.

"That's all anyone sees."

"*Oui*. But being a leader isn't a beauty contest."

Inga made a sound of disgust. "Tell them that."

Levet clicked his tongue. He was attempting to comfort her. Why was she making it so difficult?

"When times are good then a pretty smile and shallow charm is fine. A shiny bauble is all the people need," he insisted. "But when times are troubled they need strength. A leader who has overcome obstacles and endured hardship. Like a finely tempered steel blade."

"More like a battle-axe."

"If you insist," Levet readily agreed. He always found battle-axes formidable weapons. "When it comes time to enter a fight I want a battle-axe, not a shiny bauble. Eventually the mer-folk will understand your worth."

A sad smile touched her lips. "Your hope may spring eternal, Levet, but I'm much more realistic." There was a note of finality in her voice. "They will never accept me. Not as long as I look like an ogress."

Levet sighed. There was no point in trying to convince her that her value as a queen wasn't based on her physical appearance. Not when she was in a poopy mood. Instead he would give her what she desired.

Permission.

"Then look like a mermaid."

She made a shocked sound, turning her head to gaze at him with a wary expression. "What?"

Levet reached to touch her hand. "You can wear the ring as long as you desire. Forever if it makes you happy."

A vulnerable expression rippled over her pretty face. "Do you think I should?"

He wanted to stomp his feet and scream in protest. Of course he didn't think she should. Why destroy her rare perfection with shallow ordinariness?

"The decision is yours, *mon ami*," he forced himself to say. "You be you."

She tossed her head in frustration at his refusal to give his opinion. A mistake as the wind caught the golden curls and sent them spinning across her face.

"Argh." She reached up to try and clear away the mess. "Why would anyone want so much hair?"

* * * *

Locke motioned for Kyi to remain near the door as he crossed the flagstone floor of the demon club. He didn't worry about the handful of customers scattered around the narrow space, not even the two trolls drinking grog in a shadowed corner. None of them could match a vampire in brute strength.

But the club wasn't one of the five-star establishments on the island. In fact, it probably rated a negative one star. It was created out of a decaying villa that had damp crypts dug beneath the pitted marble structure. The interior was stuffed with a jumble of furniture that had been pillaged from local hotels, and splotches of mold adorned the walls.

Locke had chosen the establishment to avoid meeting up with any vampire who might recognize him. No demon would willingly stay at this sleazy club unless they were hiding from something. Or someone.

He wanted to spare Kyi from spending more time than necessary in the disgusting place.

Heading toward the end of the room, Locke approached the mongrel goblin slouched on a stool. Locke doubted he was the proprietor, but he was surveying the common room as if he was in charge.

"Yes?" the creature demanded as Locke halted in front of him. He was a good six inches taller than Locke, with bulging muscles beneath his filthy T-shirt and jeans. He had coarse black hair, brutish features with a heavy brow, and eyes that held hints of crimson fire. There was a smug swagger in his manner that assured Locke the creature was accustomed to being the biggest, baddest demon in the club.

Good. An inflated ego made demons careless.

"I want a room," Locke said, keeping his disgust out of his tone.

The goblin sucked air through his pointed teeth, as if considering whether or not to allow Locke to stay.

"A sun-free room is extra."

"Fine."

"Do you want dinner?"

Locke shuddered, unable to imagine what the goblin considered dinner. "Just the room."

The goblin glanced over Locke's shoulder, a sudden leer twisting his lips as he caught sight of Kyi. There was even a bit of spittle at the corner of his mouth.

"Ah. You have your own snack. There's a service fee for bringing take-out unless you're willing to share—"

Fury burst through Locke before he could leash it. Not that he would have tried, even if he could.

Snapping out his arm, he grabbed the demon by the throat and lifted him off the floor. Behind him the customers released shouts of alarm as the air snapped and sizzled with his power.

"Give me the key before I use your head to ram open the door," he said in a cold voice.

The goblin struggled, as if too stupid to realize his survival was hanging in the balance. "We haven't negotiated the price."

Locke tightened his fingers, intending to crush the creature's throat. Then, with an effort, he gained control of his temper. It seemed unlikely any of the customers would rush to this male's defense, but he couldn't risk a potential battle that would leave Kyi vulnerable.

With a flick of his hand, he tossed the creature against the marble wall, taking a childish satisfaction in the idiot's grunt of pain.

"It doesn't matter." Stepping back, Locke watched with a derisive expression as the goblin struggled to salvage his balance. "Send the bill to Styx."

The goblin blinked, as if he was having trouble comprehending what Locke had said. It was possible his brain had been rattled when he hit the wall, or more likely he was horrified by Locke's words. Evoking Styx's name had a tendency to spread terror far and wide.

"Styx? The An...Anasso?" the goblin stammered.

"I'm one of his Ravens." Locke reached up to touch the scar on his neck, as if it was some sort of symbol of authority. The goblin would have no idea he was lying. "If you want to haggle the price you can call the King of Vampires."

The male was shaking his head before Locke finished speaking. Reaching into the pocket of his jeans, he pulled out a handful of keys. Choosing one, he tossed it toward Locke.

"Just take it, spoilsport."

Locke flashed his fangs. "I try."

Turning, he nodded toward Kyi, who warily joined him. Together they walked through the arched doorway that led to the stairs heading down to the crypts.

"Winning friends and influencing people?" she murmured once they were out of earshot of the glaring demons.

Locke shrugged, allowing the last of his anger to drain away as her sweet scent perfumed the stale air. Just having her near was soothing. One of many reasons he was eager to keep her close to him.

"I don't have your charm," he told her.

"Charm?" Kyi released a humorless laugh that echoed through the spiderweb of tunnels as they reached the bottom of the steps.

Locke arched a brow, leading them through the middle tunnel toward the back of the crypts. He didn't need directions to know that any demon club placed the vampire rooms as far away from the other demons as possible. It couldn't prevent all accidents if a vamp lost control, but it gave the other customers a chance to escape.

"You don't believe me?" he demanded.

"I've spent the majority of my life alone in my grove. I don't have any practice at being charming."

"Then you're a natural."

They reached the end of the crypts and Locke halted at a wooden door. Using the key, he led them into the small room, pleasantly surprised as he glanced around. It was sparse. Just a bed shoved against a stone wall and a chair near the door along with a wooden stand that held a pitcher of water. But it was dry and basically clean. Unless you counted a stray cobweb.

Closing the door behind them, Locke leaned against the rough wood as Kyi paced the cramped space in the middle of the room.

"How long will it take?" she demanded.

Locke shrugged. He'd contacted Jagr as soon as they'd arrived in Cyprus. The vampire had promised he'd search for any information on gateways he could find.

"It could be a few minutes or several hours. I'm going to guess it's the latter," he warned in dry tones. "Jagr tends to forget what he's supposed to be doing when he's in his library." He nodded toward the bed. "You might as well make yourself comfortable."

She continued to pace. "I can't."

"What's wrong?"

Her jaw tightened, her steps jerky as if she was straining against a fierce emotion.

"I've always known my mother was evil," she suddenly burst out. "Even before she tried to kill me. But my father..."

Her words trailed away, her scent of bougainvillea suddenly subdued, as if her sadness was muting her very essence.

Locke resisted the urge to step forward and pull her into his arms. She wasn't ready to accept comfort. Not until she'd worked through her complicated emotions.

"No demon is perfect," he pointed out in low tones. "Not even me, as hard as that is to believe."

Her lips twitched, but she couldn't conjure a smile. "I don't expect perfection." She grimaced. "Just basic decency."

Locke considered his words. He'd lived among vampires who had their own value system. He wasn't offended by Kahn's desire to take over rival tribes. But he was deeply offended by his underhanded way of doing it.

It made it hard to know exactly how to ease Kyi's distress.

"He was obviously ambitious," he finally said.

"Ambitious?" She glared at him. He'd apparently said the wrong thing. "He made a deal with the devil for power, and then tried to kill the devil."

"Climbing to the top of the demon hierarchy is usually a bloody business," he reminded her. "But you have good memories of him, don't you?"

Her lips tightened, as if she wanted to deny Kahn's good qualities, then, with a sigh, she slowly nodded.

"Yes."

"Tell me."

She bent her head, allowing the sweep of golden hair to hide her profile. "Every morning he would take us to a small spring in the center of a nearby meadow so we could play in the water," she said, her voice so soft it was hard to make out the words. "And he always pretended to forget how to get back to the village so either Cleo or I could lead the way back home. It made us feel..."

"Feel what?"

"Special."

Locke could no longer resist his instincts. Pushing away from the door, he wrapped his arms around Kyi and pulled her against his body.

"You *are* special." He brushed his lips over her furrowed brow. "Special enough that your father was willing to sacrifice his life to protect you."

She melted against him, laying her head against the center of his chest. "Yes."

With one fluid motion, Locke swept her off her feet and carried her toward the bed. He sank down on the thin mattress, cradling her slender body in his lap.

"Hold on to those memories, Kyi." He gazed down at her, letting her see his regret that he'd allowed his bitterness toward the Anasso to turn his back on the Ravens. They'd been his brothers and he'd walked away. "Nothing else matters."

She released a shaky breath, raising her arms to wrap them around his neck. "Locke."

Chapter 17

Kyi didn't struggle against his possessive hold. She didn't *want* to struggle. After endless centuries of solitude, the sensation of being wrapped in strong arms was a balm to her weary soul. She'd been so utterly isolated. Now she eagerly snuggled against him.

Locke pressed his lips against the top of her head. "Why were you alone in your grove?"

"I was afraid," she admitted, revealing her long-hidden secret.

"Of Xuria?"

"Yes. Not only for myself, but I couldn't risk allowing anyone else to become collateral damage," she said.

It had been a constant fear that her mother might arrive without warning and harm some innocent bystander. How could she risk having a lover? Or even a friend?

He lifted his head to gaze down at her, his lips twitching. "Collateral damage?"

She shrugged. "When I'm bored I like to watch human television to pass the time. My favorite is Arnold Schwarzenegger movies."

Locke paused, as if searching his memory. "'I'll be back,'" he at last quoted in robotic tones.

She snorted, although she was pleased that he'd seen the movie. As if it proved they had something in common beyond their hatred toward Xuria.

"That's a terrible impression," she teased.

He dropped a kiss on the tip of her nose. "What else do you do to pass the time?"

Desire spread through her. A slow, relentless flood of need that she'd kept trapped for too long.

"I read and tend to my trees," she managed to say, her mind clouded with the tingly sense of anticipation.

His lips skimmed over her brow. "And create traps for unwary vampires."

She smiled. "Every girl has to have a hobby."

"You don't need any cages to trap this particular vampire." He nuzzled the tender skin at her temple.

She sucked in a deep breath of his coppery scent. "What do I need?"

"Your smile." His lips brushed over her cheek, the faint scrape of his fangs sending shudders of pleasure through her. She wasn't a demon who craved pain with her sex, but the fantasy of feeling those fangs sinking deep into her throat was intensely erotic. "Your scent." He pressed his lips against hers. "Your taste." Kyi readily parted her lips to allow the sweep of his tongue into her mouth. An electric shock tingled through her. "Your heart."

Kyi plunged her fingers into the cool, silken strands of his hair. It felt oddly decadent, but then everything about Locke was decadent. His astonishing blue eyes rimmed with gold. His bold features and the chiseled body that held such enormous power. And the electric sizzles that crackled through the air.

Decadent and sexy and utterly fascinating.

Just what she needed to drive away her aching sense of betrayal.

He deepened the kiss, his fangs pressing hard against her lower lip as his hands smoothed up the curve of her back. A tremor raced through her.

Lifting his head, Locke sent her a quizzical glance. "Kyi?"

"You make me tingle," she murmured.

"In a good way?"

She allowed a slow smile to curve her lips. "In the best way."

Locke growled, swooping down to bury his face in the curve of her neck. At the same time he allowed his power to dance around his fingers as he smoothed them down the length of her bare arms.

"Is it time?" He pressed his lips against the rapid pulse at the base of her throat. "No more teasing?"

She snuggled closer, heat exploding through her at the feel of his hard erection pressing against her hip.

"Not unless you ask very nicely."

Locke's eyes shimmered with enjoyment as he laughed in startled appreciation.

"I'll get on my knees and plead at this point," he promised.

Kyi lowered her arms, slipping her hands beneath his leather jacket to explore the hard, sculpted muscles of his chest.

"I'm not averse to having you on your knees," she told him in a husky voice.

With a speed that stole her breath, Locke was lifting her off his lap and setting her on the edge of the mattress. Kyi shivered. Not from the cold. The air in the crypt was surprisingly warm. No. It was a fear that Locke was rejecting her.

Swallowing a sudden lump in her throat, Kyi tried to speak, but before she could say a word, Locke was sliding off the bed and onto his knees.

"Your wish is my command," he assured her.

She watched with painful anticipation as he gently tugged her legs apart and slid his hands along her inner thighs. Jolts of pleasure ignited, bursting through her, like the fireworks she'd seen the humans shoot into the sky.

"I thought only jinn could grant wishes," she gasped, leaning back on her elbows as Locke lowered his head and followed the path of his fingertips with soft lingering kisses.

"I have all sorts of talents."

Kyi believed him. Right now, however, she was focused on his skill at stirring her hunger to a fever pitch.

Had she forgotten how glorious it was to feel the touch of a male? No. A shudder raced through her as his mouth found the sensitive apex of her body. It had never been like this. Never. It wasn't just the pleasure that sizzled and zapped through her. It was the heart-pounding certainty that this was special.

That Locke was special.

With a low groan, Kyi tilted back her head and closed her eyes. She wanted to savor the sensation of his tongue as it slid through her slick heat. Her breath hissed through her clenched teeth, her back arching as he found her sweet spot.

"You taste of summer," he murmured, chuckling as her moan echoed through the cramped room. His tongue dipped inside her heat, thrusting deeper and deeper. Kyi released more moans, her head twisting from side to side. "Bougainvillea."

"Locke." Kyi reached down, her fingers tangling in his hair as a delicious pressure started to build. As anxious as she was to satisfy her aching desire, she wanted her arms wrapped tightly around her lover.

Easily sensing her need, Locke straightened and stripped off his clothes with quick, efficient movements. Kyi watched in silent admiration. almost wishing he would slow down so she could thoroughly appreciate the unveiling of his magnificent form.

Almost.

Right now, she was as anxious as Locke to be rid of their clothes so she could feel those hard muscles pressed against her.

As he approached the bed, she did have a few seconds to savor his perfection. The broad chest where her amulet glowed. Someday she would demand he return her property. Or maybe not, she silently conceded. She liked the thought that he carried a part of her with him wherever he went. Her attention moved to the tapered waist and the long solid length of his legs. His skin was a pure ivory that had more to do with his Nordic ancestry than the centuries as a vampire.

He was every inch a conquering Viking.

Then her gaze locked on the proud thrust of his erection and her mouth went dry.

Yes. She needed him.

Now.

Reaching down, she grabbed the hem of her dress, but before she could pull it over her head, Locke was brushing away her hands.

"My honor," he insisted.

Locke leaned forward, gently tugging the straps of her dress off her shoulders and down her arms. Then, careful not to rip the soft fabric, he shimmied it down her body, tossing the garment aside. His eyes widened at the sight of the knife that was nestled between her breasts, kept in place by a hidden leather strap. Slowly, he removed the weapon, then pulled off her slippers to gaze down at her with a strange expression.

Kyi shivered. "Is something wrong?"

"I thought Xuria bewitched me," he murmured.

Kyi frowned in confusion. "She did."

"No." He shook his head as he placed one knee on the edge of the mattress. "She blinded me with magic. You…" He urged her to lay back on the mattress. "You bewitched me."

His husky words pierced her heart, shattering the barriers she built to protect herself. If she didn't care about anyone, then she couldn't be hurt or betrayed.

Now she eagerly welcomed Locke as he at last settled on top of her. The cool press of his body was paradise. Kyi released a sigh of bliss, wrapping her arms around him. Still it wasn't enough. Hooking her heels over the back of his legs, she allowed him to settle between her legs, positioning the hard length of his cock in the perfect position.

Locke gazed down at her, his eyes shimmering like sapphire fire.

"Bewitched," he murmured, then with one smooth motion he thrust deep inside her.

Kyi hissed at the intensity of her pleasure, her back arching off the bed as she met him stroke for stroke. Sharp moans filled the air as copper-scented lightning danced over her body.

Bewitched. Yes.

Chapter 18

Locke was caught between the delicious lassitude that came after amazing sex, and the fierce realization that he would never be truly sated. Not until he bound this female to him by the most primitive means.

A mating.

Still, he wasn't going to complain. Not when he was holding Kyi tightly in his arms, their naked bodies pressed together as she brushed her fingers lightly down the side of his neck.

Pausing as she reached the star-shaped scar, she tilted back her head to send him a curious gaze.

"Does this still hurt?"

"At times," he said, although he'd never been sure if the throbbing pain was from the physical trauma he'd suffered or the mental. He only knew that it was a constant reminder of his past. At least, it had been until he'd been caught in a cage by a fascinating nymph who smelled of summer. "It feels better when you're near."

She blinked in confusion. "I don't possess the skill of healing."

"Yes, you do." He bent his head to brush his lips over the plump softness of her mouth. "For me, everything about you is healing."

Without warning, she reached up to touch the tip of his fang. "You didn't bite me."

The fierce need seared through Locke, wrenching a groan from deep inside. "Are you disappointed?" he rasped.

"Curious," she corrected, although her blush revealed it was more than just curiosity. A part of her had wanted his bite. Perhaps ached for it.

The knowledge helped to ease a portion of Locke's frustration. "There's nothing more I desire than to taste your blood."

"But?"

He gazed down at her beautiful face, oddly certain he would never get used to having her so near. It was going to feel like a miracle every time he opened his eyes to find her wrapped in his arms.

"But I'm not sure you're ready," he said.

She frowned, clearly confused by his words. "I'm not afraid of you."

"Are you afraid of eternity?" He grabbed her hand, pressing it over his unbeating heart. "Because once I sink my fangs into the temptation of your delectable flesh, I will belong to you heart and soul."

The color in her cheeks darkened, the warm scent of bougainvillea wafting around him, like fragrant velvet petals brushing over his skin. He shivered in delight.

"You're sure?" she whispered.

Locke grimaced. He understood her wariness. Less than a week ago he'd been certain that Xuria was his mate and that this female had been her killer.

"Trust me." He held her gaze, willing her to accept his sincerity. "Magic clouded my mind once, but a true mating is unmistakable. It consumes me like an inferno."

His power sizzled through the air, creating tiny bolts of lightning that sizzled near the ceiling.

Kyi's eyes widened as she watched the impressive display. "Oh."

"Now are you afraid?"

She smiled, lifting her head off the pillow to press a kiss on his cheek. "No."

Locke believed her. She seemed so fragile, and yet she had the power of a full-sized troll and the courage of a warrior. An amazing female.

He brushed his lips over her furrowed brow. "Eternity can wait until we have managed to destroy Xuria," he assured her.

"*If* we manage to destroy Xuria," she muttered.

Lifting his head, Locke gazed down at her with an expression of pretend outrage. "Are you doubting my skill?"

Her lips twisted into a humorless smile. "Never but after centuries of trying to kill my mother, I'm beginning to wonder if it's even possible."

"It's possible," he assured her. "First we destroy the gateway and then…" His words trailed away as the ring of his cellphone echoed through the room. "Ah. Jagr on cue." Rolling over, Locke grabbed the phone off the floor where he'd left it and pressed the screen. "Tell me," he commanded.

* * * *

Troy had a yucky feeling in the pit of his stomach. Not a "bad-hair-day" yucky feeling. Or a "someone-wearing-the-same-outfit" yucky feeling.

This was a "run-away-screaming" yucky feeling.

Standing on the sweeping veranda of the massive villa, he tilted back his head to study the arched door that loomed in front of them.

"Should we knock?"

Cleo clicked her tongue. "Don't be an ass."

Next to her, Llewen unsheathed his sword. "I'll go first."

"An excellent decision," Troy commended the male, clapping him on the back hard enough to make him stumble forward.

Llewen whirled, clearly intending to stab Troy. Cleo, however, quickly motioned him to stand down.

"Ignore him," she snapped. "It's the only way he's bearable."

Troy shrugged. "If you want to get rid of me I'm ready, willing, and eager to return home. Just open the gateway and I'll be gone."

"Not until you fulfilled your debt," Cleo warned.

"Levet's debt," Troy reminded her in sour tones.

She nodded toward the crow etched onto the back of his hand. "You wear the marker."

"Exactly when am I going to pay my debt?" Troy demanded.

"Soon."

Cleo turned back, waving toward the door. Immediately Llewen rushed forward to push it open and dart inside. The uniformed warriors followed behind him, their weapons held ready to use.

Troy waited, prepared to take off at the first hint of battle. He was a lover, not a fighter. Especially when he had no reason to join the skirmish. When nothing happened, Cleo stepped over the threshold, glancing over her shoulder until Troy reluctantly joined her.

Troy wrinkled his nose. It was a typical Roman villa. Lots of marble. Lots of fluted columns. A mosaic tiled floor and coved ceiling and walls painted with brilliant frescos. But despite the elegant surroundings, there was something...off about the place. Like they were standing in an oversized mausoleum, not a home.

Seemingly impervious to the weird vibe inside the villa, Cleo tilted back her head and sniffed the air.

"Mermaids," she said in surprise, hurrying toward a nearby hallway lined with columns.

Troy strolled behind her, considering the meaning of the faint scent of salt in the air. Time-travel was a nuisance. There were always paradoxes and cosmic anomalies. But there was always one certainty.

"This is the focal point," he muttered.

Cleo's quick pace never slowed. "What does that mean?"

"It pins this villa to a specific point in time," he said. "Otherwise whoever created the gateway would just hurtle back and forth through various centuries. There has to be an anchor."

Cleo considered his words before slowly nodding. "Yes," she finally agreed, stepping into the inner courtyard of the villa. "That makes sense."

Troy stumbled to a halt, a shudder of horror racing through him. "I'm glad something does," he rasped, taking a slow survey of his surroundings.

Again, it looked like a normal villa. The long space possessed a shallow pool that ran from one end of the room to the other. On each side were marble benches that lined the pool and overhead there was an opening to allow in the night air.

What had captured his attention was the numerous servants who drifted around the space. They were all wearing matching robes in a material so thin it was easy to see their slender bodies as they carried around trays of food and drinks or played instruments that filled the air with music. It was as if there was a party going on with no guests.

That wasn't the most bizarre part of the tableau, however. It was the strangely blank expressions of the servants that made Troy's mouth go dry.

Warily he stepped toward a nearby mermaid who was absently waving a palm frond toward one of the empty benches. She ignored him. He moved to step directly in front of her. Still nothing. Troy waved a hand in front of her face.

"Hello?"

"They can't hear you," Cleo told him, motioning for her warriors to spread through the courtyard, standing guard as she moved toward a nearby statue of a naked male.

Troy grimaced. "What's wrong with them?"

"They're bespelled."

Magic had turned the demons into robots? He'd seen humans under compulsion. And a few vampires could compel lesser demons. But he'd never seen dozens of creatures being manipulated at the same time.

"By who?" he demanded.

"Xuria."

Troy made a choked sound. A human had the power to do this? Unthinkable.

"The sorceress?"

"Yes."

Unable to conceive the amount of magic needed, Troy turned to study the dew fairies that twirled and danced in time to the music.

"Why would this sorceress need so many?"

"I assume some are here to work." She nodded toward a brownie who was repairing a crack in one of the marble columns. "And some are here for protection." Cleo shrugged, moving toward the next statue, as if she was searching for something. "The fey creatures are here to provide the magic Xuria needs to stay alive."

Troy turned his attention to the nymph, watching as she bent down to inspect the feet of the statue.

"Humans can't use fey magic."

Cleo straightened and moved to a framed portrait of a female that was placed on an easel made from gold and studded with gems. A smug smile spread over her face.

"They can if they have a secret weapon."

"What secret weapon?"

"This one." Cleo pointed toward the base of the frame. "Come here."

Troy didn't want to. The sense of evil that pulsed through the villa seemed to originate from that precise spot.

"I don't have a good feeling about this," he warned.

Cleo made a sound of impatience. "You should. Once I have what we came here to retrieve then you'll be free to return to your home."

Troy reluctantly moved forward. "Who is that?"

"What do you mean?"

"The portrait. Who is it?"

"Xuria." A hard expression tightened Cleo's features. "This is how she looked once upon a time. Before she became incorporeal and started taking over the bodies of other creatures."

Troy frowned as he studied the portrait of a young woman with a cloud of raven black hair and ice blue eyes. Her features were bold with a wide brow and narrow nose and strong jaw that was tilted to an arrogant angle. Her pouting lips were shaded with a bright red color that matched the silk robe that was wrapped tightly around her lush body. Gold jewelry encircled her throat and rubies dangled from her ears. She was stunning. As long as you didn't mind the cold, ruthless glitter in her eyes.

"You look like her," he abruptly announced.

"I should," Cleo drawled. "She was my mother."

Troy hissed in shock. She was the daughter of a sorceress? Then slowly he realized that he should have suspected the truth from the beginning. What other nymph had managed to control an entire neighborhood in London for centuries? It wasn't because she'd been there before Victor, the vampire clan chief. "Of course she is."

Cleo jerked, as if his words had somehow manage to penetrate her thick skin. "Why do you say that?"

"I sensed there was something different about you from the beginning."

She sniffed. "It isn't my heritage that makes me different. It's my power."

Troy glanced toward the nymph soldiers who were staring at the blank-faced slaves with obvious wariness. They didn't know what was happening, but they could sense the evil in the air.

"Do your warriors know you have human blood?" he asked Cleo.

"My warriors don't care as long as they are generously rewarded," Cleo snapped.

Troy smiled with wry amusement. Her sharp tone revealed she wasn't nearly as certain as she wanted him to believe. Most demons readily accepted mongrels. Only purebloods cared about protecting their pedigrees. But no demon would be happy to discover that their leader was a child of a sorceress.

He narrowed his eyes. "Do *you* care?"

Cleo shrugged, pretending not to understand the question. "Care that I have to generously reward them? Of course not. You get what you pay for."

"Care that your mother is a sorceress," Troy pressed.

Cleo glanced toward the portrait, the smell of figs thick in the air. "I care that the bitch tried to kill me when I was a child."

Troy grimaced. "Charming."

"Not really." Her lips twisted into a bitter smile. "But I do admire her willingness to destroy anything that stands in her path."

"The apple doesn't fall far from the tree," Troy murmured.

Cleo looked pleased by his accusation. As if she gloried in the thought of being ruthless enough to destroy others.

"What is the point in being alive if you don't seize the day?"

Troy arched a brow. "And that's what we're doing? Seizing the day?"

"Exactly." With a smug expression, Cleo pointed toward the bottom of the frame, where a small gem was mounted in the wood.

Troy leaned forward, not sure what he was supposed to see. The stone was a murky white, like a common agate. But as he watched, he realized that deep inside there were pinpricks of color that pulsed as if it was alive.

Hissing in disbelief, Troy took a step back. “Holy crap. Is that a starlyte crystal?”

Cleo sent him a startled glance. “You recognize it?”

“Only from history books.” Troy clenched his hands into tight fists. Long ago the crystals had been used by the Chatri in battle. They’d filled them with their combined powers so they could replenish their strength whenever they needed. There were also rumors that it could be used to steal the souls of their enemies. “Where did your mother get it?”

“From my father.”

Troy felt his eyes widen in disbelief. “Your father is a Chatri?”

“No, just an overly ambitious nymph who was stupid enough to think he could use and betray a sorceress.”

“What happened to him?”

“He’s dead.”

Her voice was thick with disgust, but Troy didn’t miss the pain that vibrated in her voice. Clearly she had daddy issues. But why? He couldn’t be any worse than her mother.

There was a brilliant flash of light from the crystal and a soft moan was wrenched from the throats of the gathered servants. Across the courtyard one of the dew fairies plummeted toward the ground, hitting a marble bench with a sickening thud. Troy watched in horror as its dazzling wings drained of color before they turned to ash.

“Shit,” Troy rasped, turning to glare at Cleo. “Xuria is not just using the crystal to absorb the power of her slaves. She’s destroying them.”

“Yes.” Cleo nodded, her expression impassive, as if she didn’t notice the demons dropping around them like flies. And maybe she didn’t. “The magic keeps her immortal.”

A sick sensation curled through the pit of Troy’s stomach. He was a very old imp, who’d traveled the world and seen some terrible things. A few that still gave him nightmares.

But this…

The level of evil was off the charts.

“That’s why she kidnapped the mermaids,” he breathed. “They’re not slaves. They’re…food.”

Cleo nodded in a careless gesture. “She’s been draining the life from demons for centuries.”

Troy swallowed, as if he could get rid of the lump forming in his throat. Gazing at Cleo’s impassive face, he recalled the moment he’d first caught sight of her.

He'd been dazzled by her beauty, and the potent sensuality that had swirled around her with a poisonous temptation. He'd sensed she was dangerous, but that didn't scare him. Dangerous women were always the most fun. But he drew the line at evil.

Even he had standards. Dubious standards. But standards.

Chapter 19

Kyi held out her hand, watching as Locke reluctantly pulled her amulet over his head and dropped it onto her palm.

It hadn't taken long to travel from the demon club to the cave at the bottom of the sheer cliff, but during the short journey, Kyi managed to come up with a plan.

Not a great plan. She wasn't a trained sorceress. What little magic she'd managed to learn was undisciplined and occasionally unpredictable. But after Locke's friend had called to reveal the only means of destroying the gateway, she knew that she had to take the chance.

Clearly as dubious about her scheme as she was, Locke studied her with a worried expression. He was once again wearing his leather jacket and the faded jeans that molded to the long length of his legs, although they looked as if they'd been freshly ironed. And his hair lay as smooth as silk to brush his wide shoulders. Even his coppery scent was fresh and crisp as it swirled around her.

Kyi grimaced. She didn't want to imagine her own appearance. There was a good chance she looked like a bedraggled sea hag.

"You're sure this will work?" he demanded, glancing at the amulet that glowed against her skin. "Jagr specifically said to use a crystal to… to overload the gateway."

Kyi's lips twitched at his stumble. A vampire discussing magic was as awkward as a harpy discussing a long-term relationship. It made them itchy.

"A crystal doesn't have magic," she slowly explained. "It's a tool used to absorb and manipulate power."

He frowned. "Then what makes the starlyte crystal so special?"

"Each crystal or focal point has a different capacity for holding power. Most can only absorb a small amount and only for a limited time," she explained. "The starlyte is capable of holding vast amounts of magic."

"I assume they're rare?"

Kyi nodded. "Which is why I don't know much about them. There are rumors they were created by the breath of dragons. And another that they are the tears of unicorns."

"Unlikely," Locke said in dry tones.

"The only thing I know for sure is that no one but the Chatri have the ability to find them."

"So how did your father get ahold of it?" Locke asked.

Kyi considered the question. Her father had claimed it'd been given to him, but Quell had told her that he assumed that Kahn had found it the crystal. Neither one seemed a plausible explanation.

"I have no idea." She paused before giving a shake of her head. "I don't suppose we'll ever know for sure."

Locke nodded toward her hand. "Does this amulet do the same thing?"

"Actually, it does just the opposite."

Locke's eyes narrowed. "Opposite?"

"The amulet reflects magic."

"What does that mean?"

"It can protect the owner from malicious spells."

Locke arched his brows, as if struck by a sudden thought. "Ah, I was right. The amulet was the reason Xuria couldn't muddle my mind with her magic this time."

"Yes."

Without warning, his eyes darkened with annoyance. "Why did you allow me to keep it? You should wear it for protection."

She allowed a small smile to curve her lips. "I like to see it against your naked chest."

He made a strangled sound, as if she'd managed to shock him. Then, stepping forward, he wrapped her in his strong arms.

"Kyi." His voice was husky with an unspoken promise. "You continue to astonish me."

She tilted back her head, feeling a familiar zing of heat darting through her. This gorgeous Viking knew how to stir her blood.

"I don't want you to get bored," she teased.

"I have no fear of that. Not as long as you're near." Lowering his head, Locke brushed her lips with a light, lingering kiss. "We'll finish this later."

She shivered in anticipation, tingles dancing over her skin. "Mmm."

With an obvious reluctance, Locke dropped his arms and stepped back. "How's the amulet going to overload the gateway?"

It took a second for Kyi to clear her mind. Locke had the ability to scramble her brain with a single touch. Not that she was complaining. She liked a good brain scramble as well as the next female. But right now she needed to concentrate.

She cleared her throat. "As I said, it reflects magic. Which means it should ricochet the spell."

"Like skipping a stone?"

"Something like that," she agreed. "Usually the spell bounces off the amulet to dissipate harmlessly in the air."

He grimaced. "I still don't understand."

Kyi paused to consider the best way to explain what she intended to do. It would have been easier if she'd had actual experience.

"The gateway also reflects magic."

Locke glanced over his shoulder at the middle of the cave, as if searching for the gateway that was invisible to vampires.

"How do you know?"

"I don't for sure, but it's the only logical way to prevent stray creatures from entering her private dimension. Like locking a door to your house." Kyi pointed toward the center of the cave. "So if I place the amulet there and concentrate my spell on it, the magic should be able to bounce between the two reflective surfaces until it reaches a critical point and..." She spread her arms in a gesture of a huge explosion. "Boom."

His golden brows drew together. "*Should* be able?"

"In theory," she grudgingly conceded.

"Wait." Lightning crawled over the ceiling as Locke struggled to leash his burst of temper. "You've never done this before?"

Realizing he was about to be unreasonably stubborn, Kyi stepped around Locke to head toward the gateway.

"I've never had any reason to."

"Stop," Locke commanded as Kyi bent down to place the amulet on the rough stone floor.

"Why?" She glanced toward the male towering beside her, but she lowered herself to her knees as she prepared to cast her spell.

"We'll come up with a new plan," he told her.

Kyi shook her head. "This is the best plan."

Locke folded his arms over his chest, his features tight with tension. "Why not just cast your spell directly into the gateway? I saw what you did to the nymphs. It was impressive."

Kyi blushed, tucking away his words to savor later. She treasured the knowledge that Locke considered her a strong, competent female. It would have been way too easy to spend her life as a victim after her mother's attempt to kill her and the death of her father. That was exactly why she moved from the protection of the dryads into her own grove. She had to build a life that wasn't cowering behind the protection of others.

"But not nearly powerful enough to destroy the gateway. The amulet will amplify the spell." Tilting back her head, she met his worried gaze. "Trust me."

She watched his internal struggle ripple over his face, clearly torn between the urge to keep her safe and the knowledge that she needed him to have faith in her decision.

"I do," he at last assured her, squaring his broad shoulders. "What do you need?"

"I have it here." She reached into her pocket to pull out the remaining bundle she'd created before leaving her cottage.

It looked harmless enough. Twigs from a cypress tree, juniper berries, dried hyacinth petals soaked in lavender oil and bundled together by a piece of cloth soaked in salt to keep it stable.

"That's a dangerous pocket," Locke murmured.

"You have no idea," she teased. Then, spreading the ingredients next to the amulet on the ground, she waved a hand toward the opening of the cave. "You might want to stand back," she warned. "I'm not entirely sure how long it will take before it explodes."

"Kyi..."

"I'll protect myself," she muttered, already distracted as she concentrated on the amulet.

"You promise?"

"I promise."

She heard Locke's slow footsteps head toward the opening, the scent of copper thick in the air. She didn't have to glance at him to know he wasn't happy. Thankfully, he did as she asked, giving her plenty of space to complete her spell.

Shutting out everything but the magic that bubbled through her like uncorked champagne, Kyi bent forward. In the shadows of the cave, the amulet shimmered with a bronzed fire. Was it already responding to the magic of the gateway?

Only one way to find out.

Swallowing a lump in her throat that she assured herself wasn't fear, Kyi parted her lips and whispered the words of the spell. Power bubbled out of her, spilling toward the items she'd spread on the ground.

There was a faint scent of lavender, followed quickly by warm juniper as the air heated. Kyi repeated the words again. And again. She was about to complete the spell when there was a sharp crack of stone behind her.

"Kyi. Look out!" Locke shouted.

Jumping to her feet, she whirled around in time to see a huge slab of rock split off the roof to land directly on Locke.

"No."

Horrified, she rushed to his side. What the hell had happened? Was the gateway reacting to her magic? Or was it a trap that had been left by her mother?

Dropping to her knees, Kyi desperately pulled aside a layer of rubble to reveal a glimpse of Locke. Through the dust and rocks she could see that he was unnervingly motionless with blood pouring from a deep wound on his forehead. He looked like a corpse, she realized as horror clenched her heart. No. She grimly wiped the image from her mind, continuing to frantically clear away the rubble. She had to believe he was alive. Otherwise…

"How touching," a voice drawled from the entrance of the cave.

Kyi froze. Damn. She'd made the one mistake that could ruin everything. She'd allowed herself to be distracted.

Cursing her stupidity, Kyi reached beneath her dress to grab her dagger. She should have realized her mother had caused the ceiling to collapse.

Once she had the weapon gripped tight in her hand, she straightened and turned to face the woman who'd caused nothing but grief in her life.

As expected, she didn't recognize the intruder. The female sylph had short silver hair and skin that was tinted green. Her slender body was covered by a flowing gown that looked like spiderwebs, revealing more than it concealed. But it was the white eyes that captured Kyi's attention.

Eyes that were all too familiar.

"Xuria." The name came out as a curse.

The sylph released an eerie laugh. "Not Mommy?"

Kyi shuddered. Even if the sorceress hadn't tried to kill her, there was no way she'd ever felt anything but disgust for the woman.

"Never."

Xuria smiled, strolling into the cave to study the vampire lying unconscious on the ground.

"He really is quite lovely, isn't he?" she drawled. "I enjoyed having him in my bed."

Kyi narrowed her eyes. Xuria was trying to piss her off. Why? She couldn't fear that Kyi's magic was any match for her own, could she? No. Even with Kyi's fey blood she couldn't create the sort of lethal spells that would destroy a sorceress.

It wasn't until the shimmering white gaze darted toward the gateway, that Kyi realized the sorceress was trying to distract her. Her mother didn't want to fight, she wanted to escape.

"Liar," Kyi retorted. "You might be a powerful sorceress, but not even your considerable magic could force Locke to desire you." Holding the dagger in front of her, Kyi cautiously inched toward the center of the cave. Not only did she need to get close enough to finish the spell, but she wanted any potential battle to be as far away from Locke as possible. "Pathetic really."

"Is that what he told you?" She clicked her tongue. "What a gullible fool you are."

Kyi shrugged. She didn't doubt Locke's assurance he'd never had sex with this female. Not for a second.

"Better than a jaded hag who sold her soul for a cheap bauble," she taunted.

"Jaded?" Xuria pretended to consider the accusation, waving a slender hand in a casual motion. A blast of magic exploded an inch from Kyi's feet, forcing her to jump backward. Xuria smiled in satisfaction as the scent of sulfur tainted the air. "Yes. I've learned that you can't trust anyone. It's probably a blessing you won't survive long enough to become equally... jaded."

Kyi didn't dare risk trying to move. She had no idea what might prompt an attack. Her only hope right now was for Locke to wake up. Or for Xuria to make a mistake.

"Did you learn that lesson before or after you killed my father?" she taunted. Xuria wasn't the only one who needed a distraction.

"Oh, long before. I was once young and happy, you know."

Kyi snorted. "I believe you were once young. Happy? Not so much."

The sorceress shrugged, taking a step forward. She was preparing to escape through the gateway. Kyi used her nymph power to create a silvery thread of magic and tossed it like a lasso. Hissing in anger, Xuria dodged to the side to avoid being wrapped in the unbreakable strand.

Kyi braced herself, prepared for a magical counterstrike. It never came. Why not?

Did Xuria sense that Kyi had a spell prepared to destroy the gateway? She might fear any attack would trigger the magic. Or was it something else?

"It's true," Xuria said between clenched teeth, as if forcing herself to speak. "I was raised by the Oracles—"

"You were raised by Oracles?" Kyi interrupted, her curiosity momentarily overcoming her fear. "Why?"

"My parents tried to burn me at the stake when they discovered I was a magic-user."

The words were said with a cold indifference, but they hit Kyi with unexpected force. Not that she felt sorry for the woman, she sternly told herself. Xuria had destroyed any hope for sympathy.

"So trying to kill your offspring is a family tradition. Nice," Kyi said in dry tones. "Did the Oracles teach you to become a sorceress?"

Xuria grunted, as if outraged by the question. "When I said I was raised by the Oracles, I meant that they endured my presence in their caves. They were too occupied with their visions to care for a young child."

There was an unmistakable bitterness in her voice. She obviously resented the Oracles' lack of nurturing. Was that why she'd become such a selfish bitch or had it just come naturally?

She was betting on the natural method.

"Then how did you learn?"

"They had a library."

"I didn't know Oracles studied books," Kyi said, genuinely surprised. The Oracles were elusive creatures who rarely left their caves, but she'd assumed they were devoted to seeking prophecies. "I thought they looked to the heavens for their inspiration?"

"They didn't collect the books to read."

"Then why?"

Disgust twisted the sylph's delicate features. "They buried them to keep them out of the hands of humans."

Kyi was puzzled. It was one thing not to have any use for books and another to deliberately ban them. Then, she abruptly realized why a demon would try to keep information from humans.

"Dark magic," she muttered.

"Yes."

"And you found them."

Xuria looked smug. "I've always been curious. I knew they were hiding something in the deepest caves. It took me years, but eventually I found a means to get past their illusions and enter the library."

"So you repaid the kindness of the Oracles by betraying them?"

"They shouldn't have tried to keep them from me." Xuria shrugged, seeming to sincerely believe she had every right to break the trust of a family who'd taken her in. "Magic was my only means of protecting myself."

"Did they agree with you?" Kyi asked.

"No." The shimmer in the white eyes momentarily dimmed. "They tossed me out of the caves."

Had it hurt the young Xuria to be rejected by the Oracles? It seemed hard to believe that she ever had a heart that could be wounded, but stranger things had happened.

"So you decided to become an evil villain?"

"Evil?" The female quickly recovered her mocking arrogance. "Why would you say such a thing about your own mother?" Xuria punctuated the question with a blast of magic that sent shards of ice blasting through the air.

Kyi danced back to avoid the projectiles. She was being herded away from the gateway, she realized. She had to do something or Xuria would escape and it might be decades, or even centuries, before she returned.

"Because it's true."

Kyi released another strand of fey magic, but this time she aimed it at the ground beneath Xuria's feet. As the magic struck, the limestone began to melt into a soupy quagmire. The effect was temporary, but the sorceress was forced to back away from the spreading bog.

She glared at Kyi in blatant frustration. "I'm not evil," she snapped. "Just determined to take control of my future."

"Is that what you call it?" Kyi mocked. "I call it abuse, betrayal, and attempted murder. But whatever lets you sleep at night."

Surprisingly, Kyi's words seemed to strike a nerve. Xuria stiffened, her eyes smoldering with white-hot anger.

"How easy for you to judge when you're a demon," she sneered. "You might feel quite different if you were facing your own mortality."

Kyi couldn't argue. A demon could be destroyed, but they didn't have a ticking clock from the second they were born. She had no idea how she would feel if she were mortal. She hoped she wouldn't be desperate enough to spend centuries sucking the life from other demons to stay alive. Right now, however, she was more interested in Xuria's determination to kill her.

"Did you always intend to murder your children after you got what you wanted?"

"Of course," she admitted without shame.

Kyi made a choked sound. Her mother's casual willingness to destroy others, even her own family, was a continual source of shock.

"Why?" Kyi stared at the sylph in confusion. "Did you fear we would take the crystal from you?"

Xuria waved a dismissive hand. As if Kyi's question was too stupid to contemplate. "You are no match for my powers."

Again, Kyi couldn't argue. "Then why not leave us in peace?"

"Because of the Oracles."

Kyi waited, expecting her mother to finish the sentence. When she just stood there, Kyi shook her head in frustration.

"Is that supposed to make sense? I have no connection to the Oracles."

"After I made the trade with Khan—"

"Babies for the crystal," Kyi clarified. She'd be damned if she let this woman pretend it was some harmless negotiation.

Xuria rolled her eyes. "Yes. After I made the trade, one of the Oracles visited my villa."

"I thought they turned their back on you?"

"They did, but they're compelled to share their visions," the sorceress said.

"They had a vision about you?"

"And you." Xuria's lips twisted with an unmistakable bitterness. "Or at least one of my daughters. They couldn't tell me which one."

Kyi's mouth dried. She'd deliberately avoided Oracles and soothsayers. She had no interest in peeking into the future. What was the point in dreading a looming disaster when you couldn't do anything to change it?

Unfortunately, she couldn't stick her head in the sand. If the vision included her mother, she needed to know.

"What was the vision?" she reluctantly asked.

The stench of sulfur filled the cave. "That you would kill me."

Kyi's eyes widened at the blunt confession, then tilting back her head, she laughed with overwhelming delight.

Chapter 20

Inga gripped the Tryshu tight enough it turned her knuckles white. She had a bad feeling about the villa perched on the top of the hill. On the surface it looked fine. More than fine. It was magnificent. The sweeping veranda was at least twenty foot wide and framed with fluted columns. High, arched windows reflected the moonlight and the sparkling water from the nearby fountain. The roof was sharply slanted to drain the rainwater to the atrium at the side of the villa, while marble statues of Roman soldiers stood guard along the winding pathway.

Appearances, however, were often deceiving, as she knew from painful experience. Beauty could hide a poisonous soul.

Unfortunately, she didn't have the luxury of listening to the voice of warning that whispered in her ear. She was here to rescue her people and if that meant entering a villa that gave her the heebie-jeebies, then that's what she would have to do.

End of story.

Squaring her broad shoulders, Inga forced herself to step forward and push against the heavy wooden door. As if to ramp up the creep factor, the hinges released a loud screech as it swung open and the stench of sulfur threatened to gag her. Inga held the Tryshu in front of her, expecting the sorceress to leap out of the darkness.

A second passed. And then another.

Nothing.

"Let me go first," she finally muttered, forcing her heavy feet to take a step forward.

"*Non.*" Levet was swiftly at her side. "We go together. That is what partners do, is it not?"

A portion of her unease melted as she gazed down at the small gargoyle. She'd been alone her entire life. First as a slave, and then as a guardian to Lilah in the isolated glades of Florida. There was no one she could depend on to guard her back or share her burdens. Not until Levet.

It was no wonder she had no idea what to do with the charming, aggravating, utterly unique creature.

"Yes, that's what partners do," she agreed in soft tones, taking another step forward. This one was easier with Levet at her side, as if his presence offered her a courage she was lacking. Then, glancing around the vestibulum, she felt a shudder race through her body. "Ugh."

Levet lifted his hand, a fireball dancing just above his palm. "What's wrong?"

"More marble," Inga groaned.

"Oh." Levet reluctantly allowed the fireball to sizzle and die before he glanced around the large open space. "You have a distaste for marble?"

Inga wrinkled her nose. "It's white."

"*Oui*."

"And cold.

"*Oui*," Levet agreed again.

"And smelly."

Levet tilted back his head, sniffing the air. "Sorcerous magic," he announced.

Inga shivered. It wasn't from the smell of sulfur. She'd been prepared for the stench. No. It was the heaviness in the air. And a sinking sense that the entire structure might collapse into a steaming pile of perversion.

"Is more than that," she muttered.

Easily detecting her distress, Levet reached up to grasp her free hand. "What's wrong, *mon ami*?"

"This." She waved the Tryshu in a vague gesture.

Levet frowned. "The marble?"

"No." Inga made a sound of impatience. She didn't know how to explain the brooding sense of doom. "At least not entirely."

Levet tightened his grip on her fingers, tugging her toward a bench set near the wall.

"Let us walkie-talkie."

Inga didn't bother to correct him. Instead, she moved to settle on the bench. A wry smile curved her lips as she waited for the groan of protest from the marble. As an ogress she discovered human furniture wasn't created for a female with her grand proportions. More than once she'd broken a chair and landed on her tooshie. But this time there wasn't so much as a creak. Levet hopped up beside her, his wing brushing softly against her arm.

It was delightfully comforting.

Inga sucked in a deep breath, trying to ignore the smell of sorceress magic. "There's decay," she said. "A deep decay. As if this place is rotten to the core."

Levet glanced toward the floor, as if expecting it to suddenly crumble beneath them. "You are right. I can sense it."

Inga's shoulders slumped. "How does it happen?"

Levet glanced around the vestibulum, as if searching for the answer. "The sorceress, she has infected the villa with her evil," he said. "It spreads like a cancer, infecting everything it touches."

Inga wanted to believe him. If the rot infiltrating the place was the result of an evil heart, then she had nothing to fear. She might be an ogress, but she wanted what was best for her people.

Unfortunately, she couldn't fool herself. Not anymore. "I think it's more than that."

Levet's wing brushed against her back. "Inga."

"I think the villa is decaying from the weight of the unhappiness that fills it," she told her companion. "Eventually it will collapse into a black hole of misery."

Levet frowned. "Why do you say that?"

"I have ogre blood."

"*Oui.*" Levet smiled, as if she'd just confessed some wonderful secret. "And it is glorious."

Inga snorted, even as she inwardly preened at his words. She'd spent the majority of her existence apologizing for being an ogre. It was lovely to occasionally take pride in her father's ancestors.

"Hardly glorious, but it does give me the ability to connect with the stone." She laid her hand flat against the cool marble of the bench.

"Royal ogre blood," Levet murmured. He was right. Only an ogre with royal blood could truly communicate with the earth. That was why she'd been so valuable as a slave. Rare gems buried deep in the mountains sang to her like a chorus of angels. "What does a marble tell you?"

Inga shuddered. "It speaks of a darkness."

"Dark magic?"

"A corruption of the soul," she corrected. This wasn't magic. It was a reflection of those who inhabited the villa. "It comes from an unhappiness that is rotting this place from the inside out."

Levet studied her, as if attempting to peer into her head. She could have warned him that her skull was too thick to see through. The gargoyle, however, managed to uncover her mounting fear.

"That troubles you," he said.

Inga licked her lips, afraid to speak the words. Would saying them out loud make them come true? Then, silently chiding herself for her foolishness, she turned on the bench to face her companion.

"What if this same thing happens to my castle?"

Levet looked confused. "What thing?"

Inga waved the Tryshu around the empty space. "This thing."

"Do not be ridiculous—"

"Listen, please," she interrupted his protest. Levet always saw the best in everything. It was one of the things she loved best about him. But this once she needed him to be realistic.

The gargoyle reluctantly nodded. "Very well."

"I know that you believe the mer-folk will eventually accept me as their queen."

"They will," Levet insisted.

"What if they don't?"

"In time—"

"Levet, what if they don't?" she once again interrupted.

Levet's wings drooped as he was forced to imagine a future where the mer-folk continued to treat her as the enemy.

"I do not know what to say, *mon ami*," he finally confessed.

Inga sighed. For months she'd tried to be patient. She told herself that it was understandable that the mer-folk would be wary of her. Not just because she looked like her ogre father, but because she'd de-throned the former king. Adjustments in leadership always took time.

But as the days passed, nothing improved. In fact, they were getting worse. The nasty whispers when she walked past, the jaundiced glares, the refusal to obey her simplest commands.

And it wasn't like it was all the fault of the mer-folk, she conceded. She'd been a slave since she was a baby. What did she know about being a queen? She didn't want to sit on a throne, and the crown gave her a headache, and trying to be diplomatic was worse than walking barefoot over hot coals.

Her only true asset was that she controlled the mighty Tryshu.

Oh, and her fierce determination to protect her people.

She heaved a heavy sigh. "It isn't hard to imagine my people will become increasingly rebellious, and in time I will in turn become bitter," she admitted the dread that kept her awake at night. "It's a toxic brew."

Levet clicked his tongue. "It is this place that is making you feel so pessimistic, *mon ami*," he insisted. "Even my moony attitude is dimmed by the heaviness."

"Sunny," Inga absently corrected.

Levet sniffed. "Not for me. The moon is my friend, not the sun."

"Okay." With a wry smile, Inga rose to her feet. "Maybe you're right," she conceded, trying to shake off her foul mood. This villa would give anyone the willies. And besides, now wasn't the time to dwell on "what-ifs." The sooner she could get the mer-folk out, the sooner she could get away from this place.

Levet hopped off the bench, waddling toward the open door. "I'm always right," he reminded her. "Now, let us get out of here."

"Not without my people," Inga said.

Levet halted, his tail twitching as he reluctantly turned to face her. "I was afraid you would say that."

Inga closed her eyes, sucking in a deep breath. The stench of sulfur was overwhelming, but with an effort she caught the faintest hint of salt.

"This way."

Inga headed across the marble floor to enter the hallway, her hand tightening on the Tryshu as she realized there were more than just mer-folk in the villa. She caught the scent of pixies and fairies and nymphs, among other mongrels. There were even a few brownies and trolls. Hurrying forward, she was vaguely aware of Levet just behind her as she stepped into the open space of the inner courtyard.

She glanced around, taking in the sight of the various demons moving around the long, narrow pool. A frown tugged her brows together. They were obviously slaves as they carried trays or wafted palm leaves toward empty benches, but they didn't appear distressed. In fact, they looked…dead.

"Dear goddess," she muttered. "What's wrong with them?"

"They are bespelled," Levet said, his tone laced with disgust.

Inga took a step, her gaze locked on the closest mermaid, who was holding a tray of fruit. Without warning, she was distracted by a familiar scent. With a blink of shock, she turned her head toward the side of the courtyard where an imp was standing next to a large painting.

"Troy?" she breathed in disbelief.

The male frowned, momentarily confused by her magically altered appearance. Then his eyes widened in shock. As a royal imp he could see through any illusion.

"Inga," he breathed, seemingly unable to decide if he was more shocked at her delicate beauty or by the unexpected encounter, but even as he stepped toward her, his eyes abruptly narrowed as he caught sight of Levet. "You."

Levet smiled, wiggling his fingers in a mocking wave. "What are you doing here?"

Troy clenched his hands into tight fists. "I'm—"

A female nymph appeared from behind Troy, her eyes glowing with a golden fire.

"Cleo," Levet murmured in seeming pleasure.

The nymph ignored his greeting, instead gesturing toward the armed guards who were spaced around the pool.

"Kill them."

Levet cleared his throat as the nymphs rushed in their directions. "Umm. Perhaps we should run, *mon ami*."

Chapter 21

Kyi wrinkled her nose as the acrid stench of sulfur blasted through the cave. Obviously Xuria didn't find the situation as amusing as her daughter. In fact, her eyes were blazing with a white fire.

"You think it's funny?" the older woman hissed.

Kyi shrugged. "It certainly answers a few questions," she admitted.

And it did. If the sorceress was convinced one of her children was fated to kill her, she would naturally be eager to try to destroy them. It also explained why she had always tried a sneak attack to accomplish her goal, and why she even now remained at a wary distance. She was afraid that this was her moment to die.

Unfortunately, the prophecy hadn't clarified if it was Kyi or Cleo who was destined to strike the killing blow. Which meant Kyi had to remain cautious.

"I'm pleased to be of service," Xuria said between clenched teeth.

She didn't sound pleased. She sounded pissed.

"Doubtful," Kyi drawled.

Xuria inched to the side. She looked as if she was trying to get closer to her daughter, but Kyi wasn't fooled. The white gaze flicked toward the nearby gateway with increasing urgency.

"What are you doing here?" the sorceress asked.

Kyi battled back the urge to glance toward her spell in the middle of the cave. So far Xuria hadn't noticed the bits of sticks and dried petals on the floor, but Kyi knew it was only a matter of time.

Her lips twitched. They were both trying to get to the gateway and at the same time to keep the other one away. It was almost funny. Or maybe it was tragic.

Hard to know at the moment.

"I'm waiting for you," Kyi smoothly lied.

"Why?"

Good question. "I thought it was time for a mother-daughter chat."

"Doubtful." Xuria threw Kyi's taunt back in her face.

Kyi opened her lips to offer another insult, only to swallow the words as she caught a glimpse of movement out of the corner of her eye. Locke was stirring. An overwhelming relief jolted through her, along with a stab of fear. She had to keep Xuria focused on her. If her mother realized that Locke might be a danger, she would finish him off.

Quickly shuffling through her brain for a legitimate excuse to be in the cave, she recalled the last time she'd seen her mother. On the mountain in the Canadian Rockies, with a group of mindless pixies.

"Okay, I've decided that I'm not going to let you enslave any more demons to fuel the crystal," she told the woman, then she halted, glancing toward the opening of the cave. She'd been so shocked by the unexpected arrival of Xuria, that she hadn't noticed what was missing. "Wait, where are the demons?"

Xuria shifted another step toward the gateway. "I don't know what you're talking about."

Kyi narrowed her eyes. The pretense of innocence touched a raw nerve. She doubted that Xuria had ever been innocent.

"We both know that you came here to collect victims that you intend to suck the life out of to keep you alive. So where are they?"

Xuria lifted a hand to cover her mouth, as if stifling a yawn. "Has anyone told you that you're very dramatic? You must take after your father."

Kyi flinched, waiting for the pain. It didn't come. There was a vague pang of loss and wistful sadness, but she was becoming used to her revised memory of her father. He was far from perfect, but he'd cared for her and Cleo. Until the bitter end.

"I hope so," she murmured.

Xuria's brows snapped together. Was she annoyed that Kyi didn't hate her father with the same burning intensity as she hated her mother?

"You think he was any better than me?" Xuria confirmed Kyi's suspicion. "He had every intention of enslaving his enemy."

Kyi released a choked laugh. The woman was not only evil, but she was a nutbar.

"He saved my life from you," Kyi said dryly. "So yeah, I think he was better."

The sorceress sniffed. "If he'd been warned by an Oracle that you were destined to kill him, I promise he would have destroyed you without one second of regret."

Kyi shrugged aside the accusation. Neither of them knew the full depths of Kahn's heart. And right now she was more interested in the tingles that crawled over her skin. It had to be Locke. A second later she caught the faint scent of copper.

Stiffening her spine, Kyi stepped to the side, drawing her mother's gaze toward the rear of the cave.

"You really are pathetic, you know," she taunted, speaking louder than necessary. "I used to fear you, now I just feel sorry for you."

"I am Xuria," the older woman snapped, lifting her hand in warning.

"You're a perpetual victim." Kyi continued, watching the white fire flare in Xuria's eyes. It was never smart to provoke a sorceress. The trade-off, however, was giving Locke the opportunity to sneak up behind the bitch. "Nothing's ever your fault."

"You know nothing about me," Xuria snarled.

Kyi shrugged. "You admitted yourself that you broke the trust of the Oracles and blamed them when they threw you out. You sold your babies for a crystal because you're not immortal. And then tried to kill us when some chick had a dream that showed we might be a threat."

Xuria hissed in fury. "I am a survivor."

"Victim."

"There was a time when I might have felt regret about your death." The sorceress lifted her hand over her head in a dramatic motion. "Now I'm certain it's going to give me a great deal of pleasure."

"You've tried before," Kyi goaded her mother even as she backed away. It wasn't that she was afraid…well, that wasn't the only reason she was drifting toward the far side of the cave.

She'd caught sight of a shadow moving behind Xuria. Locke was not only awake, but he was on the hunt. She just had to keep her mother occupied so he could strike a blow before Xuria realized the danger.

"This time I won't fail." Xuria murmured low words, creating a spell.

Kyi could sense the power building, but the sorceress didn't lob the magic toward her. Instead she stepped to the side, as if trying to get a better angle. Kyi frowned. Why was she waiting? Did the woman sense the approaching vampire? Was she attempting to lure him into a trap?

No. Kyi's stomach clenched with fear as she realized that the sorceress wasn't planning to attack. The spell was nothing more than a diversion so she could make a last-second dash toward the gateway.

"Now, Locke," she called out. There was a time and place for stealth. This wasn't it.

Xuria snorted, obviously assuming Kyi was trying to trick her. "How stupid do you think I am?"

"On a scale of one to ten?" Kyi pretended to consider the question. "An eleven."

Sparks danced around Xuria's fingers as she prepared to hit Kyi with the magic. Kyi darted to the side as Locke leaped from the shadows, knocking the woman to the ground.

"Argh." With a speed that clearly caught Locke off guard, Xuria rolled onto her back and released the spell.

The magic caught Locke in the center of the chest, knocking him backward with enough force to smash him against the wall of the cave. There was the scent of singed leather and with a furious cry Kyi rushed forward. She'd managed to get within inches of her mother when the floor in front of her exploded. The rubble pelted her skin and the dust momentarily blinded her.

"Idiot," Xuria snarled. "When will you learn you are no match for me?"

Kyi blinked away the grit, expecting another bolt of magic. Her mother, however, was turned toward Locke, who was cautiously circling her.

"Never." He smiled, his fangs glinting as the air tingled with electricity, as if a thunderstorm was approaching.

"A shame," Xuria drawled, seemingly oblivious to the currents dancing through the cave. "Vampires are always so pretty and yet so stupid."

"Did you hear that Kyi?" Locke glanced toward Kyi, a hint of warning in his fabulous eyes. He was silently telling her to stay back. "She called me pretty."

"Mmm." Kyi wisely halted her approach. She had no desire to get caught in the crossfire. "And stupid," she added.

Locke shrugged, his smile refusing to falter. It might have been to goad Xuria into some stupid mistake, but Kyi suspected he was hiding the full extent of his pain. They needed to overpower Xuria. Quickly.

"No one's perfect," he murmured.

"Stay back." Xuria sent another burst of power toward Locke, driving him toward the entrance of the cave.

"Locke, she's trying to get to the gateway," Kyi warned.

Xuria muttered a curse, spinning toward Kyi. A homicidal rage burned in her eyes, and Kyi had a jarring flashback to when she was just a child. She'd been crouched in the tree, peering through the leaves at the dark-haired woman who'd stormed into the grove, her eyes blazing with hatred.

Kyi hadn't wanted to look. She'd spent her early years surrounded by love and kindness. The realization that the intruder could feel such a violent animosity toward her was shocking. Cleo had obviously felt the same. She'd cowered behind Kyi, as if hoping her sister would shield her from the looming attack. For a horrifying moment, Kyi had felt as if she was alone with the enraged madwoman. Then, as the sorceress had lifted her hand and pointed it in Kyi's direction, her father had abruptly appeared. He'd stepped directly in front of the spell, absorbing the magic that drained the very life from him.

Lost in the terrifying memory, Kyi was frozen in place. She couldn't move, she couldn't even scream as her mother conjured a spell and sent it flying across the cave. She watched in silence as the fate that had been postponed—but never forgotten—hurtled toward her.

This time it wasn't her father who saved her. It was Locke.

In a blur of movement he'd jumped in front of her, releasing a burst of power that surrounded them with electricity. Her mother's magic smacked against the shield, sizzling and zapping until it was burned to a crisp. Kyi shivered, thankfully jolted out of her strange sense of paralysis.

Xuria lifted her hand again. "I've had enough of you, leech."

This time Kyi was prepared. "Locke," she muttered, warning him to be ready, as she called on her fey magic and created two shimmering bands.

Flinging the strands toward her mother, she didn't aim for her head. Instead she skipped them along the ground to wrap around the sorceress's ankles. Xuria stumbled, her concentration shattered. It was only for a second, but it was enough for Locke.

With a roar, he rushed forward. Xuria hissed, tossing a hasty spell in his direction as she struggled to regain her balance. Locke dodged to the side, unable to see the magic, but knowing it was headed his way. Then, glaring at the woman, he released a bolt of lightning. It missed the sorceress, although she was forced to stumble backward to avoid being skewered. A cold smile touched his lips and he released another bolt. Xuria hissed, jumping back again.

Kyi frowned. Was he deliberately missing the sorceress? Why? Kyi wanted to see the bitch turned into a crispy critter....

Oh. Kyi muttered a curse, wanting to kick herself for her stupidity. He couldn't be sure his powers would kill a sorceress. Not when she was connected to the starlyte crystal. Instead he was herding Xuria toward the entrance of the cave so Kyi could complete the spell and destroy the gateway.

Licking her dry lips, Kyi cautiously moved toward the center of the floor. She was desperate to sever her mother's connection to the crystal, but she didn't want to risk attracting Xuria's attention.

She'd managed to reach the gateway when the sorceress glanced in her direction, the white eyes widening with the first genuine terror that Kyi had ever seen on her mother's face.

"No," Xuria screeched, turning away from Locke to rush toward Kyi.

There was a blur of motion as Locke leaped to block her path, grabbing her by her arms. Kyi hurriedly dropped to her knees, holding her hand over the ingredients of her potion. Then, bending her head, she closed her eyes and struggled to concentrate. Her fey magic was natural. It came without any need to perform a ceremony or to use words of power. But human magic was far more difficult to manipulate. Especially when she could feel her mother's desperate fury pounding against her.

She'd managed to form the spell in her mind when the sensation of spiders crawling over her skin distracted her. What the hell?

"Kyi," Locke's voice was harsh as he called out. "She went into stealth mode."

Damn. There was no way to stop Xuria while she was in her spirit form. Her only hope was blocking the sorceress's exit before she could retreat to her lair. Keeping her head bent and her eyes squeezed shut, Kyi desperately spoke the words and cast the spell that she'd been holding. It released from her body with a wrenching explosion. She wasn't sure why. Maybe because adrenalin was screaming through her body. Or it might have something to do with her mother's magic that filled the cave.

Whatever the cause, the spell hit the amulet with a sizzling force and reflected toward the gateway. Step one…complete. Now to see if her sketchy plan would actually work. Her heart lodged in her throat as she set back on her heels and watched the sparkles of magic dance around the copper amulet, beginning to twirl in an increasingly large funnel. Like a tornado that was posed to wreak havoc.

Barely daring to breath, Kyi felt a small quake beneath the cave as the spell at last reached the gateway. It hit with a loud hiss before being reflected back to the amulet, just as Kyi had hoped.

Was it possible that this might actually work?

The cautious flare of hope had barely been ignited when a hot breeze brushed past Kyi's face, heading directly to the gateway.

Xuria.

"No!" she cried out, surging to her feet.

She didn't know exactly what she intended to do. Once a human spell had been cast it couldn't be altered. It couldn't be increased in power and it certainly couldn't be stopped. It was what it was. Still, she couldn't prevent herself from holding out her hand, as if hoping to hurry the spell along.

A mocking laugh echoed in the air before the breeze was gone as it entered the gateway. For a second there was nothing. Just her spell blazing from the amulet and bouncing toward the gateway. Then, without warning, a screech of pain shattered the silence.

Kyi flinched, her hand lifting to shade her eyes as a glow filled the cave. She narrowed her gaze, trying to peer through the bright light.

Was that a human shape? Yes. It was a woman. Slowly Kyi could begin to make out the long black hair and a lush body that was covered by a long silk robe. It was Xuria. Only she was in her own body and young again.

Not that she looked particularly happy to be back in her original form. She was floating several inches off the ground and her arms were spread wide with her head tilted back. Her lips were parted, her screams of pain continuing to reverberate through the cave.

Kyi pressed a hand to her thundering heart, realizing that her mother had become trapped in the ricocheting magic.

Was it killing her? Or—horrifying thought—making her stronger?

The answer came a second later when the glow became a blinding blur and the scream reached a piercing crescendo. Then, the world seemed to stop as a dark force sucked everything toward the center of the cave. Like a black hole that threatened to consume them.

Kyi felt Locke's arms wrap around her, pulling her away even as the quakes beneath their feet intensified. At last, with a force that would have killed a mortal, a shocking explosion sent both of them flying through the air to land in a painful heap near the entrance to the cave.

The light was gone and the shadows shrouded them in a thick silence.

* * * *

Troy wasn't caught by surprise very often. When an imp lived as long as he had, it was difficult for many new things to happen. But he had to admit that the sight of Inga in a magical disguise along with Levet had rattled him.

He'd sent the warning that mer-folk were being imprisoned, but he'd never expected the two of them to enter the gateway. Not without…ah. Troy grimaced. The Tryshu. It had obviously allowed them to follow the mer-folk to this place.

He was still struggling to accept that he hadn't imagined his friends when Cleo ordered her warriors to attack.

"No." Troy hastily stepped to the side, blocking Cleo from following.

It would be hard enough for Inga and Levet to battle against the guards; they wouldn't have a chance if Cleo joined the battle.

The nymph sent him a glare filled with icy warning. "Stand aside or I will destroy you."

"I don't think so."

Although Troy was an arrogant creature who believed he could kick the ass of anyone stupid enough to challenge him, he was also smart enough to cheat whenever the opportunity presented itself.

Leaping toward the portrait, he wrapped his fingers around the starlyte crystal and wrenched it out of the mount drilled into the frame of the portrait. He whirled around, expecting to fend off a furious Cleo. Instead she was staring at him with a smug satisfaction.

"I knew it," she rasped.

Troy grimaced. If the nymph was happy that was probably bad news for him.

"Knew what?"

Her cognac gaze remained locked on the crystal clutched in his hand. "That your royal blood would allow you to touch the crystal."

Ah. He bounced the gemstone against his palm. Cleo wasn't the first female to try and manipulate him because of his royal blood, but he'd never been used to grab an oversized pebble.

"Tell me what Xuria does with it," he commanded. "The truth, this time."

"I told you the truth." Cleo clenched her hands. She was a female who was accustomed to being in charge. It was clearly an effort not to reach out and slap him. "My mother uses it to make her immortal."

Troy had heard of fey magic being used to lengthen a human's life, but not from a Chatri. It was a dangerous gamble to play with that sort of power.

He shook his head, dismissing Xuria's desperation. Sorceresses were notorious for sacrificing whatever necessary to achieve their goals. Even if it was themselves.

"You're immortal," he pointed out the obvious. "Why do you want it?"

Cleo shrugged, her expression wiped of emotion. "Someone has to stop Xuria. Why not me?"

"Hmm. Very altruistic," Troy drawled. "I don't believe a word of it."

Her lips twisted into a bitter smile. "You should. I've spent the majority of my life dreaming of the day I could kill the bitch."

Okay. That Troy believed. He glanced down at his hand. "You need the crystal to accomplish your goal?"

"Yes."

"But you can't touch it?"

"Not until I remove her magic."

Troy pursed his lips. He didn't have to ask how she intended to remove Xuria's magic. There was only one way. To kill her.

"And after that?" he demanded.

The scent of warm figs wafted through the air. The thought of owning the crystal obviously pleased Cleo. A lot.

"Then the crystal will belong to me," she said.

Her vague answer warned Troy that she didn't want to admit her plans. "And?"

"And nothing."

Troy wrapped his fingers around the crystal, hiding it from her greedy gaze. "Tell me what you intend to do with it."

Her eyes flared with annoyance. "What it was meant to do."

"Not good enough." He met her glare for glare. "Explain."

"I don't take orders from you," she snapped.

"Explain," Troy stubbornly repeated.

She muttered a curse that he suspected she'd learned from a human sailor as if she was reluctantly conceding defeat; at the same time, however, she took a small step forward.

Was she intending to try and overpower him? No, that didn't make sense. Not if she couldn't touch the crystal. She must have some other nasty surprise she was plotting.

"The crystal is intended to store power," she told him.

"I know that much."

She took another step forward. "To use in battle."

Troy was genuinely confused as he studied her lovely face. Fights and even full-out wars weren't uncommon among demons. But nymphs rarely instigated violence. Not unless it was against another nymph tribe.

"Who are you planning to battle?" he asked.

"As the leader of a tribe of nymphs surrounded by vampires, I must always be prepared to protect my people."

Troy snorted at the smooth explanation. "You've obviously existed with Victor for centuries…ah." Troy released his breath on a low hiss. How had he been so stupid? He should have suspected the truth from the minute she admitted she craved the power of the crystal. "You're not satisfied with your territory."

She tilted her chin. "Why shouldn't I be allowed to expand?"

"Umm." Troy tapped the finger of his free hand against his chin, as if considering the question. "Because it belongs to the vampires?"

"Who made them boss?"

"Nature. They're stronger, deadlier, and utterly ruthless." Troy shrugged. "You don't like having them as neighbors, then move."

"They can move," she snarled, revealing the emotions that seethed just beneath her cool façade. "I was there first."

"You want to rule all of London?"

Her eyes darkened with an all-consuming hunger. "For a beginning. After that I'll decide what other cities I wish to claim as my own. Perhaps Paris."

Troy made a sound of disbelief. No demon was stupid enough to challenge a vampire. Certainly not a clan chief. And now she was talking about taking on more than one.

Insanity.

"How do you intend to fuel the crystal?"

She hesitated, as if deciding whether or not to lie. Then, perhaps sensing that Troy would easily see through any pretense, she glanced toward the portrait behind him.

"I possess the same magic as my mother."

Troy considered what exactly that meant. Human magic. It was obviously possible to manipulate the crystal with it. Xuria had proved that much. But beyond making her immortal, exactly what could she do with it?

It was the distant scent of salt that allowed the truth to crash into him with stunning force.

The sorceress used the essence of the fey creatures to extend her life. But if an immortal could capture that essence, they could use it to battle their enemies. Even a vampire.

A sick sense of disappointment twisted his stomach. He'd already suspected that Cleo was a ruthless, immoral creature. But to think she would willingly sacrifice countless demons to fuel her power-grab was unforgivable.

"You intend to do this?" He waved a hand toward the fey who circled the space like mindless robots.

She didn't bother to glance toward the slaves. As if they were so far beneath her notice that they might as well have been invisible.

"Empires are always built on the backs of the weak," she told him.

He glared at her. The beautiful face surrounded by the glorious midnight curls. The cognac eyes and the plush pink lips.

Belladonna.

So exquisite. And yet, so poisonous.

"That's your excuse for enslaving demons? Because you have to crack a few eggs to make an omelet?"

"Not all of us were born into power, Prince Troy," she sneered, something that might have been jealousy sharpening her voice. "We have to snatch it with our bare hands."

Troy curled his lips in disgust. As far as he was concerned, she burned her last bridge.

"Actually, I'm the one doing the snatching," he taunted, holding up the crystal.

Her jaw tightened, her body vibrating with the force of her need to grab the stone.

"You asked for an explanation, I explained." She pointed toward the entrance of the courtyard. "Now let's go."

Troy took a step back. "I don't think so."

"What?"

"I'm not going to let you spread Xuria's evil through London."

"Weren't you listening?" The scent of charred figs hung thick in the air. "She won't be spreading anything. I intend to kill her."

"No, you intend to become her."

Cleo flinched, as if his words had managed to strike a raw nerve, and a cruel smile touched her lips.

"I won't tell you again." She released a burst of power and the brand on Troy's hand seared his flesh with a sudden heat. "Let's go."

Troy clenched his teeth, the agonizing pain nearly sending him to his knees. "No."

Cleo stepped forward, raising her hand as if she intended to hit him. "You—" She bit off her words, her eyes widening as her gaze locked on the crystal in his hand.

Troy glanced down, confused by her fascination. It wasn't until he noticed the crystal was no longer glowing that he sensed something was wrong. He shook it, as if that might get it going again.

"What's happening?" he demanded.

The cognac eyes darkened with a fierce emotion. Not anger. Not joy. But some weird combination of the two. Then, with the speed of a striking viper, she reached to snatch the crystal out of his hand.

"It would appear that someone has taken care of the bitch for me," she grated, a gloating expression on her face as she tucked the stone into the bodice of her gown. "Bad luck for you, Prince Troy."

Troy blinked, not fully understanding what she meant. Then it hit him. Xuria was dead. That's why the magic had drained from the crystal. Which meant that Cleo no longer needed him.

"Shit." Troy whirled on his heel and darted toward the nearest exit.

Chapter 22

Not for the first time, Levet cursed his short legs. They were designed to crouch on the edge of buildings, or to squeeze into small spaces. And of course, they perfectly framed his elegant tail. But they weren't much good when he was being chased by nymph warriors determined to skewer him with arrows.

Beside him, Inga held her Tryshu in one hand as she raced through the seemingly endless hallways.

"I thought you said that Cleo was a friend of yours," she panted.

"She is." Levet wrinkled his snout, accepting that he wasn't being entirely honest. The truth was that he'd done a favor for Cleo centuries ago and she'd been in his debt. Once it was paid off, she'd obviously considered their relationship at an end. "It was transitional in nature."

"With friends like yours, who needs enemies?" Inga muttered, making an irritated sound as the long skirt of her gown threatened to trip her. "This dress is ridiculous. How am I supposed to run in it?"

"We cannot run forever, *mon ami*," Levet retorted, not bothering to point out that most females in long dresses had no plans to flee from their enemies. "I am built more for comfort than speed."

"Tell the warriors to stop shooting arrows at us," Inga suggested.

Levet cursed as an arrow whizzed past his horn, smacking against the marble wall before it dropped to the ground.

"I do not believe they will listen to me."

"Then we run."

They turned into a narrow corridor. It was different than the others. Not only had the marble been replaced by brick walls and a flagstone floor, but there were no windows to allow in the moonlight. Instead, a row of burning torches were stuck into iron brackets in the wall. They were obviously headed toward the slave quarters at the back of the villa.

Levet's heart sank. He'd been in enough slave quarters to know there was never, ever an exit.

Which meant they were going to be trapped.

He cleared his throat. "This feels like the appropriate moment to remind you that you possess a love for bashing creatures on the head with your big fork, *ma belle*."

Inga glanced over her shoulders at the warriors who were slowly closing the gap. "There's too many. I can't fight all of them."

"I am not helpless. I can—"

"No!" Inga rudely interrupted. "The magic in this villa is unstable. If you start lobbing fireballs it might collapse."

Levet snapped his wings at the insult, but before he could argue, he felt a weird sensation ripple beneath his feet. It wasn't magic. Or at least, it wasn't a spell directed at them. It was more a sense of magic fading. As if it was being sucked out of the villa by some unseen force.

"*Oui*," he breathed. "You are right."

"You don't have to sound surprised," she groused. "I have seen the disaster you cause with those things."

"*Non*. I am not talking about my magnificent fireballs." Levet pursed his lips. He found this female fascinating, gloriously powerful, and occasionally charming. But he was not convinced that she fully appreciated his own special qualities. "Although I do demand we have a discussion of your unreasonable jealousy of my balls."

She ignored his chiding, sending him a puzzled glance. "Then what do you mean?"

"The villa." Levet pointed toward the ceiling where a spiderweb of cracks was visible. "It is starting to collapse."

"Oh." She slowed her pace, as if concentrating on their surroundings. "Yes. The magic is fading. Something's happened."

A portion of stone fell off. What started as cracks were rapidly turning into chunks. Never a good thing.

"We need to get out of here before we're buried beneath the rubble."

Inga stubbornly shook her head. "Not without—"

"*Oui*, not without your people," Levet broke in, shaking his head even as he caught sight of a narrow opening carved into the wall. "Let us try down here."

He dashed forward, feeling an arrow bounce off his backside before he managed to leap through the opening. Thankfully he had buns of steel, although he was fairly certain it was going to leave a bruise. Behind him, Inga grunted, as if she'd been hit as well. About to turn his head to make sure she was okay, Levet caught sight of the heavy iron door that blocked their path.

"Stop," he called out.

The word had barely left his lips when there was a hissing sound followed by a thunderous explosion that knocked the door off its hinges and sent it toppling backward. Levet coughed at the cloud of dust that filled the narrow hallway, his ears ringing.

"Some warning the next time you intend to use that magical fork, *mon ami*."

"Sorry," she muttered, although she didn't sound sorry. She sounded distracted.

Levet understood why. The pungent scent of salt and fruit and goblin was mixed with the dust floating in the air.

They'd found the slaves.

Brushing past him, Inga jumped over the twisted and charred pile of iron, not bothering to admire her handiwork. Levet followed behind, although he did pause to appreciate small pools of liquid metal where the door had taken the main impact from Inga's Tryshu. Impressive. Then, entering the large, open space his nose curled with disgust.

Slave pens always smelled the same. Fear, filth, and rank desperation.

Staying near the entrance to fight back the guards who'd been chasing them, Levet risked a quick glance at the numerous fey creatures and goblins that shuffled around the room. From a distance they appeared to be in the same strange zombie-mode as those in the courtyard. Then a closer look revealed that they were starting to blink and glance around in confusion, as if they were slowly waking from a dream.

Or a nightmare.

Inga marched to stand in the center of the space, her voice ringing through the air.

"Follow me."

The motley crew craned their necks to stare at Inga, their eyes still unfocused from the lingering compulsion spell.

At last a tall, slender merman dressed in a gauzy robe with his bluish-tinted hair pulled into elaborate braids stepped forward.

"Who are you?"

Inga held out the Tryshu. "Your leader."

The male frowned. Not at Inga, but at the nasty room that was crowded with demons.

"Where are we?" he demanded. "How did we get here?"

Inga's lips parted, as if she intended to answer, but Levet loudly cleared his throat. He couldn't see the guards, but he could hear their approaching footsteps.

"You might wish to hurry this along," he warned.

A nearby pixie turned to see who was speaking. Her blue eyes widened and without warning she released a piercing scream.

"Monster!"

"Monster? Where?" Levet hastily glanced around. He didn't see any monster. Well, not unless you counted the imp who stripped off his robe and was strutting toward Inga with his dangling bits exposed.

Raising his hand, Levet intended to lob a curse at the outrageous male, but Inga distracted him with her loud snort of annoyance. Not many females could snort like Inga.

"Oh blessed goddess." With a wave of her trident, she released a burst of magic. "Follow me."

The gathered demons stiffened, their eyes glazing over as the power washed through the room. Then, as one, they turned to follow Inga as she headed toward the doorway.

Levet waited until they were out of the nasty slave pens and marching through the narrow hallway before he spoke.

"That is a handy-dandy fork," he congratulated his companion. "You are like the Pee-pee Piper leading your people to safety."

"Pied Piper," she corrected, turning toward him to reveal the fear in her eyes. "And he didn't lead people to safety. He lured the children away from their families."

Levet scowled. "That is a terrible story."

She nodded. "I'm hoping for a better ending for ours," she said. "But the warriors are going to be waiting for us."

Levet squared his shoulders. "I am ready."

She hesitated, as if struggling against some fierce instinct. Finally, she nodded toward the demons marching ahead of them.

"Fine, you lead."

Levet spread his wings, a surge of pride racing through him. At last. He'd been waiting forever for Inga to accept that he possessed the skills and brains to be a true partner. Now was his opportunity to prove his worth.

Shoving his way through the crowd, he managed to get ahead of the bespelled demons. Almost immediately, however, he winced when a stupid goblin stepped on his tail. Being the head of the pack wasn't easy. Or pain-free.

Ignoring his throbbing appendage, Levet concentrated on the shadowed hallway. He could sense the guards before they came into view, but he hadn't been expecting them to be lined up to block their path.

Hmm. He was going to have to clear the way. With a smile, Levet held up his hand and conjured his favorite fireball. Desperate times called for desperate measures, right?

Besides, they were so pretty.

Lifting his hand over his head, he reared back and tossed the fireball toward the uniformed nymphs. It exploded with enough force to tumble the guards backward. Unfortunately, it also created a shower of rocks bouncing down on their heads as the ceiling threatened to collapse.

"Levet!" Inga cried out.

"Sorry."

Levet swallowed a sigh. Perhaps it wasn't the best time to toss around his beautiful balls.

But he had to do something. Already the guards were crawling back to their feet, their expressions revealing they weren't particularly happy. Maybe because their hair was singed and their uniforms covered with soot.

Once again raising his hand, Levet released his magic. This time it wasn't a fireball. It wasn't even a weapon. It was a massive illusion of a dragon that was large enough to brush its head against the ceiling and wide enough to fill the passage from side to side. It had shimmering green scales and green eyes that were smoldering with hunger. Smoke curled from his long snout and the ten-inch, razor-sharp teeth dripped with acid that sizzled as it dropped to the floor.

The guards nervously shifted from foot to foot, their bows lowering as they took in the beast. No doubt they suspected that it was a trick, but the tiniest possibility that it might be real had them backing away.

"Hold firm," a male voice called out, obviously the leader of the warriors. "It's just a—"

Levet didn't give him the opportunity to find their backbones. Like a skilled puppeteer, he opened the dragon's jaws to release the illusion of spewing flames. The guards shrieked as the fire billowed toward them, dropping their weapons and scrambling over one another to flee down the hall.

Deeply pleased with his success, Levet turned toward the gathered crowd that blankly stared straight ahead.

"Now that is a monster," he crowed, snapping his fingers. "Ha. Did you see my…argh."

Lost in his self-congratulations, Levet was oblivious to his danger. It wasn't until a hand wrapped around his horn and snatched him off the ground that he realized that not all of the guards had fled. Kicking his feet, he swung around to glare at the nymph holding him captive. The male had golden hair pulled into a braid and pale eyes that were hard with anger. He was also wearing a uniform that was drenched in gold trim. Tacky.

There was a thudding sound of demons being shoved aside before Inga was abruptly standing next to the nymph, her eyes blazing with crimson fire. Levet's heart swelled. There was his ogress.

"Let him go," she commanded, pointing the trident at the center of the nymph's chest.

The male took a hasty step backward, pressing a dagger against Levet's throat.

"Lower your weapon or he dies."

Levet clicked his tongue, not particularly scared. Unless the blade was cursed it couldn't kill him.

"Why are demons forever hauling me around like a sack of yams?" he groused.

"Potatoes," Inga automatically corrected.

The nymph lifted him high enough to study Levet's face in puzzlement. "What are you?"

Levet clicked his tongue. Obviously the fool hadn't been around when Levet had retrieved Cleo's magnificent emerald. Otherwise he would recognize him as a legendary hero.

Holding out his hand, he prepared to create another fireball. "Your worst nightmare."

Inga sent him a warning glare. "Levet, no."

Levet pouted. Someday very soon they were going to have a discussion about his balls. Waiting for Inga to destroy the nymph with her mighty weapon, Levet was distracted by the sight of a shadow looming behind the nymph.

There was something familiar about the shape. In fact...

There was a loud thud as a heavy object smashed into the back of the nymph's skull, knocking him unconscious and sending Levet flying through the air to smack against the wall.

"Actually you're *my* worst nightmare," a male voice drawled.

Levet shook his head, clearing away the cobwebs before he forced himself to his feet and glared up at Troy.

"Where did you come from?"

The imp gestured over his shoulder. "A hidden passage."

"Oh." Levet's annoyance was forgotten as his wings fluttered in anticipation. "I adore hidden passages."

Before he could check it out, Inga reached down to grab him by the top of his wing.

"Does it lead out of here?" she asked Troy.

The male shrugged. "That's the hope."

Levet didn't try to pull away from Inga's grasp. He liked it. His wings were very sensitive.

"Where's Cleo?" he asked the imp.

The male's elegant face twisted with revulsion. "Probably headed toward the gateway. We need to get there before her."

Inga gave a sharp nod. "You and Levet lead; I'll follow behind the prisoners to make sure no one sneaks up on us."

Without giving them time to object, she hurried back through the demons, taking her position at the back. No doubt she intended to herd them like mindless sheep.

Levet fell into step beside Troy as he led them into the cramped tunnel. After a few minutes he clicked his tongue in disappointment. It wasn't nearly as exciting as he'd hoped. In fact it was dusty, narrow, and it smelled faintly of a cesspit. No self-respecting sorceress would hide her treasure in such a disgusting place.

Accepting there was nothing to discover, Levet turned his attention to the male beside him.

Troy was wearing the same clothing he'd had on when he'd left the mer-folk castle, including the ghastly leopard-print cape. But his usual elegance was tarnished by a layer of dust that covered him from head to…

"Hey." Levet's eyes widened as something sparkly in Troy's tangled hair caught his eye. "Are you wearing a tiara?"

"Isn't it lovely?" Troy reached up to touch the ornament. "My cousin might be a cold-hearted bitch, but she has excellent taste in jewelry."

Levet wondered if he should consider a tiara to emphasize the beauty of his stunted horns. Hmm. Something to think about. But not now.

"Why do we have to stop Cleo?"

"She has her mother's starlyte crystal," the male revealed, his long, impatient strides making it hard for Levet to keep pace. "She intends to challenge Victor for control of London."

Levet snorted, assuming it was some stupid joke. Troy had a twisted sense of humor. Then, glancing toward the male's rigid profile, Levet realized he was speaking the truth.

"Has she gone locomotive?" he demanded. Cleo had always been ambitious; the fact she'd refused to move when the vampires had taken over London was proof of that. But she'd never been suicidal.

"Worse," Troy said. "Power hungry."

Levet heaved a sigh. "A shame. I always admired her."

"Yes. She could have been..."

Levet tilted his head as he sensed the strange emotion that vibrated around his companion. "She could have been what?"

"Special." The word sounded as if it was wrenched from Troy's lips.

Ah. The imp had been enchanted by Cleo. Not surprising. She was a fascinating, powerful, tragically flawed female.

"True." Levet offered a wise nod of his head. "It is a fine line between special and psychotic."

Troy made a choked sound. "Sometimes you are remarkably astute, gargoyle."

Levet preened. "*Merci.* You are a nice fruit as well."

For some reason, the imp rolled his eyes. "I wonder how many years before Inga turns you into gravel with her Tryshu," he muttered.

"Could she?" Levet considered the threat. "Hmm. Probably. But why would she want me turned into gravel?"

"Blissful silence."

"Rude." Levet sniffed, flapping his wings as Troy picked up his speed.

Behind them the demons marched at a brisk pace, squeezed together as the passage narrowed. They were eerily silent except for the heavy trod of their feet. Levet shivered. It was like being followed by a horde of mannequins.

He *hated* mannequins.

Concentrating on forcing his exhausted legs to keep moving, Levet was vaguely aware of exiting the villa through a hidden door and skirting around the slumbering city. Then, at last, they were back in the vineyard where they'd first entered this timeline.

Next to him, Troy slowed his pace, and Levet caught the scent of figs. A few steps later they crested a hill to discover Cleo standing in the moonlight, her arms spread wide.

"There she is," Troy whispered, coming to a halt.

Levet watched the female as she weaved her hands in strange patterns. She was attempting to open the gateway.

"I will attempt to stop her," he announced, sounding more courageous than he felt.

There was no way to know what powers the nymph might be able to conjure now that she had the crystal. Still, they had to do something to keep her from returning to London.

He didn't particularly care if she wiped out the vampires in London. He had no love for the bloodsuckers. Especially Victor, the clan chief. But there were bound to be innocent creatures caught in the crossfire. Including Juliet, Victor's mate, who was part human.

"Okay, go for it." Troy waved a hand toward Cleo, who had seemingly sensed their presence and was turning to face them.

"Thanks," Levet muttered, his heart sinking to his toes as Cleo narrowed her eyes and reached into the bodice of her gown to pull out a small stone.

The starlyte crystal? Probably. Would it kill him? Probably.

"Stay back," she ordered.

He pasted on a smile, taking a cautious step forward. "There is no need for us to fight, *ma belle*," he said in soothing tones. "I'm certain that we can…argh."

Levet jumped to the side as the ground exploded beneath his feet.

"I told you to stay back," Cleo snarled.

"Enough of this," a female voice muttered from behind Levet and a second later, Inga appeared at his side.

Cleo narrowed her eyes. "Who are you?"

"I am Inga, Queen of the Mer-folk." Lifting the Tryshu, she launched a blast of energy that sent the nymph reeling back.

Inga stepped forward, releasing another blast. This one hit Cleo with enough force to knock her off balance. Toppling backward, the nymph windmilled her arms, trying to avoid falling flat on her ass.

Instead, she collided with the gateway.

There was the sound of sizzling, as if someone had just thrown a steak on a hot grill. Levet pressed a hand against his rumbling stomach. Mmm. Steak. Struggling to dismiss his hunger, Levet forced himself to concentrate on the female nymph.

He expected her to fall through the gateway or bounce off the magic and stumble forward. Instead, she was lifted off her feet by an invisible force. Higher and higher she rose, her mouth parted as if she was screaming, although no sound could be heard.

Levet grimaced. Cleo was starting to arch and writhe as if she was being pelted with unbearable power. Was it the magic of the Tryshu? Or the gateway? Not that it mattered.

Seconds later, Cleo's head dropped to an awkward angle, her body limp.

Troy took a step forward, as if intending to go to the female, but Inga reached out to grasp his arm.

"Not yet," she warned.

The imp frowned, but before he could protest, a strange heat prickled in the air, crawling over Levet like the sensation of an early morning dawn, threatening to turn him to stone.

Seconds later, a shattering explosion sent them all flying backward.

"Oof."

Levet landed on top of a goblin. He winced, rubbing a cracked rib. The ground would have been softer. Before he could complain at yet another battle injury, Inga was reaching down to yank him to his feet.

"The gateway is collapsing," she said in a terse voice. "We have to get everyone through."

Rubbing his aching side, Levet nodded. "What do you want me to do?"

"I'll have to go through first," she warned, holding up the Tryshu. "I need you and Troy to make sure the prisoners follow me. Otherwise they'll wander off."

"Very well," he agreed without argument. He could feel the tiny quakes coming from the gateway. He suspected they had mere seconds to get through before…kablooey. They were all toast. "Lead the way."

Squaring her shoulders, Inga marched forward, ignoring the sparkles of ash that were the remnants of Cleo scattered across the ground. The female nymph had chosen her fate. Then, surrounded by a sudden glow of power from the Tryshu, she stepped through the magical opening.

The demons shuffled in her wake, still under Inga's compulsion. Not that it was an orderly escape. They all tried to go through the narrow opening at once, knocking each other to the ground and turning some away. Muttering beneath his breath, Levet hurried to tug the stragglers forward, while Troy tossed two pixies over his shoulders and ran toward the gateway.

"It's going," he growled. "Jump."

With a quick glance to make sure there were no lingering prisoners, Levet tucked his wings tight and charged forward, like a speeding train toward the opening.

Perhaps not a speeding train, he conceded, as the magic enveloped him. But he was pretty sure he could give a drunken slotva demon a run for his money.

* * * *

For the second time in less than an hour, Locke was forced to dig his way out of a pile of rubble. Not his favorite hobby, he grimly acknowledged. In fact, if he never had a ceiling fall on him again, he would be a happy vampire. Or at least a less grumpy one.

Once free, he glanced around the partially collapsed cave. Fear slammed into him. Where was Kyi? It was the muffled groan that led him out of the cave. She was so tiny, she'd been tossed onto the beach by the explosion.

Dropping onto his knees beside her, Locke gently cradled her head in his hands, brushing her tangled hair out of her face.

"Kyi," he rasped. "Are you okay?"

Her eyes blinked open. "I'm not sure." Her voice was hoarse. "Are all my parts still attached?"

Locke allowed his gaze to slowly inspect her slender body. She was covered in dust, and her dress was torn in several places, but he couldn't see any injuries.

"All attached and all perfect," he assured her.

She released a shaky sigh. "Xuria?"

"Gone." Locke paused, wanting to insist it was time to return home, but knowing it was too important to risk allowing the sorceress to escape. "Or at least I assume she's gone," he conceded.

As he feared, Kyi's expression hardened with determination. "I need to make sure."

Locke didn't bother trying to convince her it was too dangerous. He was becoming familiar with that particular gleam in her eyes. Best to agree with her so they could get this over with ASAP.

Helping her to her feet, Locke kept an arm wrapped protectively around her shoulders as they returned to the cave. Once inside, he pulled her to a halt, inspecting the cracks that spread across the ceiling. The cliff above was mere minutes away from crashing down.

"We have to hurry," he warned in stark tones.

She nodded, and together they moved toward the charred spot in the center of the floor. Kyi shuddered, no doubt realizing that the smear was the residue from the spell that had destroyed her mother, but with the courage he'd come to expect, she didn't back away. Instead, she reached out her hand and closed her eyes.

A full minute passed before she lowered her hand and opened her eyes. "Her spirit isn't here." Turning her head, she sent him a weary smile. "*Hasta la vista*."

"Baby," he completed, leaning down to brush her lips with a light kiss. "What about the gateway?"

"It's still there, but—" Kyi cut off her words, her body stiffening.

Locke dropped his arm from around her shoulders and stepped to the side. He wanted room in case he had to fight.

"What?"

"It's shivering."

Shivering? That didn't sound good.

"What does that mean?" he asked.

"I'm not sure," she admitted. "I hope it means that it's about to collapse."

"Should we be here when it does?" He lifted his hand to his forehead, where he could feel the latest wound that was dripping blood down the side of his face. "We've both taken a beating tonight. I prefer to avoid another one."

"Yeah, it's probably not a bad idea to have a little space…" She reached out to grab his hand, her eyes widening. "Locke."

"What?"

"Something's coming."

Locke widened his stance, preparing to destroy whatever was headed their way. "Xuria?"

She shook her head. "I smell salt. And fruit. And…granite."

Granite? Locke wondered if the blast had rattled Kyi's head more than she realized, then there was a distant rumble. It sounded like a herd of buffalo was headed their direction.

"Look out," he muttered, wrapping his arm around Kyi's waist to pull her out of the path just as the stampede burst through the gateway.

Chapter 23

Kyi and Locke were laying naked on her bed, wrapped in each other's arms as they recovered from their stormy bout of lovemaking. Genuinely stormy, she wryly acknowledged. She had smoking gouges in the ceiling of her cottage from his jagged bolts of lightning.

They'd returned to her private grove after leaving Cyprus. It'd been Locke's insistence that they put off a visit to his lair in Iceland for a few weeks or even months. He claimed he had a temporary aversion to caves.

It was fine with Kyi. After the trauma of the past few days it was soothing to be surrounded by her beloved trees.

Of course they couldn't hide forever. She still had questions about what had happened to her sister. The pandemonium that had filled the cave after the Queen of the Mer-folk along with a horde of demons had crashed through the gateway had made it impossible to discover what exactly had happened. She knew that Cleo had forced the imp to travel to their mother's hidden lair to steal the crystal. And that the queen along with the strange gargoyle had followed to rescue her people. After that it was a confusing story of zombies, magical dragons, and hidden passages.

The only thing she knew for certain was that Cleo was dead, and that the crystal was lost behind the gateway that was now obliterated. The last remnants of her mother's evil was hopefully destroyed. And for the moment, that was enough.

Heaving a sigh, she lifted her hand to touch the copper amulet that she had draped around Locke's neck after they returned to the cottage. Not only did she want him protected from magic, but she liked seeing it nestled against his bare chest. It was like a badge of ownership.

He smiled as he studied her with his stunning blue eyes, the circle of gold shimmering in the firelight.

"You might have to consider a larger bed," he murmured. "My feet are hanging over the bottom of the mattress."

"Hmm." She pretended to consider his request. "You shouldn't be so big."

He slid his hands down the curve of her back, cupping her backside to press her against his stirring cock.

"That wasn't what you were saying a few minutes ago."

"Locke." She laughed. He was right. He'd been exactly the right size when he'd been moving deep inside her, making her scream with pleasure.

Holding her gaze, he allowed his teasing smile to fade. "How are you?"

"Satisfied. In case you were worried."

He blinked, caught off guard by her answer. "I wasn't. Until now."

She laughed again, reaching up to touch one of the numerous wounds on her poor head.

"I'm fine. All healed."

"I know you're healed here." He bent his head to brush his lips over her forehead, then with exquisite care, nibbled a path of kisses to the valley between her breasts. He paused directly over her racing heart. "But what about here?"

"What do you mean?" She asked the question to give herself time to prepare an answer, not because she didn't know what he wanted from her.

He lifted his head to gaze down at her with a somber expression. "You lost both your sister and mother."

"I'll mourn Cleo," she slowly admitted. "And I'll always regret that we drifted apart after she left the grove. But I'm relieved she didn't have the opportunity to use the crystal. It would have corrupted her soul."

He thankfully didn't press for more. She hadn't had time to truly process the knowledge that her sister was gone.

"And your mother?" he instead asked. "It couldn't have been easy to destroy her."

"It was…" Kyi found the words stuck in her throat. Probably because of the huge lump.

His features tightened with concern. "Kyi?"

She cleared her throat, forcing herself to continue. She needed to be honest. Locke had a right to know.

"It was easier than it should have been," she forced herself to say. "And that bothers me."

"Why does it bother you?"

"I don't want to be like her."

Locke jerked, his eyes blazing with a fierce disbelief. "You have nothing in common with Xuria." Electricity sizzled through the air, raising the hair on her nape. "Nothing."

Kyi shivered as the prickles crawled over her skin. She was rapidly becoming addicted to the sensation.

"What sort of creature takes satisfaction in the death of her mother?" she demanded.

"One who was used, abused, and hunted by that mother," he responded without hesitation.

"That's true."

A part of her accepted that he was right. Xuria was obsessed with her need to kill her daughters. If Kyi hadn't stopped the older woman, then eventually she would have found a way to destroy both of them. And probably Locke as well.

Still, there was a part of her that was terrified that she'd inherited more than her magic from her mother.

Easily recognizing her fear, Locke wrapped her even tighter in his arms. If she'd been human he would have crushed her. Kyi sighed. It was exactly what she needed.

"I felt the same," he told her.

"You didn't kill your mother."

"Not that I know of," he conceded, and Kyi was suddenly struck by the notion that a vampire didn't recall his human life. It was weirdly possible he might have killed his mortal family. Before he was turned, or even after he was a vampire. "But I did watch my master descend into madness. And when Styx destroyed him I walked away, telling myself I couldn't serve a traitor." His jaw tightened. "In truth, I didn't want to accept my overwhelming relief he was gone."

She smoothed her hands over his bare chest. "And now?"

"Now I'm not only prepared to put the past behind me, I'm eager to grasp my future." The scent of copper swirled through the air. "*Our* future."

"I've already been grasped," she teased, even as a dangerous sensation threatened to melt her heart. "More than once."

His lips twitched. "You're welcome." His eyes darkened with a blatant need. "But I want to make it permanent."

"I'm not going anywhere," she breathed.

"I want you to be my mate."

Her fingers drifted up his neck to trace the line of his jaw. "How can you be sure?" She asked the question that was gnawing deep inside her.

He turned his head to press his lips to the center of her palm. “I don’t have the words to explain how I feel.” He glanced back at her, his fangs peeking past his lips. “It’s like describing the beauty of the northern lights against a winter sky. Or the majesty of a raging thunderstorm. Or the soft quiet of the first snowfall.”

She released a shaky breath. Who knew her Viking was a romantic? “That’s not bad.”

“I could continue, but I need to know if becoming my mate is something you desire,” he rasped.

She hesitated before giving a slow, cautious nod. “Yes.”

Locke frowned. “You could try to sound a little more enthusiastic.”

“I’ve been alone for so long. My mother abandoned me, my father died, and my sister disappeared as soon as she could leave the grove.” She slid her thumb to press it against the tip of his fang. Locke had taken great care not to break her skin during their long bouts of lovemaking. Now her entire body ached to feel the slide of those fangs through her willing flesh. “I’m afraid to hope that you might stay.”

A low growl rumbled in his chest. “You’re never getting rid of me, whether we’re mated or not.”

“Is that a promise or a threat?”

“A pledge. You’re never going to be alone again.”

His soft words settled deep inside her, shattering the last of her defenses. Why was she fighting the inevitable?

This was what she wanted. What she needed. From the very depths of her wounded soul.

“Neither of will ever be alone again,” she promised, wrapping her arms around his neck.

With a groan, he rolled on top of her, pressing her into her feather mattress. “I like the sound of that.”

“Me too.”

“Are you ready?” His fangs were fully extended, gleaming snow white in the firelight.

“I think I’ve been ready my whole life.” She tangled her fingers in the satin softness of his hair. “I just didn’t realize it until you tried to kill me.”

“You never have to worry about that again. Not only can’t I bear to lose you, but you’re a very dangerous woman,” he retorted, genuine pride glowing in his eyes. “When you reach your hand into one of your pockets, I never know what’s going to happen.”

She smiled with smug satisfaction. “I like to keep you on your toes.”

“That’s exactly how I want my future to be.”

"On your toes?"

"With you." He grabbed her hand, pressing her nails against his chest and raking them downward, hard enough break through the skin. "Drink," he urged in rough tones.

Kyi lifted her head off the pillow, using the tip of her tongue to lick the droplets of blood that formed in the shallow wounds. Immediately she was hit by an avalanche of power. Not just the primitive mating magic that flowed through her, but Locke's exhilarating presence. As if a part of him was nestled in the center of her heart.

"Amazing," she breathed. "I feel…you."

"And now, my turn." Lowering his head, Locke struck with a blinding speed. Kyi hissed as the fangs pierced her skin and slid deep into her throat. It wasn't from pain. There was nothing but pleasure as he sucked her blood. An erotic bliss that made her toes curl, her back arching off the bed. The rumors were right, she fuzzily acknowledged. A vampire could cause an orgasm with just his bite. Eventually, he pulled his fangs from her flesh and lazily licked the tiny wounds. "Summer. Warm woods. Magic," he murmured. "The perfect combination."

Kyi brushed her fingers through his hair, her gaze distracted by the crimson tattoo that now scrolled beneath the skin of her forearm. It was a visible sign she was mated to a vampire.

"Oh. It's beautiful."

"*You're* beautiful." He gazed down at her in wonderment. "My mate."

She wrapped her legs around his hips and smiled in invitation. "For eternity."

* * * *

Levet stumbled through the portal, quickly moving out of the path of the demons who crowded behind him. A quick glance around revealed they'd entered the throne room in the mer-folk castle. Not a surprise. The power demanded for Inga to create a portal for so many creatures to pass through was daunting. She would naturally choose a location that was the most familiar. Plus, when Inga wasn't there, it was kept empty. It was the one place they wouldn't be worried about attracting unwanted attention.

Circling the demons who were slowly beginning to wake from the compulsion, he moved to stand directly in front of Inga.

"You did it, *mon ami*." He clapped his hands together. "You have saved your people."

There was the scent of fruit before Troy appeared next to Inga, standing far too close. So rude. Had he never heard of personal space?

"Very impressive," he commended.

Still in her disguise, Inga leaned heavily against the trident, as if she was struggling to stay upright.

"It wasn't me." She glanced toward the Tryshu. "It was this."

"*Non*." Levet firmly shook his head. "I have researched your oversized fork since you became queen."

Inga blinked. "What sort of research?"

Levet didn't want to admit that he'd spent endless hours in Jagr's massive library and that he had even traveled to Ireland to search through Cyn's private collection of rare manuscripts. He was renowned for being a *laissez-faire* sort of chap.

"I wanted to discover if it would have any adverse side effects," he told her, pointing toward the Tryshu. "There is a *derrière*-load of power running through it. I did not want you to be in danger."

"Oh. I never thought about it." She grimaced. "What did you discover?"

"That the Tryshu possesses its own magic, but it draws on the power of its owner," he revealed. "It is such a formidable weapon because of you."

Inga frowned, her lips parting to argue. She could never believe that she had any special talents. Or that fate chose her to be queen because she was the best choice.

"He's right," Troy overrode any protest she might try to offer. "I didn't do research, because you know..." He shrugged. "Boring. But I do know that any artifact is only as good as the wielder."

Levet scowled. Idiotic imp. "She is not a welder. She is a queen."

Troy slowly turned in his direction, his eyes narrowing. Uh oh.

"That reminds me. I have a bone to break with you."

Levet scratched his horn. That didn't sound right.

"I believe it is a bone to pick with you," he corrected, pleased for once to be the cliché police. "Not break."

"Oh, I'm going to break a few bones." He stepped toward Levet, towering over him. "Because of you, I was branded, forced to obey a cold-hearted bitch, hauled back in time, and nearly destroyed trying to prevent her from starting a war with the vampires."

Levet flapped his wings. What a baby. "You should be pleased."

Troy's face flushed with anger. "Pleased?"

"For once you were the Knight in Shining Armor," Levet pointed out in perfectly reasonable tones. Unlike Troy, he didn't overreact to a teeny tiny bit of trouble. "Not that you possess my own flair, but...argh."

Levet's words were cut off when Troy grabbed him by the throat and lifted him off the marble floor.

"I'm going to kill you," he growled.

"Troy," Inga protested.

Unfortunately, she had no opportunity to bang the annoying imp over the head with her big fork. Instead she whirled toward the double doors that were being thrust open to reveal Rimm and a half dozen mer-folk guards.

"Nobody move," Rimm commanded, lifting his hand. "Surround them."

Chapter 24

Inga watched in confusion as the armored guards swiftly jogged to circle the demons, who were now awake enough to realize there was a new danger. They babbled in fear and Inga forced herself to push through the mass to confront her Captain of the Royal Guards.

"It's okay, Rimm," she assured him.

The male frowned, aiming his trident directly at the center of her heart. "Who are you?" He stiffened, his eyes widening as he caught sight of her weapon. "The Tryshu," he rasped. "What have you done to our queen?"

Inga groaned. She was so tired she'd forgotten that she hadn't removed her ring. Of course, Rimm didn't recognize her.

"Are you blind," Levet demanded, waddling to stand at her side.

Rimm's frown deepened, the scent of salt thick in the air. "Levet? Where is Inga?"

Levet pointed toward Inga. "Here."

"A trick," the male snarled. "Guards. Stand ready."

There was the sound of tridents being pulled from holsters, then, much to Inga's surprise, the demons she'd brought through the gateway rushed to surround her, as if trying to protect her from the guards.

She glanced around, a strange sensation tugging at her heart. She'd never had anyone come to her rescue. Well, except for Levet. And perhaps Troy.

This was…

Astonishing.

Briefly savoring the sense of being appreciated, Inga shook her head and forced herself to concentrate on the danger that sizzled in the air. At any moment the guards were going to attack. She couldn't risk anyone getting hurt.

"Rimm. Lower your weapons," she commanded.

He stubbornly shook his head. "Not until you tell me what you've done to our queen."

"She's here." Holding up her hand, Inga removed the ring and tossed it toward Levet. She felt a tingle of magic as she was returned to her usual size, with far less pain than when she'd been originally transformed. A second later the demons around her gasped and stumbled to back away. She smiled with a wry resignation. "Yes, it's me. Inga."

Pushing his way past the cringing demons, Rimm moved to stand directly in front of her, his expression chiding. "I was worried about you."

She offered a sad smile. This male might not respect her, but he was loyal to the throne. She never doubted that he would do everything in his power to protect his queen.

"My people were in danger," she reminded him in soft tones. "It was my duty to rescue them."

He stubbornly shook his head. "No, that's my duty."

"Right?" Levet piped in. "She will never listen."

Exhaustion crashed over Inga, nearly sending her to her knees. She needed to rest before she collapsed.

"All's well that ends well," she muttered, heading toward the open door. "Excuse me, I need a bath."

"Inga!" Levet called out.

"Later."

Not giving anyone the opportunity to halt her retreat, Inga marched across the room and into the hall. It was thankfully only a short distance to her private quarters and in less than half an hour she was soaking her aching body in a tub she'd had custom designed to comfortably fit her extra-large size.

It was exactly what she needed, she decided with a groan. A shame she didn't have a tankard of grog to wash away the dust that clogged her throat.

Her skin was shriveled and her hair sticking up in damp tufts by the time she dried off and pulled on her favorite muumuu. It was a vivid pink with dancing polar bears wearing grass skirts. She sighed as she pulled it over her head.

Unlike that gauzy bit of nothing she'd been wearing, this actually covered her body and fell just below her knees. She could move without tripping over the hem.

She was in her main sitting room, pondering whether to seek out something to eat or fall into her bed and sleep for the next week, when there was a soft tap on her door.

"*Mon ami*. It is I." There was a pause. "Levet."

Inga grimaced. If it'd been anyone else she would have told them to go away. She didn't feel like being queen. Not tonight. And probably not tomorrow. But Levet was her only friend and she wasn't going to risk driving him away with her foul mood.

Pulling open the door, she gestured for him to enter. "Come in."

Levet waddled over the threshold, his wings sparkling and his tail shining, as if he'd just given it a good polish.

"Are you hiding again, *ma belle*?"

Inga stuck out her lower lip, feeling peevish at the gentle chiding. "I just traveled through time, changed shape…twice, and killed a crazed nymph. I feel like I've earned a few minutes of peace and quiet."

Levet tilted his head to the side, regarding her with a mysterious smile. "It will have to wait."

"Wait for what?"

"I have something to show you," he said.

Inga swallowed a sigh. Levet had many fine qualities, but he often found the most trivial things of vital importance. Only a week ago he'd insisted she join him in the dungeons so she could watch him juggle fireballs in the inky darkness.

"Does it have to be now?"

"*Oui*. It cannot wait," he insisted.

"Levet…"

"Now."

With his mysterious smile firmly intact, the gargoyle waddled back out of her quarters and into the corridor. Inga hesitated, glancing longingly over her shoulder at the comfy sofa and stack of books just begging her to return and enjoy. Then, grudgingly grabbing the Tryshu she'd left propped against the wall, she followed him down the hall and then up a flight of steps.

"Where are we going?" she demanded in confusion.

"Patience, *ma belle*," he urged.

Inga wasn't feeling patient. They'd reached the formal section of the castle where she was forced to play at being queen day after day. She wanted to turn and scurry back to her rooms.

They had reached the top of the stairs when she was distracted by an unexpected scent.

"I smell…" She sniffed. "Roast pig."

Levet sent her a glance that was too innocent to be real. "Do you?"

"Have you been raiding my kitchens again?" she demanded, her heart sinking to her toes.

The last time the gargoyle had snuck into the kitchen there'd been an uprising from the chefs. She'd fervently promised them it would never happen again.

"You shall see." Halting in front of a massive door that was decorated with intricate carvings and an abundance of gilt, Levet reached out to push it open. "*Voila*!"

Inga blinked. "The ballroom? Why are we here?"

The gargoyle waved his hand in a dramatic motion. "See for yourself."

Warily stepping forward, Inga stood in the doorway, her eyes widening at the sight of the long tables that were covered with silver platters of food and drink and surrounded by elegantly dressed mer-folk.

"What's going on?" she asked in genuine confusion.

"A feast."

"I don't understand." She shook her head. "A feast for what?"

From the nearest table, Rimm rose to his feet. "For the return of our people," he said in a loud, booming voice. "And in honor of you." He raised a golden goblet in a toast. "Queen Inga."

Inga blinked, her breath lodged in her throat as the mer-folk rose to their feet and lifted their glasses.

"To Queen Inga," they said in unison.

Levet reached up to grasp her hand. "Queen Inga," he whispered softly.

Printed in the United States
by Baker & Taylor Publisher Services

Printed in the United States
by Baker & Taylor Publisher Services